How to Seduce an Angel in 10 Days

How to Seduce an Angel in 10 Days

Saranna DeWylde

KENSINGTON PUBLISHING CORP.

www.kensingtonbooks.com

BRAVA BOOKS are published by

Kensington Publishing Corp.
119 West 40th Street
New York, NY 10018

All Kensington titles, imprints, and distributed lines are available at special quantity discounts for bulk purchases for sales promotions, premiums, fund-raising, educational, or institutional use.

Special book excerpts or customized printings can also be created to fit specific needs. For details, write or phone the office of the Kensington special sales manager: Kensington Publishing Corp., 119 West 40th Street, New York, NY 10018, attn: Special Sales Department; phone: 1-800-221-2647.

BRAVA and the B logo are Reg. U.S. Pat. & TM Off.

ISBN-13: 978-0-7582-6917-1
ISBN-10: 0-7582-6917-X

First Kensington Trade Paperback Printing: March 2013

10 9 8 7 6 5 4 3 2 1

Printed in the United States of America

CHAPTER ONE

The Wedding Reception

"Where you going, witchling?" Falcon Cherrywood, looking damn good in his tux, suddenly appeared between Drusilla "Tally" Tallow and the broom check service—his massive body like a brick wall. "You can't duck out of your best friend's wedding. Especially since you were the witch of honor."

A very hot brick wall. Heat radiated from him, but Tally couldn't tell if it was because his skin was really that warm, or it was the blush flooding her cheeks at being in such close proximity to him. She'd had a thing for Falcon for as long as she could remember and just sitting next to him made her thighs clench.

Tally fought for control of herself. Inappropriate reactions to her best friend's brother were the last thing she needed. "Midnight and Dred are gone, on their way to their honeymoon. All that's left is drinking, crying, and hookups everyone will regret in the morning." *Or tears in my beer for the future that I wanted, but can't have.*

"My mother will hex me to the innermost ring of Hell if I leave. Don't tell me you're going to abandon me to suffer through the rest of this alone?" He arched a black brow as if leaving was the worst sin he could fathom.

The thought struck her as both the funniest thing and the saddest. Tally had really managed to step in shit this time and there was no scraping it off her shoe and forgetting about it. After everything that had happened, Tally had been terrified to even show her face at the wedding, but Middy said that she'd wanted her there—needed her, even demanded she be her witch of honor. Middy was one of the ones she'd hurt, but she loved Tally anyway. So Tally couldn't do anything but agree to whatever her best friend wanted.

She suddenly realized Falcon fell into the same category. There was history between them, and it wasn't pretty.

"I guess since I almost killed you, I could stay and buy you a drink to dull the pain." She flashed him a halfhearted smile.

"Doesn't count. The reception has an open bar."

"Well, it's either that or sexual favors." Sweet Merlin, why had she said that? She rushed to cover her blunder. "And we all know those are a no go since everything with a penis this side of the Abyss is probably in mortal fear of me." Shit. That wasn't fixing it. By the way his eyes narrowed, she knew it was more like throwing down a gauntlet. That was just the way he was wired.

"I'm not afraid of you," he claimed. "I'd fear my mother's wrath for taking you up on that offer before I'd fear you." He smiled, his hard mouth curving in a grin that was both boyish and all grown-up warlock at once.

Another blush warmed her whole body as she thought about what his taking her up on her offer of sexual favors would entail. Only things she'd fantasized about for years. "You're really kind of a momma's boy tonight, aren't you? Twice in five minutes you've mentioned your fear of her." Tally grinned and allowed him to guide her toward the bar.

"I admit it." He shrugged, but laughed lightly. "After everything she's been through, she deserves some happiness. I'm surprised she has any hair left after raising us alone.

My brothers and I aren't called The Trifecta of Doom for nothing."

Yeah, there were three of them. Identical. Most witches had no trouble imagining themselves in a Trifecta sandwich, but Tally's knickers only burst into flames around one of them—Falcon. It was his strength, his power, and his kindness, too.

Not that Raven and Hawk weren't good to her. They were, but it had always been Falcon who was her rock, her touchstone, her fantasy. At ten years old, she'd proclaimed to the world she was going to marry Falcon Cherrywood, she and Middy would be true sisters, and they'd all live Happily Ever After. *So much for that.*

"You guys weren't so bad." She smiled at him, remembering.

"That's because you were just as bad as we were, Tally." He handed her a glass of champagne that had manifested on the bar. "You were this tiny, golden ball of pixie mayhem."

"Things change so much, don't they?" Tally asked softly.

"They do. You and my sister are both witches grown and we can't protect you from everything anymore."

His words twisted something inside her. "You don't need to protect Midnight from Dred. He may have been an absolute shit at Academy, but they saved the world together. He traded his soul to save her life. You couldn't ask for a better warlock for her. And more than that, she loves him. He's who she chose."

"I know. That's why I've made very free with the open bar. It was all I could do to keep my mouth shut. I didn't want to ruin the day for her."

"Then get the bottle and let's go to one of those pergolas by the lake. We can be drunken pariahs together."

A bottle of Jack Daniels manifested and Falcon grabbed it as he offered his arm to her like a proper escort. Tally laughed and slipped her arm through his as they walked. She tried not to notice how strong and large his bicep was.

"You know, what I said about protecting Middy applies to you, too." His voice was low, almost a whisper.

"Falcon—"

"I just wanted to make sure you heard it. That's all I'm going to say about it. Well, that and let me have a look at your arm. I'm a Crown Prince of Heaven now. There's no reason for you to be walking around with a broken arm."

He laid his hand on her arm, which rested in a sling she'd blasted with faerie dust and glitter to make it more wedding appropriate. The broken arm was the only lasting effect she had from being possessed by a lamia, or "the great and terrible evil," as she'd come to call it. The warmth of his magick suffused her and Falcon gently removed the sling.

Miraculously, the bones had mended and felt as good as new. Tally didn't know what to say. So Falcon spoke again instead. "Now, we can go back to getting shit-faced and being anti-social. In fact, I wouldn't mind revisiting the topic of sexual favors."

Tally laughed again. It felt good to laugh. She breathed deeply, the fresh air filling her lungs as a profound peace settled over her. "I thought you said Starlight would hex you?"

"That's if she finds out." He winked at her playfully.

"Well, we have Middy's permission. But only for a one-night stand." Tally flung herself down on a mass of pillows that had been artfully arranged in the pergola for lounging lakeside.

"Oh, really? Well, I guess there's nothing stopping us then." He reclined next to her after shrugging off his jacket, brought the bottle of Jack to his mouth, and took a long swig. Almost a third of the bottle.

"Nope, nothing but good sense." Tally held her hand out for the bottle and Falcon passed it to her. She took her own long pull and tried not to think about the fact his mouth had just been on the lip of the bottle.

A warlock was the last thing she needed. Her failed relationships— She cut her own thought off. Why was everything about a relationship? She was the one who'd encouraged Middy to have a little fun; why not take her own advice? Tally had to start living her life sometime. Why not now? Why not with Falcon? She wanted him. Why not have him if it was what he wanted, too? Just for tonight?

"That's never been a deterrent for me." Falcon smirked.

Tally rolled on her side and handed the bottle back to him, resting her cheek in the bowl of her hand. She licked her lips, her face suddenly warm as a languid heat stretched through her. "No? Then I guess we should get started. You strip first. You have to practice—I hear you're going to be a centerfold in the *Weekly Warlock* calendar."

He scowled. "Don't remind me." He took another long drink, downing the Jack like it was water. "No, I think you should go first."

"Oh? Why is that?" For one horrible moment, Tally thought he was going to make some crack about how he really was afraid of her, of what she'd become. The lamia had been horrible, she couldn't deny that—with the body of a bird and the head of a woman and a taste for human flesh, it was some of the darkest magick known. In ancient times, it had been used as a tool to punish evildoers, but it had grown too powerful and was banished to the Abyss. Until a warlock who Tally thought loved her had summoned one, using *her* body. In essence, offering her as a portal to the Abyss. She supposed she wouldn't trust herself either if the situation were different.

"Because you already know what I look like naked." He smirked.

She giggled with relief. "I was eleven and scarred for life."

He reached out and stroked his knuckles across her cheek. Her eyes fluttered closed, and her breath caught in her throat at the tender caress.

"You don't look scarred to me."

She opened her eyes and met his stare boldly. "Then how do I look to you?"

"Like you're fishing for compliments, my dear." He still wore a smirk, but there was warmth in his dark eyes. Something she hadn't seen there before. Or maybe that was just the whiskey? It tended to make everything languid with a sweet kind of fire, even if it wasn't really that way at all.

"So what if I am? If you're trying to get under my dress, a few words comparing me to a summer's day wouldn't hurt."

"I thought the saying was get in your panties, not under your dress?"

"Not wearing any." She bit down on her lip, before her mouth curved into a sheepish smile.

His gaze was drawn down to where her dress had ruched up around her thighs. "That's a game changer."

As his study of her traveled from the length of her bare legs, up to the low-cut bodice of her dress and finally to her face, it was as intense as if he'd explored her with his hands. Her nipples tightened in expectation, breasts aching to be kneaded in his strong hands, the throb between her legs hot and demanding.

"So was the way you just looked at me." Tally exhaled heavily and the moment hung between them, gravid with possibility. Every cell in her body screamed for him to touch her, to taste her, to crash his mouth into hers and brand her with his kiss.

"Any warlock would look at you that way if you told him you weren't wearing panties."

"Falcon, I've been naked in your bed, which is a damn

sight more provocative than telling you I'm not wearing any knickers, and you didn't look at me like that."

"You were still in Academy, Tally. And you were drunk."

Tally snatched the bottle back, hoping for some liquid courage. She needed it to tell him this secret. After swallowing hard, she said, "I wasn't that drunk."

He took the bottle back from her. "Dragonshit." He snorted derisively, before drinking the last drops of whiskey.

Merlin, but he drank like he was waging war on his liver and winning.

She licked her lips before speaking, as if that could ease the way for the words she'd say next. "Falcon, I only had one shot of tequila to ease my nerves."

"Ease your nerves?" He looked genuinely confused. "If you weren't drunk, then why were you in my bed?"

Warlocks could be so stupid. Why had she been in his bed? She rolled her eyes. "I will tell you, but be forewarned: If you ever bring this up again or tease me with it, I will tell Middy to curse every litter box this side of the mortal world to stuff its contents in your mouth."

He held up his hands in surrender. "Far be it from me to ever incite the wrath of Middy and that thrice-damned cat litter curse." Falcon watched her expectantly.

He really had no clue. The words Tally had been afraid of suddenly weren't so scary anymore. She was a witch who wanted a warlock. Maybe if she'd just told him what she wanted back then, she could have had it.

"I wanted you to be my first."

"Your first what?"

"Merlin's balls!" she swore. "I was naked in your bed, Falcon. What other first could I possibly be referring to?" Tally felt incredibly stupid now for being as upset as she'd been the next morning that he'd only come into the room and passed out next to her.

Falcon's eyes widened and then he laughed.

She wished she had more Jack. "I'm glad my teen angst amuses you. I should have made you promise not to laugh, too." Tally scowled.

"Sweetheart," he drawled, no longer laughing, his gaze burning hot over her body again. "That was one of the most torturous nights of my life."

"My turn to call dragonshit. You slept like a brick." Slam-dancing fairies were having a rave in her belly— anticipation and excitement welled.

"No, little witchling, I did not. It took me hours to fall asleep."

"Why? Was I on your side of the bed?"

He arched a brow. "Now who is being obtuse?"

Had he been tempted? She wanted to hear him say it. That's the only thing that would make it real. "I don't want to assume anything, Falcon. All those years ago, I assumed if I was naked in your bed, you'd know what was expected of you. And look how far that got me."

"Tally, any thoughts I had about you then were inappropriate as hell. You were barely more than a kid."

"So you thought about me?"

"I still do," he said in that warm, languid drawl.

"Tell me," she demanded.

His hand slid around the back of her neck, his thumb ghosting softly over the curve of her cheek. "Are you sure you want to cross this line? You know I'm not a relationship kind of warlock."

"I heard somewhere once that a witch doesn't have to buy the whole pig just to get some sausage."

"Oh, really?" His laughter slid over her awareness like warm velvet.

Tally turned her face into his hand and dragged her mouth up to his thumb, where she swiped her tongue along the digit before sucking it between her lips. "Yeah, really," she said after she released him from her caress. "Now, tell me how you've thought about me."

"How about I show you?" His arm snaked around her waist and pulled her against him hard.

She twined her fingers in his ink black hair, her breath coming in short bursts. "Yes."

Falcon shifted them so she was on her back, his weight pressing her down into the sea of pillows.

"Show me what you thought about most."

"What if what I thought about most was you on your knees in front of me, your sweet mouth around my cock?"

His words were deliciously blunt, as hard as his cock jutting against her belly.

"Was it?" She imagined herself doing that very thing and licked her lips.

"I've thought about doing everything to you that one warlock could do to a witch." He brought his lips down to the curve of her neck, his mouth hot on her skin. Falcon worked his way down to the bodice of her dress and bared her breasts—filling his hands with the firm globes. His tongue darted out across her nipple and she arched up into the caress with a small cry. "That, Tally. That's what I think about." His voice was a ragged whisper. "You wet and wanting beneath me, the taste of you on my tongue, and you making just that sound begging me for more."

Oh, Circe! His words sent bolts of desire straight to her clit, her channel slick and wet for him. This was finally happening. She'd wanted it for so long. He hadn't kissed her yet, and she wanted his mouth on hers, to taste him and the whiskey on his breath, to tie her memory of this moment to something tangible, something real, so she'd know that, too, had been real.

"Kiss me, Falcon."

"I plan on it." He worked his way down her body and pushed his hands up under her dress to grasp her hips. "I'm

going to kiss you until you're begging, just like I imagined."
Falcon bent his head between her parted thighs and kissed
her just as he'd promised—the first stroke of his tongue
against her cleft had her shuddering and digging her fingers
into his back.

"You taste so good." Falcon licked her again, his tongue
working her slick folds, until he paused, his breath warm on
her mound. "Shit."

Shit? *Shit?* That wasn't what one wanted to hear with a
warlock buried ears deep in one's witchy bits. Especially
Drusilla Tallow's witchy bits. Shit? Cold panic seized her.
She'd been possessed by a great and terrible evil, and that
evil thing had transformed her body. Given her teeth where
all things male would fear to tread, a symbol of her power.
But . . . she was cured. Healed. Unless . . . Had the great and
terrible evil come back? Why wasn't he doing anything—
saying anything?

Oh, Merlin, had she killed him?

Tally propped herself up on her elbows, the formerly
arousing sensation of his weight pushing her down now ter-
rifying. What if he'd had a heart attack? What if the great
and terrible evil—? A loud rumble issued from between her
thighs. It was like the thundering of an earthquake.

She tugged on her dress, the fabric impeding her from
seeing what was happening down there. Falcon's grip on
her thighs had changed. No longer were his masterful hands
spreading her wide for his access, but they clung to her like
a favored pillow.

The rumble she'd heard was a snore.

And she realized the hastily uttered "shit" was because he
was drunk and knew he was going to pass out.

In her quim.

Shit was absolutely, positively, unequivocally right.

Not only did Tally have a comatose warlock between her
legs, but he'd left her with blue bean, and pinned under his

dead weight. Her magick wouldn't answer her call, being unruly as it was since she'd come back from the dark side. It couldn't possibly get any worse.

She gazed heavenward, a retraction on the tip of her tongue. Tally knew it could be all kinds of worse and pleaded with the Powers That Be not to prove it to her.

So of course, they did. It was only a millisecond before she heard voices that could only belong to the rest of the Trifecta of Doom.

Why hadn't she asked Falcon to at least charm the privacy curtains closed on the pergola? No, she'd had to have the damn lake view. And now, Raven and Hawk were going to have a *Tally view*. With their brother half-buried between her thighs.

Maybe they'd just keep walking? All this lounging lakeside amongst a mess of pillows was very Jane Austen and if neither of them were trying to get laid, Tom Clancy was more their speed.

No such luck. "Falcon, hey we need—shit." Hawk froze at the entrance to the pergola, looking much like he was a deer and Tally was an oncoming semi.

Raven was still talking as he came to a stop behind Hawk. "I don't even know why you're worried about interrupting. He's not with a witch he'd shag. He's with Tally and—" Rather than freeze as his brother had done when he saw the tableau laid before him, he launched himself into action. "I'll save you!"

Raven pounced on top of Falcon and hooked his arms underneath his brother's shoulders and hauled him backwards, crying out, "I won't let her get you like she did Tristan." The atmosphere crackled around them as Raven used his magick to boost his strength and sent him and Falcon both flying into the lake with a splash that caused the water to burst high up into the sky and drew the attention of all the remaining guests.

Free of Falcon's dead-drunk weight, she scrambled to pull her dress down and frantically sought out avenues of escape. She considered crawling under the linen curtains of the pergola, but that wasn't actually a viable option. Every witch and warlock in attendance had come running to see the spectacle.

Especially with Raven sputtering lake water out of his nose and crowing that he'd saved his brother from a certain doom in between the thighs of Drusilla Tallow, Great and Terrible Evil, Esquire.

"Tally," Hawk began, a look of pity on his face. "I can teleport you home."

The pity was worse than the fear. Tally hated being pitied. She squared her shoulders and drew herself up to her full five-foot-six inches and reminded herself she was a lion, not a pussycat. Emphasis on pussy.

"No. I will leave the same way I came. Through the front gates so everyone can see my ass before they kiss it."

Tally strode boldly through the filmy curtains out onto the green and the crowd took a collective step back from her. She lifted her chin and Raven shoved Falcon's still comatose body behind him.

All manner of things were on the tip of her tongue, but she decided silence was probably her best friend. She spun on her heel and stomped toward the front gates of the estate, reminding herself to never again break her moratorium on weddings.

CHAPTER TWO

The Cherub Chore

Falcon Cherrywood awoke with the most gods-awful sound echoing in his head with the force of the report of an AK-47. It sounded for all the world like Death singing in his ear.

Not the proximity of the end of all things, no, but the Angel of Death, Tristan Belledare. The one Tally had sent to his great reward not so long ago. The bastard was singing "Cupid, Draw Back Your Bow" by Sam Cooke and at an unreasonable volume. He wished Death would, himself, indeed go *silently* into that good night. Or at least shut the hell up. Tally had— Shit.

Tally. His whiskey-soaked, foggy brain latched on to that thread of a thought as he realized he'd failed as a warlock. He'd passed out like a boy at his first Beltane revel.

Between her thighs!

Falcon had to get up right now and go over to her house and prove to her he was 100 percent warlock. He had to follow through on all those promises of making her scream his name. Not only because he had to live up to his reputation, but because he wanted those things with her. He remembered the taste of her, the delicate sound she made when he thrust his tongue against her clit. . . .

"Cupid! Are you in there?" Cold fingers tapped on his forehead.

He cracked a crusty eye open. He hadn't been imagining Death. Tristan's smug face was only inches from his own.

"What the hell, man? And don't call me Cupid."

"Why not? That's your name."

"My name is Falcon."

"It's Mud if you don't get your ass up and report for duty. The Powers That Be have been trying to get in touch with you for hours."

"My sister got married yesterday." He shrugged, but was then immediately regretting the action. There was a troupe of klutzy knife-throwing circus monkeys banging around in his head.

"Yes, you should have blessed it and gone on about your business rather than getting shit-faced. Do you know how sad it is that *I* have to be your moral compass?" Tristan rolled his eyes and then pushed Falcon so he rolled off the other side of the bed. "Move it, Cupid. I'll be waiting downstairs." Tristan disappeared.

Downstairs? Falcon lived in an apartment; he didn't have a downstairs. He dragged himself up to sit on the bed and took another look at his surroundings and realized he was in his old room at his mother's house. How had he gotten there?

His *Heaven's Helper Manual* was perched obviously on the nightstand. Like it had been put there specifically for him to find. He had his own copy at home. He didn't need this one.

Fucking Cupid.

It was amazing the things one would agree to when hovering near death. The actual act, not the guy in the flesh. Although, Tristan would argue he'd gotten some witches to do some crazy things.

Falcon Cherrywood hadn't meant to smite the former Cupid in the ass with a fireball.

It had all been a grievous mistake. One he was certainly

paying for now that he had to fly a mile in the other guy's wings since the injury had caused Cupid to take an early retirement. Falcon had only been trying to save his sister from the great and terrible evil, not take over as Cupid.

The worst part of the job wasn't the diaper. He could get over that with the right amount of whiskey. It was the wings themselves. He'd had been hoping for black ones or maybe a really dark blue; that would have been acceptable. Love was Hell after all, so he could've been happy with some demonic bat wings.

But no, not only was he forced to play the Diapered Archer; he had to do it in pink. By Merlin's teeth, *pink*. If that wasn't enough to make him reconsider his man card, they were glittery, like the inside of a thirteen-year-old witch's locker at Academy. He was surprised his swaddling didn't have a unicorn print.

Bastards.

He'd thumbed through his *Heaven's Helper Manual* briefly. It had come with the wings and the Crown Prince of Heaven gig, but wasn't impressed by anything he saw. Even in Eternity, one still had to watch the employee videos about how not to pick one's nose in front of the customers. It was ridiculous. The manual actually referred to them as "customers." Who were they kidding? If Cupid chose to shoot them, then they could damn well take what they got. This wasn't Burger King; they didn't get to have it their way.

There was another problem.

He couldn't shoot a bow and arrow to save his life. Or anyone else's. He'd been hoping to find the answer in the stupid manual, but no. There was nothing actually helpful in the thing. Cupid taking archery lessons: another side of ridiculous with an entrée of Are-You-Fucking-Kidding-Me?

Falcon couldn't do much about the wings, but he was

definitely changing his outfit. The diaper thing just didn't do it for him, or for the thousands of women who were going to give it up to be shot with an arrow from his quiver. He might see what he could do about using bullets instead of arrows. Then he could ask them in all seriousness if they wanted to see his love gun.

Yes, these were the thoughts that occupied the new Cupid's mind as he sat in his new uniform of pink wings and a toga with the hangover from Hell, debating whether he should even go down the stairs. Goddess help him if his brothers saw him this way.

Well, they were bound to sooner or later, so he put on his best swagger and strutted down the stairs.

The kitchen was blessedly empty, except for Tristan, who had helped himself to a cup of coffee.

Hey, *Cherry* wood." Tristan snickered. "Finally get *it,* I mean, *yourself* up?"

Falcon rolled his eyes. He didn't need this today. Or any day, really. He would much rather have been left alone with his thoughts and his devices. "Up longer and stronger than you, Belle of the Ball Sac."

"I see angel status has done nothing for your humor, or your wit." Tristan made it a point to stretch in an overdramatic manner, splaying his *black* wings behind him.

It was a small consolation to Falcon they glittered like his own. On Tristan, it looked like some lame allusion to stars, whereas Falcon's were just pink. He was going to take that up with the Powers That Be, oh, yes.

"Black wings do not a badass make, Tristan," Falcon said, feeling testy. So what if they were black? They looked like some emo kid had been turned loose with a Sharpie. They weren't that cool.

"Neither does getting knocked off your broom by a girl." Tristan flashed a toothy grin, obviously taking great joy in reminding Falcon about how, when possessed by the great and terrible evil, he had knocked Falcon right off his broom to certain death. Or Cupidity, as it had turned out. He still wasn't sure which was worse.

But Tally had done a number on Tristan, too.

"Oh, would that be the same girl who lured you to Loudun and used your ribs for toothpicks after eating your kidneys like jelly beans?" Falcon raised a brow and gave Tristan the best holier-than-thou expression he could manage. Falcon had been honest when he'd said he didn't hold anything that had happened with the great and terrible evil against Tally, but that didn't mean he was above putting Tristan in his place.

"You're awfully testy this morning. Not getting any?"

"No. You know how your mom is." Falcon shrugged and reached for the coffeepot.

"Not really. I would say I empathize, but *your* mom has never kicked me out of bed." Tristan smirked.

Falcon growled. "Are you ready for retirement so soon?"

"What? You'll smite *me* in the ass with a fireball?"

"No, my love gun."

"I didn't know you'd come out of the closet." Tristan shrugged. "Good for you."

"You'll think good for me when you're puckered up to a donkey's ass professing your ardent love."

"Nah, remember? Your sister wouldn't have me."

Falcon scowled, but he couldn't deny Tristan had indeed gotten the last word. "She knows better. So what is it that has your cape all in a bunch that you had to rouse me out of a perfectly good stupor?"

"Not *my* cape, buddy. The Powers. They have a job for you."

Tristan plopped an envelope down on the counter. It was red.

More fucking glitter.

He needed a barrel of ibuprofen and a vat of whiskey. A

sick feeling in his gut that was more than just the hangover told him whatever was in that envelope was going to be worse than the pink wings and the diaper.

Falcon didn't want to look at it, let alone open it.

"Well?" Tristan demanded. "I don't have all day. I have my own assignment to see to and I have to stay until you open it."

Falcon opened the letter and couldn't quite process what it said. He read the words, and he knew what each word meant on its own, but there, together, jumbled in that sentence, it just didn't compute.

His assignment was to act in the capacity of a heavenly parole officer.

His parolee was none other than Drusilla Tallow.

Drusilla Tallow, who'd become a great and terrible evil. Who'd grown teeth in a scary place. Who'd knocked him off his broom, who'd killed Tristan (not that the bastard didn't deserve it), who'd been the gateway to the destruction of the Warlockian world. But she hadn't meant to do those things or to allow the lamia to possess her. So instead of punishing her, the Powers That Be had granted her a type of parole. Being possessed by the lamia was punishment enough, but only if she could prove herself. She needed a parole officer to guide her, to help her to rebuild her life, to make the right choices.

Falcon Cherrywood couldn't be her parole officer. Hell, he couldn't even be Cupid. He didn't know how to keep someone on the straight and narrow, because he couldn't do it himself. And he certainly didn't believe in love.

Putting Tally's future in his hands was a certain recipe for disaster for both of them.

What were they thinking?

"Shit." He'd been saying that a lot lately, but it was just perfect to describe the flavor of absolutely everything that had landed on his plate. "I have to find Tally."

"Whoa there, tiger." Tristan put out his hands to stop his progress. "You are the last person she wants to see right now."

"Why?"

"Falcon, do you remember nothing from the wedding?" Disbelief made Tristan's eyes pop out of his head.

"How do you know about it?" That feeling in the pit of his stomach suddenly jumped up in his throat. But he wasn't going to barf. *Don't puke, don't puke, Merlin, please don't puke.*

"*Everyone* knows about it. Hawk and Raven walked in on you two after you passed out. Raven thought Tally was possessed again and screamed he'd save you and flung you and himself into the lake. Worse, he used his magick to do it. So everyone saw the fireworks and came to investigate."

Save him? The dots all suddenly connected to paint a horrible picture. He'd passed out between her thighs and Raven had thought the great and terrible evil had returned.

Fuck.

Part of the reason for Tally to put in an appearance at the wedding, Middy had said, was to show the warlockian community that she'd been forgiven, and most important, she was just a regular witch. And Falcon had screwed that up for her. He was officially an asshole.

Roses weren't going to fix this. She'd probably never speak to him again, let alone allow him to finish what they'd started. It was just as well. This was the universe's way of reminding him to keep his dick to himself when it came to Drusilla Tallow. Something always happened whenever things were about to change between them. If this wasn't a sign, he didn't know what was.

"You're right." He nodded at Tristan. Falcon hated to admit that Tristan was right about anything, but he hated this truth in particular. Tally'd had enough pain and Falcon was under no illusions he'd treat her any better than any other warlock had. He knew himself. Out of his brothers, Falcon had always been the one most like his father. Falcon had their father's sense of humor, his laugh, his swagger, the quirk to his left eyebrow, and that same wanderlust that led his father to abandon a witch who loved him more than her own breath and the four children they had together. "But that doesn't matter. The Powers have spoken. I'm her new parole officer."

CHAPTER THREE

Bitch Kitty Deluxe Redux

Drusilla Tallow wanted nothing more than to curl up with a Jenna McCormick novel in her *Team Zan!* T-shirt, a pint of Amazon Chocolate Häagen-Dazs, and feel sorry for herself after daydreaming about a certain immortal space pirate. He could plunder her any day. He wouldn't fear her, pity her, and he most certainly wouldn't pass out before fulfilling his promise to kiss her witchy bits until she begged him to stop.

She couldn't even think about witchy-bits-kissing or Falcon right now. Although, Tally didn't know why she was embarrassed. She wasn't the one who'd passed out mid-cunnilingus.

Either way, she was determined to have the Häagen-Dazs. Walking to the corner market to acquire said Häagen-Dazs, everyone she'd passed had crossed to the opposite side of the street to avoid her. That hurt, to see mothers averting their children's eyes and shielding them from her, and warlocks watching her with an absolute certainty that any minute, something awful would burst through her skin.

Tally tried to look at the bright side. When she'd made her selections in the market, she hadn't had to wait in line or pay. They'd just wanted her out of the store as quickly as possible. The walk was nice, other than the people cringing and hiding in terror. The scent of honeysuckle hung sweetly in the air. It masked the stench of fear quite nicely.

It was quite the surprise when she returned home to find herself face-to-face with a very handsome man who'd made himself right at home on her porch. He had a strong, angular jaw and an obvious affinity for tea. He'd brought his own—a teacup filled with a steaming brew and frosted biscuits were displayed neatly on her wicker end table. Tally noticed his fingers were elegant and somehow still masculine, even as they brought the dainty teacup to his hard mouth.

He wore a gray, pinstriped suit with gray-and-white spectator dress shoes. A crisp white linen handkerchief was folded smartly in his breast pocket. He was very debonair. Tally expected to see a walking stick or something similar. She supposed these days they were called "pimp canes." This guy was vintage gangster and made of smokin' hot. In fact, he was so hot, his eyes were on fire. They blazed with the fury of Hell.

"If you'd let me know, I could have picked up a pint for you on my way over." The handsome creature nodded to her bag of ice cream.

"Well, I didn't know to expect you." Because she had no idea who he was. Tally wished fervently for her magick. She didn't know if she should run away screaming, or maybe pounce on him and ride him like a pony. He obviously wasn't a warlock and he was damned sexy. Merlin, why was she always thinking with her witchy bits? She was as bad as any warlock.

"Of course, you didn't, silly witch. You didn't read your magick mail this morning."

"I've been a little too busy with life to worry about my m-mail."

"Mmm, don't I just know it? You're such a wicked little

libertine," he said, his mouth curling into a smile she was sure had spawned the Inquisition.

"It seems you know all about me, so just who the hell are you?" Tally asked, more boldly than she felt.

He leered at her, hellfire eyes blazing. "Hell is exactly who I am. A Crown Prince of Hell to be precise." He took another sip of tea. "But you may call me Ethelred."

"Well, Ethelred, not that it hasn't been fun, but I'm sure you have other things to do besides hang out on my front porch." Part of her wanted to assume he was crazy, but those hellfire eyes didn't lie.

"I'm rather pleased you didn't go for the hysterical screaming as those with the ovaries tend to do. That's why they call it hysteria, don't you know. *Hystero* means uterus." He nodded and took a sip of tea. "I was actually rather busy drafting a contract with a gypsy prince when the Powers That Be 'called' to put me on your case. Now that the prince has time to think it over, he might change his mind and I might miss my quota for Infernal contracts as a result. I think you owe me something for my time, don't you?"

"Me owe you? For what? I'm not responsible for your quota or for you being here."

He chuckled. "Oh, you're going to like it in Hell, doll-face. We might even be able to find you a job. No one is responsible for anything down there, either. The Big Boss 'made *everyone* do it.'" Ethelred held out a second teacup to her. "Why don't you sit down and we'll have a chat about why exactly we'll be spending time together, hmm? Since you couldn't be bothered to read your m-mail that came from Merlin himself."

Tally sank into the chair, unsure if any of this was actually happening to her. He placed a chocolate banana scone on a table that manifested in front of her, a dollop of cream on top, and smiled. Tally was taking high tea with a demon.

She didn't know how she felt about it, but staying calm seemed to be the best bet. He obviously hated screamers and it was clear it would get her nowhere in any event. And he had scones and he smelled good. This might be the closest she'd ever get to anything male again, so maybe it wouldn't hurt to hear what he had to say. At least, he was honest about the fact he was evil. Martin, the evil warlock who'd sicced the lamia on her, had pretended to love her, and had pretended to be a good person. Tally preferred honest, even if it was ugly.

Ethelred took another bite of the biscuit he'd chosen, rather than a scone. He chewed carefully, precisely, silently. But Tally could tell he had something else to say. Her own food hit her stomach like an anvil. "So, little witch. You are on parole," he said finally.

"Parole?" she squeaked.

"Yes, doll. *Parole.* The Powers That Be decided that being possessed by the lamia was prison enough. But still, you did commit a crime. You tore open a hole in this dimension, allowed evil to pass through, hurt people—and you know the Powers frown on all of that." Ethelred nodded as if he'd just shared a great secret with her.

"What—" she began.

"Hush. Questions will be answered after the lecture. You will have two parole officers—one Infernal, that's me, as I'm sure you've figured out, and one Heavenly, and that's Cupid. Only the Powers know why, of course. With your weights and balances, I don't think Merlin himself could change the chains on your soul. Things aren't looking good for you. If you were hit with a runaway broom right now, you'd sink instead of swim." He nodded, almost apologetically.

The demon on her porch had just told her she was going to Hell.

Tally didn't see how it was possible to remain in the non-hysterical category.

"I can sense your internal temperature creeping up toward Bitch Kitty."

"I don't want to go to Hell. I don't want to sink!"

"While that is completely up to you, it's really not all that bad. I'm surprised Midnight was able to keep her mouth closed."

"What does Middy have to do with it?"

"I'm afraid I can't say." He didn't sound at all disappointed.

"Then you shouldn't have brought it up." Tally huffed.

"Touché, my dear. Touché." He grinned and that pissed her off even more.

"Further, I don't know you. I was already led astray by a man once. Why should I believe I'm on parole? That smells a lot like dragonshit to me."

He laughed. "I'm not a man. I'm a demon, but I do like you. You're going to be fun."

"You think so? Let me ask you this then. Would a demon be afraid of the great and terrible evil from the Abyss?" She eyed him critically.

Tally was officially desperate. She knew at the core of her being he was a demon and someone she should steer clear of. She consoled herself with the fact she hadn't signed anything; she could start to worry when she asked for a contract to get a piece of fine, demonic ass. But she sensed she might not be too far away from that slippery slope. It wasn't the needs of her body that drove her, but the needs of self. It occurred to her that as much as she'd fought it, and as much as she wanted it to be different, Tally's self-worth had always been tied to sex and now no one wanted her. She didn't know how to process who she was within those parameters. Yes, she was officially desperate.

Ethelred appraised her, his hellfire eyes like sparklers on

the Fourth of July. "No, and no angel worth his salt will be, either."

Tally felt her mouth opening just as the thought formed like a newly hatched maggot in her fevered brain. "What about you? Put your money where your mouth is, Ethelred?"

The demon looked amused and she blushed hotly. Tally couldn't believe what she'd just done. She felt like an utter twat. "Never mind that. It just slipped out. I'm bored, you're cute . . . Just never mind. Really."

"You've done wonders for my ego, you adorable witch." Ethelred stood, and his presence sucked the air out of the space.

Why were all immortal men so freaking huge? She was sure she had a Fey in the woodpile, so to speak, something that had contributed to her short stature.

"Too bad I'm not into women just now. That would probably earn me admin points for shagging my charge on the next promotion board. You're delightful."

"You're gay?" she squeaked. Tally should have known. She reiterated to herself that anything male was the last thing she needed. Sex should have been the least of her worries, but instead, it was like a big, throbbing pimple in the middle of her forehead. No, more like shingles. It burned and itched just like that.

"I wouldn't say gay. I don't mind the term, but it's not totally accurate. I prefer 'omnisexual.' "

A lightning bolt ripped through the roof and burst into flames around Ethelred's feet and Tally was sure she could hear a trumpet. Or maybe it was the horn from a semi?

"Devildamn, Uriel. Get a grip on yourself," Ethelred growled at the sky and then looked back down to the place where a smoking pile of rubble had replaced Tally's wicker end table.

"Let me guess, he's your boyfriend? What an asshole,"

Tally snapped. "Look at my table. Just because I can do magick doesn't mean I can fix this for free."

"He's a little possessive." Ethelred held his first finger and thumb about an inch apart to demonstrate. "He said he didn't want a relationship and then I propose one tiny deal with one insignificant gypsy prince and he loses his mind. Men are all the same, doll. Crown Prince of Heaven or Hell, warlock or mortal."

Tally realized they were bonding over men. Was the demon her new gay best friend? Were they going to go shoe shopping next and eat Godivas and lament the size of their asses in the latest skinny jeans?

He flashed a wicked smile, as if he knew the vein of her thoughts. But that smile, it was all about the predator. It told her not to let her guard down for one minute because he'd devour her whole.

Any logical thought was quickly snuffed to a cold fear that gnawed all the way to the marrow of her bones; it was as if she could already feel his teeth tearing at her insides. It spoke to the darkness that was still inside her and reached out to coil around her spine. It was an intrinsic terror of the unknown Abyss, but it was painted with the red dye of desire.

These Crown Princes were really all about the mind fuck. Tally knew she'd have to remember that. He eyed her as he would a candy he wasn't sure if he'd get spanked for stealing. Or better yet, if it could be proven he'd stolen it.

"Perhaps another time? I think we're going to get you, one way or another, Drusilla Tallow."

We're? As in we? Tally was assaulted with visions of being had by the demon's "we" and it made her tingle a bit. All of those hot creatures paying attention to her? Talk about a head trip. It made her feel a bit slutty, too, but she couldn't bring herself to care. After all, what she did in her own brain was private.

Unless Ethelred's continued smirk was any indication.

She chose to ignore the fact that when he said "we" he meant Hell.

"Hark, is that the flutter of glittery wings I hear?" Ethelred's lips twisted into a wry smile. "If you don't believe me, I'm sure you'll believe your snoring savior. Do let the Diapered Wonder know I was here, would you?"

"My snoring savior?" So she had heard that correctly. Tally wasn't ready to look at Falcon, let alone speak to him, and that was miles from trusting him with her immortal soul.

"You did catch the part where I said you had a Heavenly parole officer, too, didn't you? Cupid? The Diapered Wonder? The Drunken Archer? If it's any consolation, I think it was a dick move on the Powers' part to not only saddle you with the new guy, but one who doesn't even believe in his office. You should petition Merlin to have him replaced."

"I thought you wanted me to fail?"

"Playing devil's advocate is applicable to all scenarios, doll. Not just the ones that are in my best interest. But I'm going to run along now. The gypsy prince requires my attention and the snoring savior requires yours. I'll see you soon." He winked and disappeared with the smell of sulfur hanging heavily in the air.

See her soon? She didn't want to be seen soon. Or at all. She didn't want to be on parole, she didn't want to go to Hell, she didn't— Well, she could just toss all that shit on the pile with the rest of it. There were plenty of things she'd never signed up for and the only thing she could do was pull out her big witch wand and deal with it.

The sulfur smell dissipated and was slowly replaced by the scent of cotton candy. The air in front of her on the steps began to shimmer pink like the first streaks of dawn and Falcon Cherrywood stood on the step in full Cupid regalia.

He was gorgeous, like a bronzed version of some Greek

statue. In fact, he looked very Greek in his short toga, the filmy material brushing the tops of his muscular thighs. It didn't look like a diaper at all. Of course, she hadn't seen what he had on under there. Not that she would ask after what had happened last time. Her eyes were drawn from his physique to his wings. She'd never seen him like this before—never seen the wings. They entranced her—simply beautiful, like glittery cotton candy. So downy and soft, she wondered what it would be like to touch them.

"It smells like burned eggs and a baby shit muddin' rally. What have you been doing?" Falcon Cherrywood demanded as he tripped when he tried to step up onto the porch. He'd clearly forgotten his wings were attached as they caught on both sides of the door and sent him sprawling in the yard.

"I don't know, Cupid. You're the one wearing a diaper," she called out.

Falcon dragged himself to his feet, his hair mussed with bits of grass sticking out here and there. "Poke fun at the diaper once more, wench, and I'll zap you in love with a closet gnome."

"That's not a very angelic attitude." Tally snorted.

"Yeah, well, I'm hoping to be reassigned to a different case."

"You?" Tally snorted again and feared she was turning into something porcine with all the snorting. "I'd say I got the shortest end of that wand, wouldn't you?"

He had the grace to look contrite as he tucked his wings and finally made it up onto the porch. "Tally, I can't tell you how sorry I am about what happened."

"Because you passed out in my witchy bits or because your brother proclaimed to the whole of warlockian society that he thought they were trying to eat you?"

"Tristan told me what happened and—"

"*He* knows?" Tristan was her ex-boyfriend and he'd hurt

her very badly. Probably not as badly as she'd hurt him when she killed him, but he'd taken the job as Death afterward, so it had all worked out. But Tally didn't want him to know anything about her humiliation, especially where Falcon was concerned. She sighed heavily.

"All I can say is I'm sorry. I can't undo it. I know that's not good enough, which is why I think it's best if I ask to be reassigned."

"Ethelred thought so, too." She inhaled deeply, trying to relax and that cotton candy scent filled her awareness.

"The demon was already here?" Falcon narrowed his eyes.

Tally didn't answer him; all she could think about was that delicious smell. "That smells so good. Is that you?"

"Is what me?"

"You smell like cotton candy." Tally was entranced. Those pink wings were calling to her. She had to touch them. Tally reached out unsure fingers and skimmed down the arch of his wing. "Does that come with Cupidity?"

They even felt like cotton candy, so soft and fey. She looked to see if her fingers were covered in glitter, but they weren't. Perhaps it was more like diamond dust, a pretty armor. . . . Tally touched again and Falcon grabbed her wrist.

"That's not a good idea," Falcon said through clenched teeth.

"Why not? They're so pretty." She was vaguely aware she sounded like a love-struck groupie.

If she'd been in her right mind, she'd have checked her backside for an errant lust arrow, especially after the way he'd left her at the wedding reception, but she couldn't help herself. She smoothed her cheek over the downy wing. Suddenly, her face was wrenched away by a fist tangled in her mass of blond curls and Falcon's mouth was hot and demanding on hers.

She wondered if he knew he *tasted* like cotton candy, too. Her fingers stroked his wings and gloried in their softness. Touching him and being touched by him felt so good.

But it was wrong.

He was her parole officer now, and frankly, she deserved better. After the humiliation she'd endured, he thought he could just grab her and kiss her because she'd touched his wings? He'd said he was sorry, but if he was really sorry, he'd have actions to back him up. Or he would have at least apologized first thing rather than talking about how her porch smelled like shit and he wanted to be reassigned.

Yes, she was desperate, and yes, Falcon was her most secret desire, but she deserved better than this. Not because he didn't want a relationship, but because he obviously didn't respect her.

That idea was an epiphany. The truth of it was cymbals smacking together with her head in between them.

Tally decided that Falcon deserved the same understanding, the same awareness. Her two open palms were nothing like cymbals, but they'd have to do.

CHAPTER FOUR

Enter the Fist

Drusilla Tallow was a small witch, with even smaller hands.

And yet, when they connected simultaneously with the sides of his head, they rattled the feeling out of his face.

"What was that for?" he demanded.

She stood there, her little fists clenched at her sides, her luscious mouth set in a hard line, and a flush creeping up the slender column of her throat. Her chest heaved with her emotion, causing her cleavage to jiggle in the most attractive way. He considered kissing her again. It would be completely worth another slap. Especially if he could get her to touch his wings again.

What was wrong with him?

Besides being a bastard? he answered himself.

He'd already hurt her and all he could do was think about was his dick. And his wings. But he'd never felt anything like that: The pleasure had been a vibration that echoed through his whole body, not just his cock.

Then he decided that maybe his wings weren't pink, they were flesh-colored.

Like his cock.

He would have laughed, if not for the missile of her hand flying through the air at his face yet again. Falcon grabbed her wrist before she could connect with his cheek. "If you strike me again, I'm going to take you over my knee like a little witchling."

Falcon knew it was a lie as soon as the words were out of his mouth. If he ever had his hands on her ass, it wouldn't be for any sort of correction.

"Did you hear anything I just said?" Tally asked.

She'd been talking? "Of course, I did."

"Then why were you staring at my tits?"

"Because they're magnificent." He was glad he still had hold of her wrist, and grabbed for the other one just as it launched itself from her side like a rocket into space.

The flush crept up to her cheeks. "Let me go."

"Stop trying to hit me."

"Stop being a bastard," she hissed.

"Fair enough." He couldn't really argue with that one. "Look, Tally, I know you're pissed at me, and I deserve it, but I don't have dental coverage yet. I'd like to keep my teeth."

She laughed, and then scowled halfheartedly. "Don't make me laugh. I'm angry."

"I know." He released her wrists and drew her against him slowly. Falcon felt like even more of a bastard when she relaxed into his embrace with perfect trust. He never should have crossed that line into his fantasies with her. But she felt so good in his arms. The way she clung to him made him feel like he could conquer the world.

Only, that was the problem. She trusted him to conquer the world, to be the hero, and that just wasn't in his DNA.

He released her reluctantly, at a loss for what to say, and struggled to keep his eyes on her face rather than her magnificent breasts, but it was a losing battle. So he surrendered.

"Falcon, do you know why I was an—" She broke off with a huff. "For fuck's sake, really?"

"I was listening!" he swore. "I heard every word you said."

Tally sighed again and did something completely unexpected. She pulled up her shirt and bared her breasts. They bounced with her movement, entrancing him further. Her nipples tightened and puckered, begging for his mouth.

Falcon froze. Merlin's teeth, what was she trying to do to him? "Tally, if you're going to slap me for kissing you, what do you expect me to do with this?"

"Well, you can't look at my face when I'm talking to you, so there. Look your fill and then maybe we can have a conversation."

"We had *this* conversation. I always look and I always hear what you're saying. Swear to Merlin."

"Fine. What did I say?"

"How do you expect me to remember now with your rack in my face? The other parts of my brain have shut down."

"Well, if you were listening . . ." she singsonged.

Fuck. What had she been saying? Right. "You wanted to know if I knew why you were angry."

She dropped her shirt. "You really were listening." Her mouth made a little "o" of surprise. On second thought, looking at her mouth and imagining all the things he could do with it—to it—was almost as much fun as her breasts. *Almost.*

"I said as much, didn't I? I've never lied to you, Tally. I may not be the most honorable warlock, but I'm honest."

"So you really have been scoping out my breasts every time we've talked?"

"We've been down that path and you've changed your mind about revisiting it, so let's talk about something else, okay?" His cock couldn't take any more, not after her wing stroking and tit flashing. He readjusted his toga.

"Okay, then answer my other question. Do you know why you pissed me off?"

"I would assume because I passed out in your sweet-meats."

She rolled her eyes. "No, I'm not actually mad about that."

Women's reasoning boggled his brain. He'd never understand them. Which was another reason why it was a stupid idea to make him Cupid. "So what *are* you mad about?"

Tally flashed him a thousand-watt smile. "I'm glad you asked. See, you were confused about the part where you thought I didn't want to revisit that path. I want to revisit it plenty, but I deserve your respect."

"Of course, I respect you, Tally." If his cock got any harder, it was going to explode. "Why did you think I didn't?" Aside from the part where he got hammered and passed out in her snatch. He understood that didn't convey the best message.

"Shoving your tongue down my throat just because I touched your wings. Not looking at my face when you talk to me. Not listening to what I have to say."

"But we resolved all that."

"Right. Now there's just the part where you're my parole officer." She pursed her lips.

"Honestly, I know I'm not your best shot at this redemption thing." He couldn't believe he was going to say what he uttered next. "But there's no one who wants you to succeed more than I do."

It was true. He cared about Tally, and he wanted her to be happy. She'd be just a job to another angel. For him, it was something more. Of course, he'd have to keep his dick to himself. His eyes wandered down toward her breasts again. He'd be doing a lot of things to his dick by himself if he kept this up, but her well-being and redemption were worth more to him than a one-off. Or even a several-off, but it was still something that would come to an end and not worth her soul.

"So you're not going to put in for a new assignment?" She looked so vulnerable and in need of that protection he'd promised her would always be there.

"Whatever you want, Tally. If you want me to see this through with you, I will. If you want someone else, I'll go put in for a transfer right now."

She wrapped her arms around his waist and tucked her head against his chest. "You, Falcon. I want you. I'm so scared. I don't want to go to Hell."

"You won't. I won't let you." Falcon knew better than to make promises he couldn't keep, but this one had fallen out of his mouth like old bubblegum. "I swear on my magick." And yet another bomb. Maybe he could have the Powers That Be sew his mouth shut?

"Don't do that!" she gasped, a look of horror blooming on her face. "What if I fail?"

"You won't fail." Fuck. His mouth just kept moving and shit just kept falling out of it. "I'll be here."

"All the time?"

"Yeah. There are some conditions to your parole. You'll be without magick in the mortal realm. I'm not leaving you to fend for yourself."

"Wait, what? Without magick?" Her eyebrows shot up into her hairline, as if they were scurrying away from the knowledge. "I can't live without my . . . no." She kept shaking her head.

"Ethelred didn't tell you that part?" He had a feeling he should have asked her what the demon had told her.

Tally stumbled backwards, clutching at her chest. Her skin went ashen; her lovely blue eyes bulged like over-weight koi crammed into brandy snifters. She shook her head, her mouth open, and again he couldn't help comparing her to a fish. This time. a gasping large-mouthed bass out of water.

"Tally?" he ventured.

She swayed for a moment before she collapsed.

Falcon was rooted to the spot, unsure of what to do. He knew he should have tried to catch her, but the time for that had passed. Now what?

The stench of burned eggs filled his nose as Ethelred materialized next to him. "I was holding off on that last bit. Thought it might be a bit too much for her to handle. Seems I was correct."

"Have you been here the whole time?"

Ethelred arched a brow and smirked. "Oh, did I hear all of your courtly protestations and vows of sainthood in shining armor? Why yes, yes, I did." Falcon growled, but before he could make any threats *or* promises, Ethelred spoke again. "Don't you think it's rather unchivalrous to leave the lady fair unconscious on the porch? She might have stopped breathing. Then where will we be?"

Falcon lurched into action, crashing down next to Tally. She was breathing, thank Merlin. He hauled her up into his arms and stood with his precious bundle close to his chest.

"Why don't you kiss her? True love and all that rot to bring her 'round."

"Why don't you fuck right off?"

"Should I really answer that?"

"Heaven gets the first bite of the apple. You have no reason to be here."

"Yes, and how ironic is that? It was our apple to start with." Ethelred laughed. "Don't forget to tuck your wings," he added helpfully as Falcon was about to step through the front door of Tally's house. He grumbled as he tucked them close against his body and took Tally to her room, where he deposited her gently on the bed.

"I think she needs CPR." Ethelred followed behind him.

"Why? She's breathing."

"Well, maybe. But don't you want an excuse to put your lips on hers? To put your hands on—"

"Are you trying to make me into a sex offender? She's passed out, for Merlin's sake." Ethelred shrugged, still wearing that same smug look. "Look, Tally's who you're supposed to corrupt, not me."

"And what would you actually know about Hell's agenda, Diapered One?"

Falcon narrowed his eyes. "I know there are rules, and you're breaking them."

"Really? That's all the ammo you've got? And you wonder why women always go for the bad boys. We're much more fun." Ethelred gave him a measured look. "She propositioned me, you know." The joy he took in those words was as blatant as a little girl's with a new doll.

Without thinking, Falcon drew an arrow and jammed it into the demon's leg. "And you'll fall in love with her if she propositions you again or you *think* about seducing her. Or anyone else you try these tricks on. I won't let you hurt her."

Ethelred looked up at him, his stone features betraying nothing as the red, glittery arrow dissolved to black ash and was absorbed by his skin. "I was mistaken. Love is always an asshole. You may get the girl yet." Ethelred laughed bitterly.

"I don't want the girl. I—"

"That much is obvious. You didn't have to skywrite it," Tally snarled as she sat up.

Ethelred grinned again, the expression bubbling into a laugh. "And that's my cue."

"Your cue was an hour ago," Falcon growled.

"You better get used to me, Candy Wings. We're all going house hunting tomorrow. You know part of Tally's sentence is living in the mortal world. So we're all going to be really close." Ethelred smirked. "Together. In the same house. So, do you want a two-bedroom or a three? She can pick which—" Ethelred snapped his mouth shut. He'd obviously been about to make an allusion to sleeping with Tally. "Oh, Cupid, you are a tricky bastard, aren't you?"

Falcon smiled slyly. "Don't forget it, Rotten Eggs."

Ethelred appraised him coolly. "You can be sure I won't." He disappeared in a puff of smoke.

"What was that about? Moving in together?" Tally's voice reached a pitch that Falcon was sure could shatter glass. "Are you two assholes trying to kill me?"

CHAPTER FIVE

Gypsies, Tramps, and Thieves

"I almost killed my sister after you left last night, demon."
Emilian Grey ran his fingers through his platinum hair
and glowered at Ethelred. Who, in turn, sighed at the over-
wrought drama of it all.

Emilian Grey was a werewolf, with a twin sister who had
escaped the curse that plagued him. He was also Ethelred's
latest assignment.

Ethelred continued to drum his fingers on the table in the
tiny trailer. "And how is this *my* problem, Princeling?" he
replied in his standard *un*affected tone. "You didn't sign
the contract and I was busy." Busy dealing with Tally when
he should have been handling this mess. Because Ethelred
was very affected. The gypsy prince's problem was, in fact,
Ethelred's problem. One that he needed to handle before
the Big Boss found out about it, if he didn't know already.

Emilian Grey was cursed. A gypsy cursed by his own
mother. Ethelred could get around that. He was a Crown
Prince of Hell, after all, but there was a tide of magick and
power that was this prince's birthright—a mantle of evil.
Emilian Grey was the bastard son of Michael Grigorovich,
a very bad man whom Ethelred had worked the long con
on. Michael's soul belonged to him for eternity, but it
hadn't been because Hell wanted him. The Big Boss and

the Bigger Boss had both agreed he needed to be imprisoned for the good of the world.

And all the dark power that had made Michael a danger to this plane of existence waited in the wings for Emilian's taking. Ethelred should have handled this when he'd made his father's contract, by eliminating the stockpile of black magick in Grigorovich blood. He would have, too, if he'd known about Emilian.

Ethelred turned his head slowly to the window, sensing another presence. "There's someone outside."

Emilian nodded, lifting his nose to the air like an animal. "It's Luminista. My sister."

"What, is she babysitting? Tell her to kick rocks."

"She thinks you're going to cheat me." The gypsy prince smiled bitterly.

"I don't want my brother to go to Hell for trafficking with your sort," Luminista snarled as she pushed through the flimsy door.

"Ah, yes. The road to Hell is indeed paved with good intentions," Ethelred agreed. "And yet, I don't see you offering to take this curse from your dearest twin." Oh, how he loved to stir the pot.

"And then put that guilt on his shoulders, too? That would torture him more than bearing the curse himself," she said as she flopped into the plastic-covered chair with a decided lack of grace.

Ethelred had to admit they were both beautiful, a matched, tragic set—white-blond hair, pale steel eyes, and lovely alabaster skin. He'd been tempted to make sex part of the Deal, but with Cupid's sodding curse, that was out. Ethelred, in love? Bah. He didn't have time for that nonsense and more important, he didn't want it. He'd seen the wages of Love on humanity and the cost was too dear. Much, much too dear. He wanted no part of it.

"So, Princess. Why aren't you cursed?"

"Does that matter?" Luminista answered him.

"Everything matters."

The twins looked at each other for a long moment and Emilian nodded. "Tell him. He's our only hope."

Ethelred was used to this kind of scene. Most people didn't summon a demon if they had any other reasonable option.

"Because my mother didn't know about me. I wasn't breathing and the midwife didn't tell her I'd been born."

Ethelred eyed her carefully. "There's more. Tell me all of it. Unless you don't want my help."

"I was dead. And born with a caul."

If Ethelred had been by himself, he would've indulged himself in a full-blown tantrum. He didn't know any way around this. If he negated the prince's curse, Luminista would become the heir and they'd still be in the same canoe up shit creek.

The gypsy prince looked up at him, his eyes full of something Ethelred couldn't and didn't want to name. There was a set determination in the lad's mouth. He looked much older than his twenty years. "What if I die?"

"No!" Luminista cried.

"No matter, Princeling. Then your sister will be cursed. There is great magick in your curse. It's not all bad." No, not all. Just ninety-nine percent of it. He sighed. "I don't think we'll be able to sign your contract today, after all."

"What? I'm sorry I didn't sign. I'll do it, I'll sign right now. Just help me save Luminista."

"No, boy. I'm not trying to punish you. I just don't know if I can help you and it would be bad for business to make a contract I couldn't fulfill."

"Look, demon—" Luminista stood, her hands on her hips. "You don't have to play hardball with us. We'll give you whatever you want."

The fine hairs on the back of his neck stood up, but Ethelred didn't notice as his demonic wheels began to churn around that statement: whatever you want. It really was the most dangerous phrase to utter to anyone Infernal.

"How about you resurrect my mother and let her have the curse? Who is she to decide who suffers?" There was a metallic edge of desperation in his voice.

"She was a hot-tempered gypsy woman. Curses fly out of their mouths the same as breathing." Ethelred sighed. "I once knew a gypsy woman who cursed her lovers in her sleep." When she'd tried to curse *him,* it hadn't gone over so well.

"Why didn't she curse Grigorovich instead? I'm *her* son, too," Emilian asked softly.

"We could ask her if you like. I'm sure she's in Hell for cursing you," Ethelred offered helpfully. "Maybe we could get her to rescind the curse—I'm not sure though because it was uttered during a time of great unhappiness. Sadness is like Infernal glue."

"I don't wish that on her." Emilian looked up at the demon, his eyes full of despair.

"Of course, you don't. Hell is subjective. It's guilt that tortures her." Ethelred rolled his eyes.

"Can I save her? I can't save myself. Maybe I could do something for someone. Something to make up for this evil I've loosed in the world by breathing."

"That's a little overdramatic, don't you think?" Ethelred asked lightly. Everything with these gypsies was overdramatic. Although, he had to admit this curse was kind of a bitch.

"Is it? I can't see any end to this, any answer." Emilian ducked his head into the safety of his folded arms.

"If you're so sure there isn't one, then there isn't," Ethelred answered. This was a tangle, to be sure, but Ethelred had been crafting contracts for millennia. If anyone could find a way around this, Ethelred knew he could. Even if it meant taking it to the Powers That Be.

"That doesn't make any sense, demon," Emilian roared.

"So, now you want to save Mom, too? What about Grigorovich, shall we add him to the list?" He snickered. "I made his deal, you should know."

Emilian's eyes lightened to a caramel, then to a uric yellow as the change hovered over him. His nostrils flared, seeking the scent of fear.

"Stop that. I'm not into bestiality." Ethelred slapped him on the nose as if he were a naughty puppy. Then he inspected his hand for werewolf snot and, finding some, wiped it off on his slacks. "If Grigorovich was sorry for what he did to your mother, would you forgive him?"

"No," Emilian confessed.

"Even if your forgiveness will break the curse?"

"Will it?" Emilian blinked, hope shining from him.

Ethelred almost hated to answer. Almost. "I don't know. I just wanted to see what you'd say." Ethelred shrugged. "Anyway, I have to get the Big Boss in on this, maybe even the Bigger Boss. I hate these bipartisan deals, but we do what we must."

What he really had to do was research. He wasn't saying shit to the Big Boss or the Bigger Boss if he could help it. Ethelred could handle this himself.

He stood and smoothed his slacks. "I'll be in touch, Princeling. For now, secure yourself in those blessed silver chains. I'll be back with a contract as soon as I have a solution."

Ethelred stepped outside, the RV shifting with the change in weight as Luminista followed him.

"Can I talk to you?" she hissed from behind.

"I don't know, can you?" He knew it was an old and overused retort, but he never got tired of it.

"Yes, I can. Glad you see it my way." She grabbed hold of his sleeve and dragged him toward a copse of trees.

"Hey, watch the threads, Princess. Just because you live like a guttersnipe doesn't mean I do."

"Ah, so your true colors are out, demon."

He smirked. "I've never hidden my *colors,* as you call them, Princess." Ethelred watched her for a moment. "I'm a demon. What part of that wasn't obvious?"

"Just because demon starts with a 'd' doesn't mean you have to be a dick, too."

"Your little fangs are precious, but sharpen them on someone else. I'm on a schedule." She reminded him of some socialite's purse dog, yipping and snapping at everything that came too near.

"Of course, you are. Look," she began, but pursed her lips. "I know we don't have much to offer you in trade for your services. We're poor, financially and spiritually. But I will do absolutely anything to save my brother. Do you understand what I'm saying to you? What I'm offering?"

Ethelred's neck prickled again and he was tempted to slap it. He wondered if it was some demonic mosquito the Big Boss had sent to fuck with him.

He knew the moment hellfire blazed in his eyes because the princess flinched, but he was pleased to see that she didn't back down. "I think the more appropriate question would be do *you* understand what it is that you're offering and to whom you're offering it?"

She straightened and pulled herself up to her full height, which was rather tall for a female. The brash princess lifted her chin. "I do."

Luminista wasn't as spiritually bankrupt as she believed. Her sacrifice for her brother was sweet and pure. It made him itch to corrupt her.

"You have strong magick. What if I wanted that?"

"Take it."

"Hmm." His schedule be damned. This was fun. Ethelred reached out one finger and ghosted it down the side of her cheek. She didn't flinch, but her spine stiffened and he smiled with the toothy joy of a predator. "Anything?"

"Anything, demon. Stop playing with us."

"But Luminista," he admonished. "What if that's what I want from you? To play? To raise your hopes and crush them? To give a little, but take everything? I'm a Crown Prince of Hell. Do you think I attained my status by being kind or giving handouts to poor little gypsy trash?"

Something inside him ruptured at those words. Something he'd never felt before. Her eyes watered, almost like she was going to cry and he felt . . .

Unwell.

"Fine. Then you can have that, too. Whatever it takes to save my brother."

That cold prickle on the back of his neck had sharpened into a stabbing sensation. Ethelred froze. Something wasn't right. Were those the twinges of regret? Oh, this didn't bode well at all.

"I read in my mother's journals that many witches attained great power by making deals with demons. Deals of the flesh." Luminista began working her fingers over the buttons of her shirt.

"Take it back!" he growled.

"What? Take what back?" she asked, desperation in her voice.

"Your *proposition!*" Ethelred demanded.

Her hands stilled. "You don't want me? I don't have anything else to trade, Ethelred."

"I don't want you to trade anything. Take it back! Right now!"

"Will you make the deal if I do?"

"I already said I would. You weren't listening. Damn it,

take it back!" By the light in her eyes, he realized his mistake. He'd played his hand. He'd shown her a chink in his armor by letting her hear the urgency in his voice. Fuck it, she was desperate; well, so was he. "You don't understand. I have my own curse to deal with. I pissed Cupid off last night and the first person to proposition me . . . I will love."

Her eyes narrowed. "Oh, really?"

"You don't want the love of a demon. It's a bad, bad thing."

She licked her lips, and Ethelred knew she saw this as the answer to all of her problems. "If you love me, you'll take care of me and my brother."

Panic bloomed. "Or I'll destroy your brother because he's the only thing you'd ever love more than me. Love with demons isn't love. I'm not even into women right now. It's— Just take it back. I said I'd help you, you awful creature."

"No, I don't think so. In fact, just for good measure—"

He clamped a hand over her mouth, but she bit him.

Rather than let go, he found he liked it. The sensation went straight to his cock. "Harder, Princess," he growled.

Lightning exploded all around them and suddenly, Luminista wasn't fighting him anymore; she clung to him.

"Look, Uriel wants you to take it back, too."

To her credit, she released him. "I don't care. There is nothing and no one worth my brother's freedom. Not you, not Uriel, no one. So he can suck it. I don't take it back. You will love me, Ethelred."

And to his supreme disgust, he found he did.

Or he'd eaten bad sushi.

CHAPTER SIX

Confounded Cupidity

Yes, Tally thought for the millionth time, the Powers That Be were trying to kill her.

No magick? She was already in Hell. Tally had never been without her magick. Some witches didn't get their power until puberty, but Tally had been flush with magick since birth. She'd even had to wear a diminishing bracelet in Academy so her power didn't outstrip her tutors'.

Now, nothing. The hardest part was that she could still feel it, tingling at the edges of her awareness begging to get out. It hadn't been reliable since the great and terrible evil incident, that was true, but to be forbidden to do something that came as naturally as breathing?

Sheer Hell.

Not even house hunting with an infinite budget had helped.

Okay, so it had helped a little, but only a very little. Tally had to live in the mortal realm. How was she supposed to do that? What was that supposed to teach her? Killing people was bad? She knew that. To be thankful for her magick? She always had been. No, this wasn't to learn a lesson; it felt more like punishment.

That she supposed she deserved.

It hadn't taken her long to choose a house. If she had to

suffer, she might as well do it with a view. She chose a large, hacienda-style home that perched on the 'Tween Waters on Captiva Island in Florida. Walking those pretty beaches had been the last good memory she had of her mother.

There was no place better for peace and introspection than the beach.

The warm Gulf breeze on her face did nothing to dispel the sensation that her angelic and demonic parole officers were both plotting her doom. The demon, sad chaperone that he was, was absent, and Falcon looked just as good, just as forbidden as ever.

She wasn't going to make it.

Tally kept reminding herself of what Falcon had said after she passed out. He didn't want the girl. So, why couldn't she leave it alone? She almost wished that he hadn't used his magick to unpack her belongings. Then she'd have something to do with her hands, busywork for her brain, rather than picking everything between them to death.

She couldn't deny that even after everything, she still wanted him. Maybe he could shoot her with an anti-lust arrow? Tally would ask him, if only she didn't have to admit she still lusted after him to get the damn thing.

Falcon had already moved his things in. They were going to watch a movie tonight. What did that have to do with being on parole? The Powers didn't move in mysterious ways; they moved in stupid ways.

It was like the whole system was designed so she'd fail.

She repeated that thought to herself again. Then she whispered it aloud. Tally knew no matter Falcon's faults, he didn't want bad things for her. He'd always been honest and he said he wanted her to succeed, so this didn't make any sense to her at all.

Tally turned her back on the amazing view and retreated

to her bedroom, looking for her granny knickers. Those things were better than any chastity belt. She wouldn't be showing her witchy bits to anyone in those.

But she knew it was just postponing the inevitable. She and Falcon had already crossed the line, and while he didn't want her as a partner, he wanted her body. And that's what she wanted from him.

"Shut up!" she hissed to herself. That devilish voice in her head sounded too much like her own desire. If it had been Ethelred's, she could have done a better job of ignoring it. If she had too much time alone in her own head, she'd convince herself that shagging Falcon was Fate and beyond her control.

It's what was going to happen anyway. She'd advised Middy to get it over with and shag the hell out of Dred Shadowins. She'd done it and now Middy was living her Happily Ever After.

Not that she assumed that's what would happen between herself and Falcon, but maybe they were just meant to fuck like rabid bears who'd gotten into a shipment of Viagra. It was possible.

Yeah, possible, but what was more likely was that she was still basing her self-worth on having sex with a guy she'd built into the perfect warlock in her head. In reality, he was just a guy.

Tally had done some self-reflection while hanging out on her balcony this morning and she'd come to the conclusion she was trying too hard. Not at being good and deserving the Second Chance, but at all of the things she'd always thought she was "supposed" to do.

Since her Academy days, Tally had always thought there was a certain order in which things were supposed to happen. When they didn't, she made them happen, even if they weren't what she wanted, even if it involved settling.

The revelation had been indeed a startling moment of

clarity and it had surprised her. In her own mind, she'd always thought she was bucking the system—she was the strong loner, determined to do things at her own pace and in her own way. The whole time she'd been overcompensating because she didn't fit in. Not fitting in was her attempt to do something the way she was supposed to, even if it was being the rebel.

Maybe this was part of the lesson she was supposed to be learning? How was she supposed to succeed if she didn't even know what her end goal was, besides not going to Hell?

Tally didn't think she could handle ten days of this. When she looked at herself, she didn't like what she saw. Shine-a-light therapy was kick-ass in small doses, but now she was ready for it to go away. It was ugly and it hurt. She knew she'd have to face it all eventually, but again, in small doses.

"Tally?" Falcon's voice echoed up the stairs.

Shit. He was back already and she still hadn't found her granny knickers. The ankle-length maxi dress would have to do. She padded down the cold marble stairs barefoot, enjoying the contrast to the heat of the day.

Seeing Falcon standing there, his wings hidden, with a Blockbuster bag in his hand, she was hit with a sudden wave of awkward. He was wearing jeans. She hadn't thought he could be any hotter than he'd been in the red leather pants she'd seen him in last Samhain, but the distressed denim riding low on his hips and the gun show that was currently playing underneath his UFC T-shirt gave her a hot flash. The corner of his mouth curled up in a lazy grin.

"Hey," he said casually.

"Incognito, I see." She smiled.

"Yeah, I figured laid-back was the tone for the evening. Plus, I can't sit on the couch with the wings."

She followed him to the front room and noticed he still

smelled like cotton candy—she was going to have the very devil of a time keeping her nose to herself. Maybe her hands, too, because the scent was just as intoxicating as it had been the other night when he'd kissed her. Tally shivered as sensation warmed in the pit of her belly. Tally hated herself in that moment. She knew what was on the line and still couldn't stop thinking about fucking her parole officer. Nothing she did seemed to help curb her desire for Falcon Cherrywood.

If you're listening, give a witch a hand, huh? I can't do this by myself.

"You can't possibly be cold." He studied her intently.

"No, not cold." She decided to be honest. "You still smell like cotton candy."

"Sorry, it comes with the job. I can hide the wings and the arrows, even that damn toga, but the scent has decided to stay." He shrugged his massive shoulders.

"It smells good. I like it."

He flashed her a wicked grin and that warmth in the pit of her belly spread through her limbs.

"Although, I do agree the toga had to go. If only because of the never-ending storm of crap you'd get from Raven and Hawk."

"I can't exactly wear this when engaging Cupidity," he said, pointing down at himself.

"No, but I think you could replace that with red leather pants."

"Merlin. Don't get started on those again."

"Why not? Is leather disagreeing with nether bits genetic? Because you know I tried to get Middy to wear a baroness costume to the Gargoyle Masque but—"

"TMI, Tally. I don't want to know about my sister and her reaction to leather pants."

"Well, I was just thinking I could draft a charm and . . ."

Except that she couldn't. Not for ten days. She growled in frustration.

"What kind of pizza do you want?" He tried to change the subject.

"Eh." She shrugged.

"You're not one of those witches who only eats a salad if someone is looking, are you? We're going to be spending a lot of time together, so you might as well let everything hang out now." Falcon dropped the case of beer on the floor next to the coffee table.

She smiled. "No, you know I eat like a horse. And I always let it all hang out." She sighed. "Do you remember the night after graduation?"

"You mean that night you'd been stealing my beer and then ditched me for Tristan Belledare? Yeah, I remember," Falcon said as he sat down.

"I think my life would have been a lot different if I'd stayed with you," she confessed.

He turned to look at her, the late afternoon sun casting a warm glow on his face and a light in the dark depths of his gaze. "Do you? What do you think would have happened?"

Was it seductive promise she heard in his voice? No, it couldn't be and if it was, it *shouldn't* be. Tally was determined to relate to Falcon without sex. He was her parole officer. Tally didn't want to go to Hell for one lay. Even one lay with Falcon Cherrywood.

The old adage that it was easier to ask forgiveness than permission gonged through her head. She flushed and turned her back to him under the guise of putting the first movie into the DVD player. "I'm sure I would have downed a few more beers, passed out on your bed, and you would have slept on the couch and saved me from myself. I could have gone home in the morning, embarrassed from drooling on you in my alcohol-induced stupor, but I think I would have made different choices."

"Then I'm sorry I didn't try harder to get you to stay." The sincere look on his face made her feel slightly guilty for making it sound like his fault. She hadn't meant it that way.

"I don't know, maybe I would've found my way to Fuckedupville anyway." Tally turned and flashed him a smile.

"Maybe not." He searched her face. "So that night you were actually drunk as opposed to the night you were naked in my bed?"

"So, what's it like being an angel?" Tally changed the subject; she didn't want to answer that one.

"I got to see mud-wrestling Valkyries the other day." Falcon popped the tab on one of the beers, a Blue Moon, seemingly content to let her control the path of their conversation. "I don't feel any different than I did when I was a warlock."

Tally sat down on the couch next to him. "Is this all there is to my parole? Movies and pizza?" she ventured, not completely sure she wanted the answer.

"For now. Which movie did you choose?"

"The Howling."

"Remember the last time you watched that?" Falcon smirked. "Raven scared the shit out of you and Middy."

"He's lucky we didn't shoot him with anything more dangerous than a flowerpot torpedo."

"Middy promised him clumpy cat litter next time."

"She always promises cat litter." Tally popped open her own beer and took a long drink.

"Yes, but I *know* she'll deliver."

Tally was comfortable now; he was just Falcon Cherrywood, older brother type. The movie started and Tally was entranced. She loved this movie, even though it scared the bemerlin out of her. Rick Baker was a makeup god. She knew she'd die a screaming fangirl death if she ever met him in the flesh. Maybe he'd do the lamia makeup when they made her biography into a horror movie.

She always found herself peeking through her fingers, no matter how many times she watched the movie. It didn't take long for Falcon's hand to close around her wrists and pull the shield away from her eyes.

"Don't be such a girl."

Tally couldn't help it. She turned her head away and Falcon just laughed and tucked her against him.

"There, the big bad wolf can't get you now."

She turned her face into his shoulder before she realized what she was doing. He smelled so good and his shoulders were so wide, it was easy to believe nothing would, in fact, get her while he was there. Her hand, of its own volition, had found its way up around his neck and she clung to him for dear life.

Until she peeked at the massive screen again.

Gods, everything was larger than life on that ginormous screen. It was like being there. She'd never had the sac to watch it on warlockian 3-D. It was like being *in* the movie. That was a little too much for her taste.

Falcon was so warm. Were all angels warm like this?

His calloused hand was on the nape of her neck, her curls tangling around his fingers as if they were sentient and seeking his touch.

She knew where this was headed. It's what always happened when a witch and warlock watched these kinds of movies. It was an excuse to pretend to be afraid and an excuse to play rescuer. It was a too-familiar trope, but that didn't stop it from happening. Just his fingers on the bare skin of her neck sent an electric awareness through her body and she needed to be closer to him, needed more. Visions of his hand sliding down her spine, or using her hair to drag her to him for another kiss assaulted her.

Indeed, it was an assault. She tried to shut and lock the door of her imagination against the onslaught, but need battered through her defenses. There was so much more Falcon Cherrywood could do with those hands than touch her hair. They could skim down her bare arms, or up the exposed line of her leg. They could dip down past the buttons of her soft, cotton dress and cup her breasts, his tanned flesh stark against her pale skin. They could push up past the line of leg she'd readily offered and delve into the hot, wet sheath that ached for him.

His hands were the tools of sin. She'd never wanted a man like she wanted this one. Tally had never been aroused like this, already wet and aching without her fantasies, without touch. Sex had always been something Tally gave like a reward after her chosen warlock had jumped through the correct hoops, after he'd made her feel what she needed to feel.

It scared her that Falcon had this control over her, because it *was* control. It was power. She feared it and she wanted it, but what would happen in the aftermath?

Her body didn't care about the aftermath; all her flesh knew was her breasts were pressed up against his chest, her nipples tight and hard at the contact. It only cared about the heat coming from his body and the promise of his touch.

Tally prayed he'd grab her and pull her against him the way he had before; he'd take away her culpability. She wanted him to demand this of her, to angle her just so and plunder her mouth and . . .

His hand slid down her spine to settle at the small of her back and the heat of his touch burned her through the thin fabric. Tally knew she could tilt her face up to his and their lips would be only a breath apart.

Or the way her body was angled, she could shift and be in his lap; his solid thighs would be beneath her ass and his cock would be, oh, so very close to where she wanted it. Did she dare?

Falcon tilted his head down to look at her. The hard line of his mouth was softer somehow and time stopped when she turned her face up to his. The air was gone and she couldn't breathe. She couldn't move.

The screen turned blue as the DVD player stopped automatically and shattered the moment like glass. Tally hopped off the couch like it was on fire and promptly put the DVD back in its case.

"My kind of girl," he said.

"How's that?" she asked, trying desperately not to blush.

"I can't stand it when witches put DVDs back in the wrong case or stack them on top of the DVD player. Drives me nuts. I'm a bit of a neat freak."

"Me, too. Do you feel like another one?"

"Sure, whatever you want to do." He gave her the same lazy grin that could charm the drawers off a cleric.

She wanted to sneak a peak at his package and see if he was really up for whatever she wanted to do. Not that she was going to act on it or anything, but it would be nice to know she wasn't the only one so affected. If she was, that would be embarrassing. She didn't want to get caught checking though. Tally chose *The Ring* this time.

"You brought a lot of good ones," she said.

When she sank back down, she sat safely on her own side of the couch. Not that she didn't enjoy being close to him, but perhaps the interruption of the blue screen had been fortuitous. She liked it a little too much and it had dissolved her good intentions like sugar in the rain.

It wasn't too long before the scenes were getting tense and things were popping out of places and making her squeal, but still she managed to keep her distance from Falcon. Until he decided to wait until she was engrossed in a scene and startle her with a poke to the ribs.

She retaliated with a slap to his arm. He made a grab for her wrist and Tally wasn't about to let him have a hold on her so easily. She poked him back and was delighted when she got a reaction. He was ticklish.

Tally narrowed her eyes as she decided on a course of action. She launched herself at him, but he caught her. He'd disabled her attack with one move. One delicious, resolve-shattering move.

Falcon brought her crashing down into his lap and he held her secure with her hands behind her back. The bastard still had one hand free. That wasn't what demanded her attention though; it was the fact she didn't have to worry about getting caught checking his package. The ridge of his jeans was pressed fully against her and there was no doubt Falcon wanted her.

"Oh," was all she could manage, unable to breathe. His eyes were dark with desire, but he didn't move. Neither did she.

"This is what happens when you play the tickle game," Falcon admonished.

"You started it." Tally shifted against him. Was that a fire hose he had in his pocket or was it a cannon from a warship?

"Are you going to finish it?" he asked as he used his other hand to anchor her against him.

"I finish everything I start."

He released her hands and she rested her palms on his shoulders for a moment before she used her thumbs in an offensive against his ribs. Falcon reared back, startled, and their combined weight brought the couch to its back legs, an unhappy venture until they both overcorrected the other way and the righted furniture sent them sprawling to the floor.

Falcon managed to roll them mid-flight so she landed on top of him, which was exceedingly thoughtful considering he'd have crushed her like an empty beer can against a frat boy's head.

Of course, the problem remained that his bits were pressed against her bits. Only now, he was flat on his back, his hands were still on her hips, and she was flattened against the wide expanse of his chest.

"Are you trying to kill me?" Falcon ground out softly.

"You're the one who flipped the couch."

"You're the one who has her bare mound against my cock."

Tally blushed hotly, her mouth suddenly glued shut.

"I didn't say it was a bad way to go," Falcon said as he tightened his hold.

She cried out at the friction on her clit when she moved. "We can't."

"I know. It's a Shall Not." He still didn't release her.

"Of course, it is. Everything that feels good is a Shall Not."

Tally gasped again when Falcon guided her hips in a measured roll and moved her against his cock.

"Do you like that, Drusilla? Look at you, so beautiful with your golden hair mussed, your sweet lips parted, and your eyes bright with desire for me. No, don't look away," he demanded when she turned her head from his gaze. "I'd see all of you if I could." Falcon undid the first button on her dress. "Will you let me see you?"

Tally had never felt so beautiful, so desirable, in all of her life. Not even in the pergola before he'd passed out. That thought alone, remembering what had happened, should have shocked her out of this haze of lust, but it didn't. She couldn't deny him, and unlike the other men she'd been with, she didn't *want* to deny him.

Fuck it. That little voice inside her head had been right: Forgiveness was easier than permission. Tally made quick work of the top buttons and bared herself to his view.

She knew her breasts would fit neatly in the palms of his hands and she wanted him to touch her, but all he did was look. His gaze was a caress, sliding over her heated skin. Falcon's touch moved from her hips to push her dress up around her waist and his hands guided her again.

He thrust up to meet her, grinding against her slit, and she wanted nothing more than to reach between them and undo the button at the waist of his jeans.

"A kiss," he said as he tangled his hand in her hair.

Tally bent down to meet him and she kissed him softly, as if it was her first. His mouth was hard and unforgiving, but so sweet. She swept her tongue across his and nipped at his bottom lip. He returned the caress with his own, and explored the hot cavern of her mouth.

The pressure built between her thighs and she was ready to come. She tried to stop the rhythm against him; but he wouldn't let her and she didn't want it to be over.

"Don't stop," he whispered his breath warm on her mouth. "Come with me, Drusilla."

She would have come right then, on command, but she had a sharp pain in her abdomen. Deep inside, it felt like someone had kicked her in the taco and was pinching her ovaries for good measure.

She'd just started her period.

Drusilla Tallow broke the sound barrier dismounting her chosen steed and barreled into the bathroom and slammed the door.

Tally could only pray Merlin was merciful and she hadn't bled all over his jeans. She'd have to kill herself with the nearest available blunt object. Or she could always drown herself in the toilet. There was no way to apologize for that or to live it down. The site of one's genital area covered in blood is not something any male would easily forget.

He knocked on the door just seconds later and he even

tried the doorknob. She thanked the Goddess she'd had the sense to lock the damn thing. What warlock did that? Followed a witch into the bathroom? Of course, he was an angel now, so maybe that changed the rules.

"Tally, what's wrong?"

"I'll be out in a minute."

"What's wrong?"

"I said I'll be out in a minute."

"Beer shits? Look, it happens. No big deal."

That insensitive asshole. It only made it worse when they thought they were being sensitive. "It's not that. I started my rag."

Oh, great. Why couldn't she have come up with something else to call it? Like she had earlier, in her own head. Her scarlet friend. Her Aunt Rosy. The Red Sea. Something. Anything besides "the rag."

She palmed her forehead. Now she really needed those granny panties. She couldn't run around with a tampon and no knickers.

"That's no biggie, either. I assume you need underthings now. Where do you keep your panties for that time of the month?"

Was he shitting her blue? Did the man just ask where her . . .

"I have a sister. I have a mother. I've had girlfriends. This isn't unfamiliar territory."

Tally was ready to die. It couldn't happen fast enough. Suddenly, the mirror over the sink shimmered and Ethelred appeared.

"You're welcome," he said.

"Do you mind?" she shrieked.

"Not usually. Don't say I never gave you anything."

"This is your doing? Why?" She stomped her foot as hard as she could while propped on the toilet.

"Otherwise, you would have broken a Shall Not. If you're going to do that, it will be with me, thank you very much."

"Hey, don't say that so loud. I don't fancy a lightning bolt to the tampon from Uriel."

"You're the least of his concerns. Now, can you imagine my shame if we get you just because you shagged Stupid Cupid? Bah. I'd rather your demise be something elegant and, of course, planned by me."

"You're a dick."

Ethelred looked thoughtful for a moment. "This isn't the first time I've heard that." A package of granny panties and a box of tampons appeared on the edge of the sink. "You can thank me later, I have to run. I hear a gypsy princess calling my name."

Ethelred disappeared before she'd had a chance to ask him if he'd been watching them. "Is someone in there with you?"

Tally sighed. "No, he left."

"Ethelred. Should have known. Are you okay?"

Yeah, Tally was fine. But was Falcon? She'd been straddling him and she had visions of red humiliation streaked over his jeans. She knew there was nothing for it but to ask.

"So, um . . . did I . . ." The words refused to leave her mouth.

"No. And it still wouldn't bother me if you had."

"Why is that?" she said snidely. She probably shouldn't have asked. A smart witch would have left it alone.

"The fact that my wings are pink doesn't mean I didn't get my red ones."

Red wings?

Tally's eyes goggled and she spluttered, choking on her own spit. She'd never be able to look him in the face again. Considering recent events, she gathered that's what the Powers That Be were gunning for.

CHAPTER SEVEN

A Bad, Bad Thing

"Good morning, Sunshine!"

Tally awoke from a dead sleep to find Ethelred wrapped in a precariously low-slung towel, sprawled across her reading chair. She'd never look at it the same way again.

"My door was locked for a reason."

The demon shrugged. "We need to talk."

Tally rolled over and pulled the covers over her head. "I don't want to talk. I want to lie here and die quietly. Alone."

He tugged on the sheet. "Look, if it's the cramps—"

Tally popped upright in the bed and fixed a look on Ethelred that would have caused a lesser being to whimper. "If I had my magick, I'd show you cramps," she snarled.

Ethelred wasn't nonplussed. "That's why you don't. Now, move it." He snapped his fingers.

"It's not even your turn," she whined.

"I'm never going to get my turn the way things are going. You're just going to crash and burn. Literally. I already told you, I don't want to win by default."

"You're perverse." She flopped back down on the bed. Tally shrieked when a bolt of energy zapped her in the ass, but she still made no move to get up.

"Get. Up."

"What are you going to do if I don't, hmm? You are not the boss of me until it's your day."

The stabbing pain in her belly intensified a hundredfold and Tally cried out.

"That's what. Maybe I'm not supposed to have you today, but I will. It's for your own good. Get up and I'll make it stop."

"All of it?" she demanded through clenched teeth.

He sighed. "Yes, fine. All of it. Can't have you swimming in the Gulf with your Aunt Flo. Might cause a shark frenzy and you'd die before I get what I want."

The pain eased. "I don't want to swim in the—" Tally broke off as the twinges began again. "Fine." He was a right bastard to use that against her, but Tally supposed she couldn't expect any better. He was a demon after all.

"Meet me down on the beach in five." He walked through her locked door as if it didn't exist.

So much for locking the damn door. Falcon could have come through it at any time last night if he'd really wanted to. Or any time. *Falcon.* Tally sighed aloud. She had to get it through her head that sexy time with Falcon equaled apocalyptic humiliation.

And it was a Shall Not.

Ethelred had done her a favor. It had been unpleasant in the execution, but it was a screwed-up world where it was a demon who'd done right by her—a demon she'd just met while the warlock she'd known her whole life was shoving her down a slippery slope with both hands.

She wasn't naïve enough to think Ethelred's motives were altruistic, or that he wasn't actively seeking her failure. But still.

Tally changed in the bathroom, thankful that Ethelred's little gift had made itself scarce, and then she wandered past Falcon's bedroom. She hadn't wanted to see him, not yet, but it still pricked her that he wasn't there. How was he supposed to see to her rehabilitation *in absentia*? Hadn't he just sworn that he'd always be with her through this? Hadn't he promised her that he wouldn't let her fail?

The simple answer would be that he couldn't do any of those things.

Tally wandered down to the beach, flitting across the road in her bare feet only to bury them in the sand. Thousands of shells lay scattered up and down the shoreline and Tally dug her toes into the warmth.

Ethelred waited for her, waist deep in the water. The sunlight fell on his golden skin, crowning him, and he looked almost angelic.

"Don't you think that's a little much?" She snorted. "I expected to hear a choir or something."

"Go big or go home, dollface. All demons are showmen." The light behind him disappeared.

"So, what is this about?" She tried to open herself to the experience. The sooner she learned what she had to do, the sooner he would be out of her face and she could get her magick back.

"Come out here to me, and I'll show you."

Doubt flared. "I don't think so."

"Look, sweetheart. We've got a lot on our plate today and we can't even get started until you come here."

She sighed and stepped into the water. Tally waded out to him carefully, the water rising up to her chest quickly. Something told her to turn around, to go back, but she didn't. He had to be on a sandbar—unless he wasn't standing at all, but was held up by some demon magick.

Tally was good at a lot of things, but swimming wasn't one of them. She'd always used magick to keep herself afloat. He continued to smile as realization dawned on her. Tally backed away from him, shaking her head in earnest, but suddenly she couldn't move. Seaweed had tangled around her legs and jerked her down under the water. She opened her mouth to scream and saltwater poured down her throat.

She flailed, seeking purchase on something solid, but there was only the water. Only the pressure on her chest and the burn in her lungs. Tally could see the surface, the bright blue sky overhead, the sun. Her fingertips broke the surface of the water, but she couldn't get free of the seaweed.

And Ethelred stood over her, watching her drown.

Just as the pressure in her chest splintered, Ethelred hauled her up out of the water and carried her to shore. She spluttered and coughed, not caring if the water she'd started to swallow sprayed over his broad shoulders.

"You're a bastard," she wheezed.

He laid her down in the sand with a cocky grin, his demon magick healing her. "I know. Now you do, too."

"What was the point of that? Besides to terrify me?" If there'd been anything within reach, she would have thrown it at him.

"You did exactly what I told you to do."

"You're my fucking parole officer."

"I am. Now, why did you do what I told you to do, even though your gut told you not to?"

"Because you told me to!" she cried. What a stupid fucking question. How was she supposed to learn anything with a demon who used circular reasoning?

"You don't understand. Maybe it's too complex a comparison."

"I'm not stupid," she growled.

"Well, that could be argued given your recent choices." He smiled at her and she couldn't help but be warmed by it, as much as that pissed her off. "No, Drusilla," Ethelred said kindly, "you're not stupid. So it's beyond me why you let the men in your life dictate your actions and your happiness."

Tally didn't speak.

"You knew exactly when Martin Vargill began to deviate from the path and yet you followed him. Why?"

"I thought he loved me." Tally didn't like saying that out loud. She knew it in her own head, but the sound of it was pathetic and it disgusted her.

"How could he love you, Tally?" the demon asked, his voice still kind and soft, but his words like razor blades.

"Yeah. We all know I'm not that witch, okay? I'm not the one who gets the white knight and Happily Ever After. I've always known that's not me." Tally hated how brittle her voice sounded. How vulnerable.

"Why have you always known that? Did someone tell you?"

"Are you my parole officer or my fucking therapist?" she snapped.

"I'm whatever I need to be. Answer the question," Ethelred prompted in a stern, but not unkind voice.

"No, no one told me. I know from experience."

"Again, I ask why you'd think anyone would love you?"

"Fuck you." She flailed at him, her open palm flying through the air with one stinging slap with his name on it, but he caught her wrist easily.

"No one will ever love you, sweetheart. Not until you learn to love yourself."

Tears threatened and Tally would have rather gone back under the water than let the demon see her cry.

He pulled her against him and hugged her. "There, there, darling. Time for that later. We have to move on to part two of today's lesson."

"How does this help your cause?" She tried not to sniff.

"That's for me to know and you to maybe find out. Although, I like that you're looking for the angle. Everyone has one, you know. No matter what they tell you." He straightened, suddenly dressed in a perfectly tailored, white pinstriped suit—Al Capone Chic. "Now, we're going to Piccadilly. I am in need of tea."

"So you almost drown me, rip me to shreds, and make me cry and you want me to go with you to buy tea?" Her voice cracked.

"Now, now. Watch that inner bitch kitty. Settle down. And why not tea? A good pot will fix you right up. Come along." He held out his arm and her swimsuit morphed into a long, white summer dress reminiscent of the Victorian era.

There was nothing for it but to go where he led—previous lesson aside. He teleported them to Piccadilly Square in England.

"Is Cupid going to be a good lay, do you think?" Ethelred asked as he took her hand and placed it on his arm like the most proper gentleman in days of yore, a hard contrast to what was coming out of his mouth. "I mean, when it finally happens?"

"Why? Uriel cut you off?" Tally raised a brow.

"Call me curious." Ethelred smiled.

"Of course, he will be," Tally said.

"You hesitated," he said lightly as he led her into The Fountain Tea Room Café. Then he switched subjects. "You should pick up a tea box for the Angel of Death."

Tally's head spun at how fast he switched between topics. It kept her constantly off balance and she was sure it was by Infernal design.

"Yes, I suppose," Tally agreed. She still wasn't sure how you told a man you were sorry for feeding him to the Abyss, but wasn't it the thought that counted? He'd gotten a good job out of it and really, before this whole mess he'd been aimless, content to be worshipped by witches everywhere as an ex-war hero.

Okay. She had to be honest with herself. It wasn't just feeding him to the Abyss. She'd known what the creature inside her was going to do to him and she hadn't been strong enough to stop it. Tally hadn't been willing to fight the pain that came when the lamia didn't get her way.

"Hmm, or not. Let's get back to the dish at hand. Cupid. Why did you hesitate?"

"I didn't hesitate. I simply wanted to know why it concerns you."

"I spoke with Falcon this morning and I was interested to see what he thought about the matter."

Tally knew what Ethelred was doing. He was trying to screw with her self-confidence and manipulate her. He kept tearing her down, only to give her the tools to build herself up again. Rinse and repeat. Like a kid who stomped on anthills. She wasn't going to respond. As if Falcon would ever talk to Ethelred about what had happened between them. Hell, the cheeky bastard had probably been watching from the bathroom mirror. Nope, it wasn't going to work.

He flashed her a mischievous grin that would have been more at home on a kid who'd won a shopping spree in his favorite toy store.

Why was he so happy?

So you'll ask him why he's happy, dumbass. Then he would proceed to pick and tear at every little thing Falcon had said. She wasn't going to play an emotional game of Chutes and Ladders. They were all Chutes that led straight to Hell, literally.

Ethelred proceeded to order for her. He'd chosen a cherry tart and Lady Grey tea. She wondered if he was alluding to something. Tally had to stop analyzing him to death; it was what he wanted her to do because his end goal was to make her crazy.

"What about Uriel?" she asked as they chose a table.

"What about him, doll?"

Tally decided he was evil. He was so casual about everything; nothing ever moved him to any sort of emotion except boredom or amusement. He was a total sociopath. Too bad everything he said was colored with sensuality. It was in the way he moved, the way he spoke, even the way the bastard sipped his tea.

"He stole Gabriel's horn to blow up my end table, so I have to know, is he good at blowing *your* horn?" Tally tossed his own devil-may-care aplomb back at him.

Ethelred's cheeks ballooned out as he fought to keep his tea from shooting out of his mouth like the spray from a fire hose. He gulped and spluttered, his gold-flecked eyes watering with the effort. He dabbed his napkin at his mouth surreptitiously.

"Oh, my. I may have to rethink my strategy with you, my dear girl."

"Tit for tat, darling." Tally smiled as she took a dainty bite of her tart.

"I really want you to fail, Drusilla." He said this with an ominous pleasure. "We'd have so much fun in eternity."

"I'd rather not."

"I know. What was it Martin Vargill did to earn your allegiance, hmm? Oh, yes, he told you that you were pretty. He made you feel special. I could make you feel very special, Drusilla."

Tally didn't want to admit how sharp his little arrows were, but she knew she'd have to face her own actions if she wanted to be worthy of her Second Chance.

"Yes, that's what he did. He treated me with respect, at first. Then he made me believe no one else would want me after he was finished. He was mostly right, but only because I let him be right."

Ethelred smiled at her. "Do you think Falcon is going to be any different? It's your fault he's Cupid, you know. He was battling with the lamia, or 'the great and terrible evil' as you've come to call her, and was knocked from his broom. He was choking to death on his own blood when Merlin found him. *Your fault,"* he said cheerfully.

Tally was horrified at the imagery of what she'd allowed to happen. How could she have thought she deserved a Second Chance? So many people had been hurt, so many had died because of her weakness, her selfishness.

Self-loathing was a fountain that had frozen in the winter of her redemption, but as she was faced with the truth, it melted into a raging sea that drowned all hope.

"Yes, there it is, my Drusilla," Ethelred said as he petted her hair the way he would a choleric child. "Taste it. Let it fill you until you can't breathe, until it chokes you."

She knew he only wanted to break her, but his strength lay in righteousness. The truth was a sword and Ethelred was a ruthless opponent.

"You're a raging cock, you know that?" she choked out. "It's our first date and already you're trying to get me to move in with you in Hell. I've been known to be fast, but so far, I'm completely unimpressed."

She took a bite of her cherry tart as if he hadn't just ripped out her heart.

He raised a brow and finished his tea.

"You're not special because you can whip out the horns and a tail," Tally drawled as if he were her harmless next-door neighbor instead of a demon who could summon raging hellfire and a thirty-two-ounce Big Gulp of whoop ass.

"I could drill you with my tail," Ethelred said conversationally. "I think that's pretty damn special."

"Boring. You're not that hot." She patted his hand with a dismissive gesture that was enough to insult his manhood.

The entire room burst into flames, the fire crawling up the walls and draping like deadly, living ivy over everything in its path. She heard the screaming and the terror of the tormented souls who grabbed for her as the walls melted.

"Hot enough for you?" he growled.

"Temper, temper, Ethelred," Tally admonished casually, even though he'd scared the sweet living Goddess out of her. "You can toss the slings and arrows, but I have to bow and scrape? I've held evil in my body even your *boss* doesn't want to deal with. Stop fucking with me."

He leaned back in his chair and crossed his legs. "Oh, this is the Tally I like. Much better. Perhaps you learned something today after all?"

"Look what you did to my pastry!" She had no idea how she was going to survive another day with him, let alone the entirety of her parole. "Can I have another one to go?"

"Do you think your hips can take it?" he asked this as if it were a serious question.

Tally gasped.

"You seem determined to make me the gay best friend. I'm simply obliging." He shrugged.

Tally looked down at her curves. "With friends like you . . ." She let the sentence hang.

"Actually, maybe we should order you two. I've been looking into Cupid's past and he seems to like witches with a little more here." Ethelred motioned to his backside. "Junk in the trunk, girlfriend." He shook his head as if Tally's rump were a shame on all rumps.

"I hate you."

"Because I'm beautiful?" He tossed his head.

Tally groaned. "Because you're an ass cookie."

"Ass cookie, huh? I don't know if I've heard that one before. At least it was creative. You know, for a female, you say 'ass' an awful lot."

"For a demon, you seem pretty concerned about my language use."

"Demon doesn't have to mean ill-mannered. You've got

a mouth that could blister the ears off an entire outlaw biker gang."

"Thank you." Tally smirked.

"I don't suppose it would matter to you if I said it wasn't a compliment?" Ethelred made a sound as if he were the most put-upon creature in creation to be saddled with such a female.

She grinned, pleased to finally move him to something, even if it was only mild irritation.

"I thought not." Ethelred shook his head. "Anyway, my dear girl, we're going to the Appalachian mountains next. I have business with a cursed gypsy prince."

"I thought you said he was a werewolf?"

"I did. That's why we're going."

"Okay, let's discuss this logic. There is a werewolf in the mountains. Therefore, we should be somewhere like Jamaica. They can't swim, can they?"

"Doggy paddle." Ethelred deadpanned.

"That was bad." Tally made a face to emphasize how bad.

"I know, but you liked it."

"I *didn't*. Anyway, I'm not going anywhere near the mountains. Werewolves are scary bastards. I don't . . . how do you say in your little Briticism . . . *fancy* meeting one."

"He's the gypsy prince," Ethelred reiterated, as if that should allay all of her fears.

"It would figure," Tally huffed. "Look, can you get laid on your own time?" She really didn't want to meet this thing. She'd just watched *The Howling* and she had to say if she went her whole life and never got to experience that brand of suck, she'd be good with it.

"I'm trying to save his life and keep the curse from infecting his sister. And before you get any silly girlish ideas, I'm still a very bad man."

"Oh, of that, I have no doubt. Which is why there is no

way in Godiva that you'll catch my ass anywhere near your gypsy prince."

"You said ass again," he sighed. "Choose your flavor. Me or Falcon."

"Falcon. Definitely Falcon," Tally said, pleased with herself.

"He's going, too," Ethelred informed her gleefully. "So you might as well go with me."

"Okay, let's look at this logically again. You aren't going to have time to take care of me. And with a werewolf around, I won't lie—I want to be taken care of. You're going to be too busy trying to get horns and tail deep in the wrong end of a werewolf. I don't want any part of that."

"I suppose I can see where you're coming from, but what makes you think Falcon will have any time for you?" Ethelred asked the question lightly, but they both knew it was sharper than a dagger.

CHAPTER EIGHT
Shall Not and the Bigger Boss

F alcon had left the house early that morning to talk to
the Bigger Boss. When he'd heard Ethelred running his
suck in the bathroom after "the incident," he knew something had to be done. This attraction between Falcon and
Tally was to the Infernal's advantage and it had tilted the
playing field.

He'd found Merlin lounging on the Riviera, looking sus-
piciously like Dionysus—the Greek god associated with
the grape harvest, who was also the embodiment of excess.
There was a harem of women around him, all dressed in
gold and silks, some stroking his hair, his feet, others feeding him delicacies of this or that, and all cooing over him
like some favored pet.

Yeah, Falcon guessed it was hard to be the boss. He
rolled his eyes.

"Where's your charge?" Merlin asked before opening his
mouth to allow one of the women to feed him a grape.

"At home. Sleeping. Or hiding." Yeah, she was probably
hiding. He knew she'd been embarrassed by what happened. Falcon had tried to reassure her that it really wasn't
a big deal, but Tally had been mortified.

Merlin looked thoughtful for a moment. "Hmm. No.
She's taking tea with Ethelred." He chewed some more. "In
England."

"What?" It wasn't even Ethelred's day, although why Falcon expected anything different was beyond him.

"Snooze, you lose, I suppose. You're really not doing a very good job," Merlin drawled.

"I know. That's what I wanted to talk to you about."

"You did?" Merlin seemed pleased. "I'll have you reassigned right away."

Reassigned? Not a chance in Hell. "Eh, no," he began, trying to keep his tone diplomatic.

"No?" He took a drink. "Interesting."

Falcon didn't care for the way he said "interesting." As if it wasn't interesting at all and what he really wanted to do was call Falcon a bastard. "I want Tally to succeed."

"Really? Could have fooled me. And Ethelred. And her."

"And Tally? Did she request a new parole officer?" Falcon demanded.

Merlin ignored him, still eating grapes and cheese and sipping wine.

"Well, did she?" he prompted.

"No, but don't you really think that would be best for her?"

"No, I don't think that would be best for her," he said, mocking Merlin's tone. Rage washed over him at the thought of another warlock, angel, or demon being anywhere near Tally.

"Boy!" Merlin's voice boomed through the air like thunder. "Do you forget whom you address?" He was no longer sprawled among the women, but nose to nose with Falcon.

Falcon was unmoved. "No. Did you?"

"You've got balls, I'll give you that," Merlin acknowledged. "So what is it you want from me?"

"I want you to repeal the Shall Not."

"I find it disconcerting that rather than have your charge assigned to another parole officer, you want the rules to change for you. Rules are rules, Cupid."

"When rules are wrong, they need to change."

"Why is it wrong? Because you want her?"

"It's wrong because it gives the Infernal an unfair advantage. The attraction was between us before I was Cupid, even before the lamia possessed her. It's not right to punish her for that." *Or me,* he added silently.

"So it's all for her, is it?" Merlin sneered.

"I didn't say that."

"Good, because then it would be a lie. Lying is also a Shall Not, if you forgot."

"I admit I want her." He shrugged. "But she wants me, too. Who better for her to be with now than Cupid? I won't let anyone else hurt her."

"Except you?" Merlin ate another grape.

Falcon didn't like what Merlin implied. "Look, I'm done talking about this. Repeal the Shall Not or I won't give Nimue her refresher love arrow."

Merlin narrowed his eyes. "You can't do that."

"I can do whatever I want. I'm Cupid. Courtesy of you."

"Which was my mistake. But regardless of that, we have a situation."

Had Merlin just said making Falcon Cupid had been a mistake? If he hadn't become Cupid, the great and terrible evil would have killed him. Nice. He refused to think about that. "And that situation would be?"

"Which do you want me to tell you first? The part where your magick is going to fail if you don't find a way to believe in love and you'll lose your job, or the part where you screwed up my Grand Plan for Ethelred?"

"Uh, both?"

"Exactly, boy. You don't have time to dally with Drusilla Tallow."

"I'm not dallying with her. I'll make sure she gets her redemption. Only repeal the Shall Not. Help me help her."

"You're fuller of shit than I am. What you're saying is that you don't care about Ethelred, or your magick, only getting your wand wet."

"Hell, no, I don't care about Ethelred." He snorted.

"You should."

"Why?"

"He was propositioned last night by a gypsy princess." Merlin sat down on a chaise and dismissed the women. "Sit down. Your wings are making me hear calliope music."

Falcon sat down, unable to suppress a laugh.

"Oh, that's funny? You've fucked up my whole plan." Merlin slapped the back of Falcon's head. "He was supposed to fall for her brother."

"Free will is a bitch, or so I've heard you say." Falcon ducked when Merlin moved to slap him again.

"You are obviously missing the gravity of the situation. Not to mention it wasn't free will. You shot him with an arrow. True Love is the strongest magick of all. Ethelred's love was the key to breaking a gypsy curse."

"I'll just shoot him with another arrow." Falcon still didn't get what the big deal was.

"No, you troublesome whelp. It doesn't work that way. Read your manual. Luminista and Emilian Grey are two halves of the same soul. But Emilian's is the half that is cursed. So he needs the True Love."

"What does that matter?"

"He comes from a long line of dark magick. The key to accessing a great power even stronger than the lamia is in his blood. And his curse. He's moon–cursed. The beast inside of him will gorge on all that evil until it's invincible. It will consume Emilian Grey from the inside out and the world will soon follow. He will become what the northmen call the wolf who swallowed the sun."

So, not only had Falcon smitten Ethelred, but he'd triggered the apocalypse. *Fantastic.* "How do I fix it?"

"Fucked if I know." Merlin sighed. "You screwed my plan in the ass like a rent boy. There is no plan B."

"Okay, so . . ." Falcon couldn't process what Merlin had just told him. He needed him to say it again so Falcon could be sure he'd heard him correctly. "We're on the verge of an apocalypse and you're hanging out on the Riviera?"

"First it was the lamia, now this. What do you want from me?"

"To do your damn job. You're the Bigger Boss. You're supposed to have this handled."

"I might say the same of you, my boy."

"Stop calling me 'boy.' "

"I will. When you pull up your diaper and stop acting like one. Today is your day to guide Drusilla, to help her and where are you? Here, talking to me about getting your wand wet. Are those the actions of a warlock grown?"

Falcon knew the answer that Merlin wanted to hear wasn't "yes," even if it was the truth. His shoulders sagged. He was a Crown Prince of Heaven. He was supposed to be better than the average warlock. Merlin was right.

"You better be very sure this is what you want. There is no going back," Merlin warned.

"No, I'm sure. Very sure," Falcon said.

"Against my better judgment, I'm going to repeal the Shall Not. But that means for Ethelred, too. She may choose his path." Merlin smiled slyly. "Especially since he's going to save her life twice in one day. You know how she likes the hero type. Yes, in five . . . four . . . three . . ."

Falcon used his angelic magick to search for Tally and found her at a small cabin in the Appalachian Mountains. What the hell were they doing there? What was Ethelred's game? As he teleported, he was sure he heard Merlin's laughter.

When he materialized, the scene before him wasn't anything he'd ever have expected—it was right out of a horror movie.

Tally was frozen with her back against a tree as if she'd turned to stone. There was a beast closing in on her slowly. It was bipedal, like a man, but with the twisted, contorted body of a wolf. A slavering maw filled with predator's teeth had curved into something that was almost a smile. Rage bloomed hot and volcanic inside Falcon. His angelic magick flared around him. The creature took another step toward Tally, and Falcon launched himself between her and the beast.

Slashing claws tore into his flesh, but he didn't feel it, not really. The wounds healed even as the beast ripped him open again. It registered in his head that Tally was screaming, but there was another woman's voice begging him not to hurt the animal.

The jaws came too close to clamping around his arm and when it snapped at him again, Falcon grabbed its upper jaw in one hand and its lower in another. He was prepared to rip it apart. His muscles bulged, fueled by angelic strength, but just as the werewolf yelped in pain, Ethelred snapped a silver collar around its neck.

They crashed to the ground, the beast a werewolf no longer, but a man—naked and shivering. The man's mirror image, but female, pulled him into her lap and Ethelred grinned.

That smug grin on the demon's face broke Falcon's thin leash of self-control. Falcon crashed into Ethlered, knocking him to the ground, his fist descending into the demon's face with impunity.

But Ethelred only smiled wider as the force of the blows broke his nose and shattered his teeth. At Falcon's cry of absolute rage, the demon erupted in laughter. He didn't stop until Falcon raised an arrow into the air and held it positioned over his head.

"Fine, I surrender." His features slowly re-formed, even as blood gushed down his face.

"What the fuck were you thinking?" Falcon's voice was as low and guttural as the werewolf's growl.

"What was *I* thinking?" The demon smiled around his broken teeth. "Where were you? It's still your day. You're supposed to be with your charge at all times."

"Is this what you're going to do with her when it's your day? Kill her so she has no shot at redemption?"

Ethelred pushed Falcon off him. "What are you going to do with her? Fuck her so she has no chance of redemption?"

Magick crackled around Falcon with his not-so-righteous angelic fury. The arrow in his hand was transformed into pure light and he hurled it at the demon.

White flames burst around Ethelred, and rather than laugh, the demon didn't make a sound as the fire enveloped him. He was obviously in pain and hellfire sparked to life in his eyes. Ethelred summoned his own bolt of energy, but his was black and heavy like tar. It dripped over his fingers.

Falcon almost didn't register the tiny fist on his chest or the small blond head between them.

"Stop it," she cried.

"I thought you'd like us fighting over you, sweetheart," Ethelred taunted. "Doesn't it make you feel all those things you want so desperately?"

Tally looked up at Falcon and for a single moment, everything inside her was bright and bare. Her need, her pain, her loneliness. The absolute surety she didn't deserve any of the things she wanted. Her truths were sharper than any sword, any talon, and they slashed at things inside him he never thought he'd feel. It left him raw and exposed. He was torn between wanting to see more and needing to get away from her.

"No," she whispered quietly.

"Why not, Drusilla? We both want you," Ethelred began. "Don't you like being between us?"

Tally's cheeks flamed at the insinuation and Falcon gently moved her out of the way.

"I'm going to end you, demon."

"Just take me home, Falcon." She tightened her arms around his waist and burrowed into his chest. "Please."

He could deal with Ethelred later. Right now, Tally needed him. But rather than teleport them back to the house, he took them to his mother's home. Ethelred wouldn't be able to enter there.

"I don't know what Ethelred was thinking," Falcon said as he washed the blood from his hands in the backyard of his mother's house. The garden gnome stood patiently with the hose while Falcon did his best to clean up any evidence of their earlier ordeal before his mother saw them.

Tally had a bit of blood splattered on her cheek. He reached out and wiped it away with his thumb.

"I'm so sorry, Tally. Are you okay?"

She pursed her lips, but not before he saw her bottom lip quiver. "Where were you, Falcon?"

Looking down at her, so ready to break, he couldn't tell her why he wasn't there. Anything he had to say for himself died on his tongue. He thought she'd be sleeping? He thought she'd be . . . It didn't matter what he'd thought. He'd promised her he'd be there.

She'd trusted him and he'd failed her just like every other man in her life had. Just like he knew he would in the end.

But it was too late for him to back out now. Merlin's words about being very sure rang in his head like a fire alarm.

"It won't happen again, I swear."

"That still didn't answer my question. Where were you?" she asked quietly. "You promised."

"Tally, I admit I was wrong to leave you. It's my day, so

I shouldn't have left you alone for a second. But why did you go with Ethelred? You can tell him no. You can tell *me* no." For the first time he wondered if she actually knew that.

"No, I couldn't. He gave me cramps and made them worse if I didn't comply. So no, I couldn't refuse him."

"He what?" Falcon demanded, rage boiling again.

"Look, you already bashed his face in, which I think he actually enjoyed. Let it go. You'll be there next time, right?" She dried her hands off on her jeans. "This is what he wants. To make you angry. To make us question everything."

"He had no right to do that to you, Tally. It was an abuse of power."

"And he wants you to do the same. He wants you to be angry. He probably thinks he can corrupt us because we have history. He'll play us against each other if he can."

"Aren't I the one supposed to be giving this speech?"

Tally laughed. "I guess it was my turn today. That would be pretty cool if we could save each other, don't you think? I mean, I kind of owe you."

"You mean like in those books Middy likes to read?" He smirked. "I'm not romance novel material, baby." But wouldn't it just be something if he was?

"Why not? We live in a world with magick. Lots of people think that's a fairy tale. So why can't I save you, too? It's not like I asked for shining armor or anything. Dred's already got that buttoned up."

Something sharp and hot flared at the comment. He didn't like it. "I can't believe Middy got him to wear shining armor for their wedding."

"Well, he was willing to die and damn himself for her, so I'd think wearing armor would be a little thing in comparison. I think he already wore the thing to a Samhain mixer at Academy, anyway. As much as he denies it, he likes it."

"As well he should. He's lucky my sister even looked twice at him."

"I know. He wasn't even put off by the Trifecta."

"That never stopped you," Falcon replied.

"You never struck the fear of Merlin into warlocks on my behalf."

"Oh, I beg to differ," he began and the garden gnome handed them each a towel.

"Really? Who?"

"Grigori Hampsteath."

"He stood me up for— You ass. I cried on your shoulder about that for half the night." She handed the towel back.

"I knew you'd be angry, but he was running his mouth about getting you to put out, so I encouraged him to steer clear of you if he wanted to keep his teeth and his balls."

"Falcon, people have always been talking about me. Ever since my father was convicted and sentenced to the Hall. Then my mother went crazy and killed herself. I was always fodder for the gossip mill. Since birth, apparently. You know I don't care what people say."

"I know. But you deserved better than that."

She wrapped her arms around his waist and tucked her head against his chest. "And here you said you didn't wear shining armor."

He found himself wishing for just a moment that he could be that warlock—the one that the shining armor would fit.

CHAPTER NINE

Cupid, Drop Your Bow

The first part of her parole with Falcon was almost over, thank Merlin.

Tally was torn between wanting to see Falcon all the time and never wanting see him again. He hadn't brought up the Crimson Tide Incident, or the Werewolf Incident. In fact, he acted like none of it had happened. She supposed that was just as well. It was a Shall Not, after all.

He'd stuck to her like a burr, as he'd promised. They spent a lot of time on the beach, walking and talking, shelling. She had a whole basket of shells that she had no idea what to do with, but had wanted nonetheless. He cooked out, she dragged him on the dolphin-watching cruise, and they did all of the tourist things the island had to offer. She'd been so nervous about being alone with him, but he treated her like she was one of the guys, or worse, his little sister's friend.

Tally couldn't make up her mind; she thought that was what she wanted, to go back to the way things had been. For him to forget everything that had happened between them because it seemed the universe was decidedly against it. That wasn't what she wanted at all, but it was what she needed. Her body cried out in protest that what she needed was to get laid—hard and fast by the sex in leather that was Falcon Cherrywood in his full Cupid regalia.

Whenever she'd pictured Cupid in her younger years, it had always been as a petulant child with a Botticellian mouth and a little bow and arrow. A stereotype? Sure, but it was what she'd been taught. Not this giant of a man with shoulders like Atlas, guns strapped to his thighs, and a mouth that could despoil a cleric with a smile.

Tally was embarrassed to admit she was looking forward to his turn in *Weekly Warlock*. He'd be 3-D pervy goodness all for her ogling. Tally wondered briefly how mortal women got along without live-action centerfolds. That wasn't something she ever wanted to know firsthand.

She'd reenact the scene from the living room, among other things. She'd dress him up like a Victorian lord, a SWAT commander, maybe even a gunslinger outlaw from the American West. He could show her how to sit a horse and she could practice on him. She licked her lips at the thought and had to cross her legs for fear of getting stuck to the chair like an industrial suction cup. Something like that ran right down her vein of luck. She'd end up having to explain to the object of her nefarious desires that she'd been fantasizing about him and had gotten so wet . . .

No. She'd just have to put him from her mind.

She popped another cookie in her mouth, and then spit it out into a napkin. Her jeans were starting to get tight on her ass and with no magick to move a button one way or another, she had to watch what she ate.

No magick definitely sucked.

Tally looked down and realized she might as well have eaten that last cookie, because it had actually been the last. There wasn't anything left but the empty package staring up at her with reproach in its little crumb eyes.

Falcon was going to be back any minute and she was wallowing in cookie crumbs in her not so skinny jeans, and hadn't brushed her hair. Damn the no magick twice on Sunday.

Tally crammed the cookie package into the full trash can and cringed. She'd never had a full trash can before. What did one do with it when it was full? The cleaning gnome took care of that. She prayed no magick didn't also mean no cleaning gnome. She wasn't sure if she could stand it. Previously, the house had just stayed clean; she wondered who did it if not the cleaning gnome?

She didn't have time to wonder further. When Falcon came through the door, she could tell something had definitely changed. Perhaps it was because he was in partial Cupid regalia. He had guns strapped to his hips and thighs and he was wearing the red leather pants.

"Hard day at the office?" she asked in a saucy tone.

"You have no idea. The Cherubim are harder to corral than sock gnomes and have sharper teeth. My brothers both got blind dates with Valkyries and the gals won't stop calling *my* WitchBerry asking when Hawk and Raven are going to call them. They're Valkyries, for Merlin's sake."

"Women are pretty universal, Falcon. Even hardass warrior chicks with big swords. I've heard stories about them though. If they get tired of waiting for your brothers to call, they might decide a raid is in order."

Falcon grinned. "As in a pillaging sort of raid, like in the days of yore?"

"Yeah. Picture Raven and Hawk trussed up like game birds and tossed over a Valkyrie's shoulder."

He pulled his WitchBerry out of thin air and started texting.

"What are you doing?"

"Telling the girls they won't be getting a call any time soon."

"Are you sure you're an angel?" Tally asked.

"Not entirely, no," Falcon admitted with another devastating grin. "I'm trying to get a transfer. Too bad Death's not open."

"See, I always knew Cupid was a dick."

"That hurts, Tally." He pretended to clutch his heart.

She snorted. "I'm sure. You're the Angel of Love and you'd rather be traipsing about the underworld? I bet no one ever falls in love ever again."

"Would that be a bad thing?"

"It would be horrible. That's one of the things about living that makes it worthwhile; makes being human worthwhile. Love shows the best of what we have to offer the universe."

"So, why do you blame it for following Vargill blithely down the primrose path?" Falcon asked as he stepped inside.

Tally slumped and sighed. She didn't blame Vargill for the great and terrible evil. "I don't. I know everything I did was my own fault. It was easier when I could blame someone else, though." After their initial rocky start, Falcon had turned out to be pretty good at the parole gig. "I guess there's a reason you're Heaven's parole officer. You've got this Big Brothering down to an art."

She was suddenly crushed against him. "I'm not your brother."

"No, but you are my parole officer," Tally reminded him gently. Her palms were on his chest, keeping the illusion of space between them.

Goddess, this was what she'd dreamed about—his hands on her body again, the electric current of skin to skin. It would be so easy to tilt her face up to his, to beg him to take her on her back on the floor, bent over the couch. . . .

"I don't want you to go with Ethelred tomorrow." Falcon still held her, his dark eyes serious.

"Don't do this to me, Falcon," she said as she looked down, her eyes on his chest rather than meeting his gaze. If she met his gaze, her lashes would flutter closed, her lips would part and she'd be writhing beneath him, just as she yearned to do, but this wasn't right for them. Not now.

"I can see it in your aura, Drusilla. I know you want me," he said as if it were only a matter of desire.

She dared to look up at him, moving her hands to his shoulders. "We can't."

"Oh, but we can. Merlin repealed the Shall Not."

"It's not just that, Falcon." Goddess, he was going to kiss her and she wanted him to; she wanted it with every fiber of her being. She wanted it too much.

"What is it then? What's changed?"

"Everything! I don't want to be the person I was before," Tally exclaimed and tried to twist away from him, but he held her firm.

"Then don't be."

Falcon tilted her chin up carefully with his thumb and forefinger. His descent was measured; a practiced stroke of seduction, but Tally couldn't fight him. She craved his lips, his hands on her body, the fire she'd never felt with anyone but him. Tally leaned into his strength, and surrendered to her desire.

Falcon's lips touched hers and the world fell away like a discarded gown to pool at her feet. Nothing was real but this, nothing mattered but this. Falcon was her only sensation; time began and ended in a single kiss.

She knew there was no stopping this runaway train between them, no matter what path either of them took. It had always been destined to come back to this moment. If she'd stayed that night Tristan Belledare had asked her out to Academy graduation, she would have fallen into Falcon's arms then. Deep inside her heart, Tally knew it to be true. She'd been fighting the inevitable for years; she'd seen it in his eyes that night so long ago and it had scared her. Tally had run right into Tristan's arms because she'd never believed that she could have something she wanted so much. Not without some terrible price.

Falcon was here right now, asking her not to leave again. Only this time, she didn't have a choice. She had to go to Ethelred, but it didn't mean that she couldn't hold on to Falcon tonight, if she dared to grasp at this thing between them.

Even if it burned hot and fast, only to flicker dark after this moment, it didn't matter. Tally gave herself over to the burn and when she opened her mouth to his kiss, the flame became a wildfire.

"Drusilla," he whispered raggedly against her mouth.

He was still asking, still giving her the choice. "Yes, Falcon. Yes."

His hands slid up her rib cage beneath her shirt, over the lace cups of her bra, and he eased her shirt over her head. Falcon pushed the straps of her bra down her shoulders and Tally found her back against the wall and his knee between her thighs.

He bent his head and undid the front hook with his teeth and filled his palms with her breasts. Falcon took a nipple into his mouth, his tongue flicking the hard peak before his thumb replaced his tongue and he touched his mouth to her throat, the corner of her jaw, and just beneath her ear.

"Tell me how you want it, Tally." His breath was warm on the shell of her ear. "Do you want it hard?" Falcon tugged roughly on her hair, but his mouth was gentle on hers before he spoke again. "Or have you dreamed of a tender lover?" He skimmed his forefinger lightly down her cheek.

She was so aware of herself, of her breasts rising and falling with her breathlessness, the throb between her thighs, the way each time he touched her the contact was an epicenter for concentric circles of pleasure that rippled ever outward.

"What have *you* dreamed of, Falcon?" She pushed her fingers through his hair and arched her body against him.

"Touching you. Seeing your face when you come for me."

"And is it rough? Do you pull my hair and fuck me hard, or are you gentle?" She worked the button free on his leather pants and sank to her knees.

She freed his cock and wrapped her hand around the hard length of his shaft. Her eyes never left his. She watched him as her hand moved in a steady rhythm. Watched even when she used her mouth, her tongue laving over the tip.

Tally liked the feel of him in her mouth and the knowledge that she pleasured him; the way his eyes went impossibly dark as he watched her with a growing intensity. His cock surged and she increased the pressure and speed of her mouth and hand.

A low groan escaped him and he stepped back from her. "You have to stop."

"Don't you like it?" Tally asked as she got to her feet.

"It's been too long," Falcon said and swept her into his arms. He held her aloft as if she weighed nothing and carried her to the bedroom, where he eased her down on the bed.

"How long?" she dared to ask, afraid of the answer.

"Two years."

He'd not been with anyone since his last relationship. Tally didn't know what to make of that revelation. She didn't want to think about what it meant, or if it meant anything at all.

Falcon settled between her thighs and unbuttoned her jeans and pulled them off her hips in a fluid motion. He pressed his mouth to her stomach just above her mound and moved lower.

"Aren't you afraid?" she whispered.

"Of what?" he said softly against her skin. Falcon slipped

one finger inside her and she cried out, clenching around the invasion. He dipped his head again, and tasted her, his tongue on her clit.

"That I—oh," she breathed.

There was no more room for coherent thought—only the awareness of his mouth on her, his tongue as it flicked that swollen nub, his fingers in her slick channel. It wasn't enough; she wanted his cock inside her.

His mouth drove her need further, demanding she open for him, that she submit to his pleasures instead of her own. He wanted to taste her, wanted her to come for his lips and hands. He told her this with every swirl of his tongue, every thrust of his fingers. It was the sweet sound of pleasure that flowed beneath his every breath and Tally swore she could feel it.

The pinnacle came hard and fast. She'd not even dared touch herself in all this time. She'd been afraid of what she'd find. Even after the night of the reception. One moment, she was teetering on that ledge between bliss and need and in an instant, she'd fallen over the edge. Darkness enveloped her. She had no sense of sight or sound and endless waves of scorching pleasure tore through her.

Just as she thought she'd reached the crest, Falcon rose above her and pushed his cock inside her sheath. Tally cried out and hooked her legs around his waist as he drove into her. That crest had only been a plateau, a place where she waited for the next rush of sensation to claim her. Her passage clenched around him and pulled him deeper and Falcon froze.

"What's wrong?" Tally's high crashed. What if the great and terrible evil had come back? What if she'd hurt him?

He didn't speak, but kissed her again, thrusting inside her, and his whole body went rigid. Tally realized there wasn't anything wrong; he'd spilled inside her.

"Shit." His lashes brushed his cheeks and he pressed his forehead to hers.

Shit? Oh, Goddess, not again!

"Like I said, it's been a long time."

"I was scared I'd hurt you," she confessed.

"My pride, maybe." He dropped a brief kiss to her lips. "Being inside you was too much after wanting it for so long."

It was only a few moments before Falcon's breathing was deep and even. He was asleep! Not that she was a cuddle in the afterglow kind of girl, but it would have been nice to have had the option.

Tally supposed it was just as well, since she didn't have any witty remarks to parry with—she'd hoped maybe he'd want to prove himself and drill her like a Craftsman. Of course, she'd gotten off just as quickly. She'd never been one of those multiorgasmic witches anyway, but it could be fun to try. Then again, she'd never really been an orgasmic witch at all, if Tally was being totally honest with herself.

She looked over at Falcon's sleeping form and decided maybe all the afterglow bullshit wasn't bullshit at all. Her face felt warm, her body tingled all over, and Tally had the most ridiculous urge to giggle. She leaned against him experimentally and found herself tucked against the hard length of his body.

Yes, Drusilla Tallow liked the afterglow very much.

CHAPTER TEN
Falcon's Folly

Falcon watched the sleeping woman next to him. She looked so fragile and small in her sleep, so utterly breakable.

He'd never known a woman to be so passionate in the bedroom when it meant nothing to her. Not that his experience was as vast and mighty as some, but he'd been with his fair share.

It was no surprise she was beautiful; no surprise he was hard again at the thought of being inside her, but what did surprise him was he found himself thinking of the future. What would happen between them when her parole was over? Or a question of a more urgent nature: What would happen when she went to Ethelred? He'd be twice damned if he was going to let her go back to Ethelred's supervision. He could take his "bloody" Briticisms and blow them out his "arse." Bastard. Tally could have been killed, something that would have concerned Falcon even if he hadn't fucked her.

He cared about her, he always had. She'd been a part of his family since his sister could talk. She'd brought Drusilla home like a stray animal and Middy had asked prettily to keep her. None of them would deny her and Tally had become a part of their family.

The thought of being without her was like a knife in his

chest. It occurred to him that since they'd crossed this line, he was destined to lose her. She'd eventually want more than what he could offer.

Falcon should have been there for her before she'd ended up with Vargill and then none of this would have happened. He realized his thoughts were at odds with themselves, which was why he wasn't sleeping, but lying awake and staring in a completely non-stalker way at Tally while she slept.

He wondered briefly how many women had done that to him, lying next to him, watching him sleep. How could he want her so much and not enough at the same time?

Tally curled against him in perfect trust, her silken hair soft under his chin. He tucked the errant curls behind her ear and gathered her closer, as if the act would stop what lay ahead for them. Falcon reveled in the moment, for in this moment, she was his. He knew it was selfish and . . .

"I hope you don't think this means she loves you, Pinky."

Falcon had to fight not to jump to his feet, wings splayed and guns at the ready, until he realized this intruder was none other than the Angel of Death. Another guy who'd gained his lofty position through Tally's antics.

"I'm kind of busy," Falcon responded with a harsh whisper.

"I know, man. I waited as long as I could, but you know how the Powers are. I thought you'd never be done. Anyway, she curled up into me like that my last night at Loudun and you see what I got for my troubles?" Tristan demanded.

"You were aimless anyway. Death has given you direction," Falcon offered, his voice still low.

"Fuck you, Cupid."

"So, what do the Powers want? The sooner you tell me, the sooner you can leave." Falcon pulled the sheet up to cover Tally's bare bottom.

"You don't need to cover it, I've seen it before." Tristan winked. "Up close and personal like."

"Let me guess. They want to see me because I've mur-
dered Death with my bare hands."

"Nope, that's not it. They need you for a vote, but
you've got to leave Tally here."

"A vote? Do you have to vote, too?"

"Yeah, it's something about that werewolf tangle the
other day."

"Damn it." Falcon tried to extricate himself from Tally
without waking her.

"Oh, it gets better. This is on the scale of apocalyptic."

"Yeah, I knew that," Falcon confessed. "I don't want to
leave Tally here alone. She's supposed to go back to
Ethelred today."

"She'll be fine. With Death and Cupid watching over
her, what could go—" Tristan was promptly cut off by Falcon's hand over his mouth.

"Don't ask what can go wrong, because, invariably, it will."

"Okay, fine. Just don't put your fingers on my mouth
again. I *do* know where they've been," Tristan said before
licking his lips. "Yep, definitely Tally."

Before Falcon could process his impulse to knock Death's
teeth down his throat as a Good Idea or a Bad Idea, he had
Tristan by the throat and had lifted him off the ground.

"That joke was in bad taste, I get it," Tristan agreed and
then laughed. "Bad taste. Get it?"

Falcon squeezed harder.

"Can't. Breathe."

"You don't need to breathe."

"Still uncomfortable."

"Show her some goddamn respect." Falcon dropped the
other angel.

"Man, it was just a joke. You've got to lighten up." Tristan rubbed his throat. "For a sissy with pink wings, you sure
do have a grip."

"I mean it, Tristan. She's been through hell and she doesn't need this shit from you."

"Oh, so she kills me, eats my organs, and leaves me to rot and I need to be considerate of her feelings? In case you haven't noticed, I'm *dead*."

"So am I and you don't see me crying about it or blaming her."

"Maybe you should."

"She blames herself enough as it is."

"Is this a pity Tally party?" Tristan sneered. "I've had enough of this shit. I've been as good-natured and accommodating as I'm going to be. We've all had enough of the Surly McHero routine, Falcon. No one needs saving, least of all a—"

"Be careful what you say. Because like you said, we've all had enough of Surly McHero. You never thought that applied to you, Tristan? *Oh, I'm the great war hero who's so tortured,* even though just between you and me, we know that you didn't save anyone. Dred Shadowins did and you took all the glory. You've always wanted what belongs to other men."

"I hope you're not referencing Tally now, because she doesn't belong to *other* men. She's pretty equal opportunity for *all* men."

This time, Falcon did have time to process the Good Idea, Bad Idea scenario, but he simply didn't care. Tristan had called Tally a whore. Falcon was going to break his face in places that would ensure the man could never open his mouth again, let alone say such hateful things about his woman.

Small fingers closed around his arm, giving him pause. He turned to see Tally standing behind him, wrapped in a sheet and her golden hair haloed by the light of the setting sun. Her eyes shimmered with tears and if her hands hadn't been on him, he would have already beaten the Angel of Death bloody.

"No, Falcon. Please."

He wanted to open his mouth and argue, but her emotions were written so plainly on her face. She felt all the guilt and self-recrimination anyone could ask her to feel. She didn't want any more violence to happen because of her. Falcon lowered his arm to his side, though it went against his instincts.

"You've fought enough for me," Tally said before turning her attention to Tristan. "I've already apologized to Falcon, but I know I owe you one, too. I was going to send a tea box, but somehow that doesn't seem to cut it. I didn't mean for you to get hurt. I didn't mean for anyone to get hurt. I'm sorry for what you suffered; if I could take it back, I would."

"You can. There's going to be a vote today to take a man's life. The werewolf who almost bit you? You could take the curse and channel it back to the Abyss and then no one has to die."

"The portal to the Abyss isn't a swinging door, Tristan."

The pain on Tally's face almost broke Falcon, but the steady pressure of her touch assured him she was holding her ground. Falcon wondered when she'd found such strength. He felt a warmth grow inside him and realized he was proud of her. She was facing her fears, her past, and her pain all on her own.

"No, it would most likely kill you. But you could atone for your sins. I'm giving you your way out, but you're too selfish to take it."

"I know you're angry and you have every right to be. All I can do is say I'm sorry. I hope one day you'll forgive me, Tristan. I've been thinking about something for a while, wondering if it would be the easy way out," she began.

Falcon didn't like the sound of this and when she moved to stand between them, he got a sinking feeling in his gut, but he knew her well enough to keep his mouth shut.

"You're the Angel of Death. If you want to pay me back in kind for what I did, I understand."

Falcon felt like he'd been gutted. Tally was offering to die.

His wings exploded out of his back and hardened into silver armor, but he made no move. He'd learned that one couldn't protect a person from herself. This was Tally's choice.

She extended her hand to Tristan, waiting for him to take it and, for Falcon, the world stopped. Time was meaningless. His existence would change forever if Tristan took Tally away. He'd kill him.

A small voice nagged at him from somewhere in the back of his head—it cried out that killing Tristan would be wrong. This was Tally's choice and if he really cared for her, he'd do what he could to help her find her redemption.

Yes, he could admit he cared for her. It wasn't love with a capital L, but he cared for her.

Tristan eyed Tally and reached out his hand to take hers and Falcon made up his mind. Her redemption rested in Tristan's hands? No. He refused to believe that and he wasn't going to lose her to a selfish man's sense of entitlement.

Tristan took her hand in his; Falcon was too late. Yet Tally still breathed, still stood in front of him. The anger was gone from Tristan's face.

"I loved you, Tally." The confession seemed to have been ripped from the Angel of Death like a vital organ.

"You never said so and you never acted like you did. You were always out with other women. You talked down to me, made me feel like I wasn't worth anything to you."

Falcon felt another sensation, a tightening in his chest. Was he having a stroke? No, a heart attack? He was angel— he couldn't have those things. Whatever it was, he didn't like it.

"I know." Tristan hung his head. "I didn't think you'd stay with me. I thought if you didn't think you could do any better, you'd never try."

"Oh, Tristan," Tally sighed. "What a mess, huh?"

"I didn't mean what I said about you being a whore. You didn't deserve that. And me? I probably deserved what I got at Loudun."

"Then why are you still so angry?" she whispered.

"I don't know."

Tally hugged him.

Falcon felt the stirrings of a certain green-eyed bastard. He was jealous! He knew he had nothing to be jealous of— Tally had spent the last night in his arms, as evidenced by the fact she was only wearing a sheet.

Pressed into the chest of a man she'd dated for years.

It was only reasonable to assume that they'd spent many nights tangled with each other. The visions that assaulted Falcon now were very uncomfortable and he wished, not for the first time, he'd beat the brain juice out of Tristan Belledare.

"I loved you, I did." Tristan said as he sank to his knees and laid his head on Tally's stomach like a child seeking comfort.

Falcon coughed. "So, I thought we had to go, or something." He shifted uncomfortably on the balls of his feet.

"Do you forgive me, Tristan?"

"Yes."

Realization hit Falcon again, but this time it was like getting hit with the wrong end of a hippopotamus. During their conversation on the beach, Tally had been asking for his forgiveness, but he'd been too stupid to figure it out. Instead, he'd kept trying to get between her thighs. He'd been concerned about demonstrating the prowess of his cock while she'd asked for redemption.

He couldn't very well say it now, not with Belledare going on all needy. It would be like the third wheel on a date saying, "Hey, pay attention to me, too. I'm included. Damn it." Tristan was being a dick and he still had Tally in his arms.

The nasty implication there was that's where she'd rather be. At least, Tristan could tell her he loved her. Even after everything that had happened between them, he could say it. And from the haunted expression on his face, it looked like he meant it.

How did they get from verbal sparring to this? It made the bile rise in his throat. It was his own fault for being so gung ho to kick Tristan's ass. If he'd ignored Belledare's fat mouth, they'd already be on their way and none of this would have happened.

But then Tally wouldn't have Tristan's forgiveness, either. Damn, but Falcon felt like a selfish bastard. It was small comfort Tally didn't return Tristan's declaration.

"Shouldn't we be going?"

"We're having a moment here. I'd think with you being Cupid, you'd be a bit more understanding," Tristan growled.

"Him?" Tally snorted and pulled away from Tristan. "Nah, he says he can enforce the party line without 'spewing' it."

"Really?" Tristan raised a brow. "So there's been no grand confession, no talk of *feelings*?"

Falcon felt the words die in his throat. Tristan had effectively crushed his windpipe without touching him, but Tally rode to the rescue.

"We don't need to talk about feelings. I know Falcon's stance on most things."

He didn't know why, but that pissed him off, too. Falcon

couldn't put his finger on it, but he found Tally's comment to be incredibly insulting.

"There you go." Tristan rolled his eyes. "He's willing to beat me stupid, but he can't tell you he loves you? I guess I'm not one to talk, but I've said it now, Tally. I love you. I still love you. When you're ready for an angel who can commit, you know where to find me."

"Tristan, no offense intended, but you couldn't commit before. I'm not sure anything has changed."

Wait, so, she wasn't saying she didn't want Tristan and that she'd stay with Falcon. She was saying that she wanted proof Tristan had changed.

This was all in one word dragonshit.

Falcon didn't want to lose her. He knew that much. He didn't want to lie, either. Not only that, but Tally would smell a lie like a six-week-old piece of fish left in a dirty jockstrap.

He fingered his guns, antsy to be away from the situation.

Tally smiled at him softly, but it didn't quite reach her eyes. His palms flattened against the guns again. He found their smooth grips to be comforting.

"I'll prove to you I've changed, Tally. If you give me the chance." Tristan looked wistful.

"You'd better go if the Pantheon is waiting," she said softly. "Thank you for your forgiveness—it means a lot. Will you do one more thing for me?"

Tristan nodded.

"Tell your mother I'm sorry. I'd do it myself, but if I were her, I wouldn't want to look at me."

Tristan grinned. "Oh, when she saw I was still alive, or angelic, she said I had it coming for being so awful to you. Of course, if I'd really been dead, she would be implementing your demise as we speak."

"Damn, Belledare. Do you ever shut up? Let's go if we're going," Falcon interrupted.

"I have a bad feeling about your going," Tally said and wrapped her arms around her stomach. Falcon wondered if the act quieted that feeling.

Falcon kissed her gently. "Everything will be fine, but stay here where you're safe."

Tally seemed startled by this display of affection. "You don't have to treat me any differently because we fucked, Falcon. Or because Tristan called you on it," she whispered in his ear before she stepped away from him. "Be safe. Both of you."

Falcon wasn't sure what to make of any of this, not the new direction his brain was determined to take, his jealousy, or this new side of Tally he'd seen. She'd been so strong and yet so soft; she was breakable and invincible all at once. There'd been a quiet wisdom in all of her words, until it had come to discussing what was between them.

She'd called it "fucking." Was that what it had been? If it was something more, what was it?

He understood now why ancient warriors didn't have sex before battle. It really did suck out one's manhood.

CHAPTER ELEVEN

A Bird in the Bush Is Worth Two in the Hand

Tally was surprised by how quickly Falcon returned. Things had either gone very well or very badly. From the sour look on his face, she imagined it had gone very badly. Or was he still irritated about Tristan?

"What's wrong?" She bit her lip.

"Aside from the fact I went to my first meeting with the Powers smelling like sex?"

"Why didn't you do a grooming charm on the way?" Tally put her hand over her mouth to try to keep from laughing.

"I never use manual grooming charms. I have them set to automatic at my apartment."

"I'm sorry, but it's funny. It's nice to see these things don't happen to just me."

"Well, that's what's wrong, Tally. It seems like you're always getting screwed. At the meeting, Ethelred convinced the Powers that the gypsy prince won't turn werewolf in his presence."

"I don't like the sound of this. Did they not see what just happened at the cabin? Ethelred was there when he turned!"

"I know that. But it's Ethelred's problem. He should have allowed for the curse when he made the deal with Emilian's father. If Ethelred had been on the ball, he would have used the deal to cleanse the entire line of magick and we wouldn't be dealing with this right now. This is his mess and The Powers want to let him clean it up."

"What does this mean?" Tally swallowed hard, fear crawling up her throat and cutting off her air.

"It means the prince and princess have to always be in his presence to keep the Beast from manifesting. The Powers want them to move in here."

"No," Tally said flatly. "No. I won't. I can't. Not after what happened at the cabin. It's not fair to ask it of me, either."

"And I'm not going to make you. The Powers suggested that you suspend your time with Ethelred until after this is over."

"Why does—" Tally didn't finish her question because she already knew the answer. She'd been about to ask why everything was always more important than she was, but even the Powers put everyone else first. She understood this was an end of the world thing, but Tally's redemption was just as important. There were other ways this could have been handled that didn't screw her. But it didn't matter. "Never mind."

"Look, I came up with something else. I told Ethelred that maybe you'd consent if he'd give up his claim on his days with you and you could spend the rest of your parole with me."

Falcon's words did nothing to soothe her fears. In fact, it sounded like he believed that if Ethelred had his shot, she'd fail. Maybe she was just being oversensitive because she was afraid of being anywhere near Emilian Grey.

"Why do I have to consent?"

"I don't know. That's just what the Powers demanded."

"Can we go somewhere else?"

"Yeah, I'll take you anywhere you want to go."

"For now, can we go back to your mother's? I know that's not living without magick, but I feel safe there."

"It's always been your home, too, Tally." He pulled her into his arms and she sagged against him with a sigh.

Until she realized he really did smell like sex.

She wrinkled her nose and gave a delicate cough.

"Yeah, witchling. You smell like that, too."

She gasped. "I don't."

"Sorry, sweetheart. You do."

Tally gasped again and slapped his shoulder as they landed on the small balcony that led to Falcon's room in his mother's house.

"Do you think we should tell your mom we're here?"

"Nah, she'll figure it out when we come downstairs."

"One of these days you're going to literally scare the life out of her. Then you'll feel bad for being such a rotten son," Tally teased.

"She's made of sterner stuff. Believe me, we tried when we were eight." Falcon snickered. "She broke a wooden spoon on my butt."

Tally couldn't resist a peek at said part and leered over his shoulder. "It doesn't look any the worse for wear."

"Wench, we'll see about that." Falcon swatted her bottom.

Tally squealed and twisted away from him into his room. "Says the boy who keeps an apartment even though we all know he really still lives with his mommy."

"Boy?" Falcon's eyebrow arched.

"Yep. *Boy,*" she reiterated.

"Little girl, you're about to be in big trouble."

"Oh, yeah?" Her voice was almost a whisper and Tally realized she sounded like she was begging for attention on the most primal level.

Their first experience hadn't been as wonderful as she'd hoped. Not that it had been bad, but Tally knew fear had held her back. She'd been so afraid of her own body, of its responses, and whether the great and terrible evil would come back. It had been quite the mood killer.

Regardless of what Falcon said about how long it had been for him, she knew it had to have been a relief that she was just a witch and didn't morph into something horrible. She knew there was wildness between them that burned hotter than any fire even the Devil could summon.

She wanted to explode with him into that possibility—to burn with him. "It doesn't feel like I'm in trouble."

"I've got to get clean before you can be in any serious trouble," Falcon said as he wandered into his bathroom, pulling his shirt off as he went. He emerged with a towel and a clean T-shirt in hand. "I'll even let you have the first shower."

"Such a gentleman," she said with a cheesy Southern belle accent.

"Not really. There's a peephole." Falcon smirked.

"If you wanted to see me naked, all you had to do was ask. In fact, you could use a grooming charm on both of us."

Falcon appraised her for a moment. "First, I like the hot water, and second, nothing's ever that easy."

"But why isn't it?"

"I don't know. I don't make the rules."

"Yes, you do. You're Cupid," Tally pointed out.

"Yes, but I'm more like a gardener. Or so the *Heaven's Helper Manual* says. I just water the 'seeds of love.' I don't plant them, unless it's a special circumstance. For those cases, I have lust bullets."

"I don't want to have that conversation now." Tally grabbed the T-shirt from him and headed into the bathroom.

"What conversation?"

"Which one do you think? You said you water the seeds

of love, nurture them, and then you said that you had lust bullets if there were no seeds to water, correct? There's a huge difference between lust and love," Tally said as she foraged for some shampoo underneath the sink. "And I was only talking about a grooming charm and some wham-bam, thank-you, ma'am. I didn't bring up that nasty 'L' word."

"Right, but sometimes people need the taste of lust to get at something that means more." Falcon held up his hands. "Not my words, the manual. You know I don't buy into the propaganda. So, no 'L' wording here. Wait, isn't that a show about lesbians?"

Tally raised an eyebrow and scowled. "Of course, you don't buy into the propaganda. But I don't see how you can be an effective Cupid if you don't believe in love. Especially when you started the conversation and now you're talking about lesbians."

"I don't have to spew the party line to enforce it—and it's never a bad time for lesbians or Valkyries."

Tally rolled her eyes. "So not going there. But I have to know, why serve the Kool-Aid if you're not going to drink it? Seems like a waste of time to me." Tally shrugged.

"Dying wasn't on my schedule the day they were handing out job assignments."

"Oh. There is that. I don't know if it matters, but I'm sorry," she said, looking down at her hands.

"It's not your fault." Falcon leaned across her to get—she wasn't sure what he was reaching for; all she knew was that he was in immediate proximity and she wanted to touch him.

Tally felt bad about perving on him while she was apologizing for almost killing him, but hey, he was the one who took his shirt off, revealing all of his rippling Cupid muscles. She wondered if all angels were built like gods, though Falcon had been eye candy before his job change.

"No, I have to take responsibility for what I did. I caused

a lot of damage." Tally left her thoughts about Tristan un-spoken.

"Heaven got two more civil servants out of the deal," Falcon said as his undid the button on his leathers. "Look, this leather is really chafing, so the sooner you hop in the shower, the sooner I can peel these off."

"I think you're dirtier than I am anyway—you go ahead. Wouldn't want you to get a rash on your *cupidity*." Tally sat back down on the bed, which had been made with military folds.

"Yeah, I'd rather not rash that up, either." He flashed a wicked grin. "I've still got to prove myself."

"What do you mean?" she asked while watching the planes of his back shift as he finished undressing.

"I know our first time could have been better for you, Drusilla." He was matter of fact.

"What are you talking about? I had my first orgasm that wasn't from my own fingers with you."

"You don't have to soothe my ego, sweetheart."

Oh, the way he said "sweetheart" made her whole body melt like chocolate on a warm day, sweet and languid.

"I wouldn't have minded if there'd been more, but I've been accused of being a greedy witch. Honestly, I've never felt anything like the things you did to me, for me. You were the first person I slept with because it was what I wanted instead of what I thought I was supposed to do."

"You didn't want Belledare?"

"I wanted him to want *me*, if that makes sense. Wow, now I'm channeling Cheap Trick. Will the torture never end?" Tally looked down at her hands.

"In essence, you're a virgin," Falcon replied.

"What? I've slept with—" She snapped her mouth closed. That wasn't exactly what she wanted to say about herself. "What I mean to say is, my experience is fairly extensive. How could you say I'm a virgin?"

"If I'm the first that you slept with out of desire, then the emotions you think you feel will be very intense."

"That I *think* I feel? Are you kidding me? You're almost as big of an asshole as Tristan. If you give me the don't fall in love speech, I swear to Merlin, I'll kick you in your chafed-up cupidity." Her leg twitched as she thought about doing just that.

"Sensitive much? I'm being honest with you."

"This raging honesty includes telling me what I'm feeling while still trying to get into my panties?"

"Tell me what you're feeling, then, if you're so sure I don't know."

He was in her space now, sucking all of the air away from her, out of her lungs and out of her mouth. She couldn't form words, but the heat of his nearness caused her to tighten her thighs. It didn't matter that he smelled like a mangy werewolf; it didn't matter that he was giving her the asshole speech—none of it did. All that mattered was the spark she felt every time he was near her.

Tally didn't know what demon possessed her, but she settled his hand between her thighs. She was so wet she knew he'd have it on his fingers even through her jeans. "This is what I'm feeling. This is what I want."

His pupils dilated at the contact, as if touching her was a hit from a drug, and Falcon's wings exploded from his back in all their angelic glory. He began to stroke the rough material and it moved against her mons; she gripped his shoulders for support to lean into the caress and give him better access to her clit.

"This is all you want from me?"

"Yes."

He rubbed harder and she dug her nails into his shoulders while she bucked her hips against him. She was going to come for his hand right here in his bedroom. Tally could see his heartbeat in the wide column of his neck. It pulsed in time with the rise and fall of his chest and she knew he was just as aroused as she was; he wanted to be inside her as badly as she wanted him there.

He didn't use magick to strip her, but his own hands. His fingers were nimble and quick, still damp with her desire as they pushed the fabric of her T-shirt up over her head and then shoved her jeans down past her hips. His touch was experienced, but unhurried and his knuckles grazed her thighs as he undressed her.

Even the barest touch of his skin to hers sent erotic awareness through her touch receptors and it was as if his hands were everywhere at once. Falcon hauled her tight against him and hoisted her legs around his waist, the leather of his pants a contrast of sensation on her bare slit.

Tally cradled the back of his head with her palm and her mouth crashed into his, almost violent with need. She tasted him, her tongue tracing his lips, and she nipped where she tasted. Her small acts of brutality invited his own and he tangled his fist in her blond curls and angled her head back to expose her throat.

He bit down on the tender skin and she jerked against his erection and he moaned. Falcon began to chant and Tally found herself lifted from him, held aloft in the air by some unseen force. Her limbs felt posed, yet cushioned. Her thighs were spread wide and her womanhood was at Falcon's eye level.

She'd never done this before, not with all the warlocks she'd been with. None had either known this magick or wanted to use it with her. Tally had a moment of fear, but she trusted him. All he'd done thus far was bring her pleasure.

He pulled her closer, used her hips to position her so that his mouth was at the apex of her thighs. The first touch of his tongue was like flint to steel. She was ignited by the spark. Tally gasped and he brought her tighter against his mouth. He explored the velvet petals of her labia with his tongue and slipped between them to taste her honey before sucking her clit into his mouth. She ached for more and wanted to be filled by him with his fingers and cock, but he kept his attention focused on her clitoris, her channel sodden with need.

"You taste so sweet," Falcon told her.

"Please," she begged.

He made one last swipe with his tongue before pulling her down from the invisible bed of clouds and turning her onto her stomach. She could see the bed below her, but still felt like she was suspended on an endless sea of velvet cushions.

Even though she was ready for him, his shaft felt impossibly large as Falcon pushed inside her. Tally stretched to accommodate his girth and she moaned with pleasure. When he was buried to the hilt, she clenched around him and he moved with long, sure strokes.

Falcon eased his weight down against her and filled his hands with her breasts. His breath was warm on her neck, the skin already sensitive where he'd bitten her. Tally shifted back to meet his thrusts when he rolled her nipples between his fingers.

He tugged gently on the stiff buds. A strange pleasure with an edge of pain coursed through her and the feeling only intensified when Falcon swirled his tongue over that place on her neck where he'd marked her like an animal claiming his mate. He tightened his arm around her waist and guided her response in time with his rhythm.

Tally was ready for more. She strained against him, urging him to increase his pace, to drive deeper, harder. He resisted her demands and stayed steady, immune to her pleas.

Falcon shifted in a smooth motion and turned them so she was astride and he was on his back beneath her. "Take what you want, Tally."

The idea of being in control of this man, of using his willing form for her pleasure was more intoxicating than any drug. Tally braced herself on his chest with the palm of her hand, her fingertips grazing a flat nipple and she leaned down to run her tongue over the tightening flesh. She moved back up to his clavicle, then down the taut skin of his chest.

Tally didn't move her hips, though she wanted desperately to come. More than that, she wanted this to last. She held herself still, but her walls spasmed around his cock as it jerked inside her, seeking culmination. The cycle of the constriction and release of her interior walls came faster now, and she couldn't fight it. She felt her own fluid drenching her thighs and his cock.

Falcon jerked his hips up in an involuntary motion to bury his cock deeper. Tally rocked her hips, expelling him from her slit only to ease back down his shaft and take him fully inside her again.

His fingertips were marking half-moons in the round part of her hips, another brand of ownership. Falcon's muscles were flexed as he fought with himself not to guide her movement, not to demand the rhythm to seek his own orgasm.

Tally heard a high-pitched sound as bliss consumed her and she realized the keening was coming from her own mouth. She rode the waves of sensation to fulfillment and, as she sank against him, she realized he was still hard.

She worked her way down his body and fisted his straining cock. With measured precision, she stroked him and took the head into her mouth. Tally tasted herself on him and he was right, she was sweet. It excited her again to know she'd marked him in her own way and when she rubbed the tip of his cock over her lips, his entire body tensed; he moaned, the sound low in this throat.

This was the first outward display of his pleasure she'd

seen in this encounter. It was only a taste, but it made her want to break his iron control. Tally jacked his shaft and swirled her tongue over the head and under the ridge. She felt it grow in her mouth, surge as his pleasure reached its pinnacle.

Tally knew he'd reached his climax and she looked up to meet his gaze while he spilled in her mouth. She counted herself damn lucky that not only did her lover taste like cotton candy when he kissed her, but so did his jism.

Chapter Twelve
A Demon's Pickle

Ethelred was not happy.

Usually, he was a rather cheerful chap and rarely did he pull out the tail and horns and the smiting. Cupid had him in a rare mood. Falcon Cherrywood was the least angelic angel he'd ever met. He stank of violence, jealousy, and guilt. He drank like an Irish pirate, fought like a war machine, and angsted like Byron. He'd never known an angel like him.

Okay, maybe that was a lie. Uriel and Gabriel were like that, but they channeled their bad for good. Or something.

Fuck. He wasn't even being erudite in his own mind, and Ethelred had a brimstone-deep love of language.

Falcon and that sodding arrow. The root of all of his troubles. Well, actually, the root of all his troubles was older than that, but his current predicament could be traced back to Stupid Cupid.

They'd voted with the Big Boss, the Bigger Boss, and all the Crown Princes of Heaven and Hell as to what to do with the new threat against the world: Emilian Grey and that damn Norse prophecy.

Stupid Cupid's rancid love arrow had him piping up when he should have kept his mouth decidedly shut. Of course, part of that was just his demonic nature, but Ethelred was sure it could have all been avoided without that arrow.

The Powers That Be had wanted to erase Emilian and Luminista Grey. Not just kill their bodies, but their souls. It was the only way to prevent the dark magick from filling them both. If they destroyed only Emilian's half of their soul, the curse would fall on Luminista.

Ethelred couldn't let that happen.

"Fucking arrow," he muttered.

Since Emilian didn't change when Ethelred was around— barring that little incident at the cabin—he'd proposed his current babysitting assignment as a short-term fix until something else could be found. But that meant both the werewolf and his sister would have to move in with him.

And Falcon and Tally.

Falcon had refused to agree and left it up to Tally because she was the one who had to live with a werewolf who'd almost killed her. Even collared, it wasn't fair to decide that for her. Or so the Diapered Wonder had said.

So the fate of the woman he loved had fallen into the hands of his parolee.

Really, it could go either way.

Ethelred almost hoped she said no. If Luminista died, maybe the arrow would lose its power and Ethelred would be free?

Then the world could go back to the way it was supposed to be and he could get back to the business at hand. Like corrupting Tally.

Ethelred was nearly ecstatic it was almost his turn with the witch.

He meant that literally. After Falcon smote him, he'd decided to seduce her. First, because it would be fun. Second, because he'd get brownie points for seducing his charge. Third, because it would piss Falcon the hell off and he'd definitely never believe in love. Which meant his magick would fail and Ethelred could stop having these imagined *feelings* for this annoying princess. Although, he was secretly glad Merlin had repealed the Shall Not. Ethelred wasn't quite done with this game. He planned on seducing Falcon, too. That would really fuck them both up.

He crept into Falcon's room. Even though it was warded against demons, he could get in because his parolee was there. Ethelred bent over Tally and used his magick to paralyze her.

"Wakey, wakey, witchy."

Her eyes flew open, and she struggled against the magick until she realized it was him. He could see every thought as it was reflected in her eyes.

"You're coming with me."

Defiance blazed on her face.

"Not to see the werewolf. To work. Come on. You'll be back before Stupid Cupid even knows you're gone."

He didn't wait for her to acquiesce, but used his magick to teleport them to a mall. Ethelred was even polite enough to dress her.

"You got me up to go shopping?" She arched a brow. "I thought we decided you weren't going to be my gay best friend."

Ethelred handed her a white mocha, the kidney-buster size. He abhorred coffee, but the witch seemed to need it. "Just drink it so you're tolerable."

"Me, tolerable? You're the one who was creeping."

"It's not the first time." He grinned.

"You know what, if you're that desperate, you deserve whatever you get."

"Thank you. I'm glad you see it my way. That will make your time with me much easier."

"Um, I thought we were postponing this? What about the werewolf?" She frowned.

"He's collared. He'll be a good boy and sleep for another few hours yet. Now, are you ready to have some fun?"

"I don't think your idea of fun and mine are the same."

"You'd be surprised."

Tally sighed. "Fine. The sooner I get this over with, the sooner I can go back to bed."

"Let's walk, shall we?" He offered his arm and she looked at it like it was on fire. Ethelred double-checked to make sure he hadn't accidentally let loose with the sulfur and the tail and horns. Finding nothing, he scowled. "Well, it's not going to bite you."

"Falcon offered his arm to me at Midnight's wedding."

"I can assure you that the outcome will be entirely different. I would never pass out in your witchy bits without making you scream in Aramaic."

"I don't speak Aramaic."

"Exactly." He winked at her.

She rolled her eyes, but laughed. "Men are all the same. Straight. Gay. Omnisexual. Warlock. Human. Demon."

"Angel," Ethelred reminded her. She was so much fun to rile up.

"What are we doing here again?" The witch took a delicate sip of the coffee and rolled the cup back and forth between her palms.

"I'm going to demonstrate to you the relativity of Hell."

"Meaning?"

"It's all relative, dear girl. In early writings, the Big Boss was referred to simply as the Adversary and he worked very closely with the Bigger Boss."

"So what you're saying is that you're not evil, you're just drawn that way?"

Ethelred couldn't stop the grin. "Yes, that's it. We're here to test you. To make you better yourselves through adversity."

"But you hurt people."

"So do doctors. To make you well. It's an end justifies the means sort of thing."

"But the end doesn't always justify the means."

"Let me show you." He led her over to a trendy store

where a girl went inside a dressing room and her boyfriend lingered, bored. "See this couple? He's thinking about giving up his scholarship to a university eight hundred miles away so he can be close to her. He'll end up working in his father's hardware store."

"Maybe he'll be happy at the hardware store." Tally scowled at him.

"He would be. Just to be with her. But the whole reason she wants to be with him is because she thinks he's her ticket out of here. He has a bright future as an engineer. She doesn't love him. She's sleeping with his best friend."

"Great. So, did you make the best friend bang her?"

"No, it's not quite so cut and dried. Free will, you know. But I can encourage the best friend to call her. And I can give the girl a little push so she asks her boyfriend to hold her purse. Just like *this*."

The scene unfolded as he said it would, leaving Ethelred feeling very pleased with himself. Until Tally slapped him.

"What was that for?"

"Did you make Tristan cheat on me?"

"Don't slap. I don't like it."

"I don't like being cheated on."

"Better it happened in the early stages of your relationship rather than after you were married and had devoted half your life to him, don't you think?" He wiggled his jaw around. "Not to mention, I didn't *make* him do anything. One of us may have presented an opportunity. If he took it, that's his sin to bear."

"You're doing nothing for your case."

"Okay, another example. Hmm." Ethelred scanned the mall for sinners. There were plenty to be had, but none that illustrated his case. Inspiration struck. "Over there"—he pointed to a child walking with his mother—"his mother is going to make a choice today. Either decision will result in her death, but one will push him to greatness and the other to some of the worst crimes humanity is capable of. Which would you push her toward?"

"Greatness?"

"Maybe. You have to look at what his crimes will do to those around him. Yes, people will suffer. But will it inspire hundreds to greatness whereas this single act would only inspire him?"

"I don't agree. What if his one act of greatness cured cancer?"

Ethelred was pleased. "Yes, now you're thinking. You have to look at every angle. Play Devil's Advocate, as the world likes to say."

"So what does your influence involve, precisely?"

"I'm the guy who distracts other drivers so they do forty-five in the fast lane. While it may inspire others to homicide, the guy behind me arrives alive and goes on to do whatever it is that we need him to do. So really, it's not a heavy hand. Unless you sell your soul. Most of them we don't really want, but it gives us something to do and people to test."

"So you don't spend your days with whips and chains and . . . other things?"

"Well, I mean, if you're into that. But no, not usually. Although, there are a few special cases. See, for all the talk of the Big Boss and the Bigger Boss, there are other hands turning the Wheel, if you know what I mean."

"I don't."

"No, I guess you wouldn't. But you will."

"I learn best by doing. Can I try it?" Tally asked.

Ethelred rubbed his hands together with delight. "I thought you'd never ask. The dad in the candy store? Keep him from leaving. Five minutes."

"Why?" the stubborn little witch asked.

"You don't get to ask that unless you have Crown Prince status. Do you?"

"No."

"Well, then."

"Okay, how do I get him to stay?"

"Think of something." Did he have to do everything?

"Can you influence his toddler to find the bottom candy on the display desperately interesting?"

"Ooh, like Jenga. I love Jenga." Ethelred exerted his influence and the boy looked up at him, questioningly. He made the candy wrapper sparkle under the bright lights and he nodded to the boy, urging him on. The boy reached out tentative fingers and tugged out the candy, causing the whole display to come crashing down. Expletives echoed throughout the store, followed by the boy crying that the Devil made him do it.

"Can you tell me how we influenced their lives now?" Tally wheedled. It was possible curiosity would be her downfall.

"Nope. If you want to know, you have to pick Team Hell."

"You're a dick." She sighed, unhappily.

"As you've told me. But time to go home now, ducks, or Falcon is going to notice you were gone. If he smells the sulfur, tell him you went out for a smoke." Ethelred laughed at his own joke.

"If he notices, I'll tell him the truth."

"That's even better. Now, you think about this later. I think you'll see that we have a great benefit package and the perks are to die for."

He blinked them back into Falcon's room, and just to be contrary, took the clothes he'd manifested on her with him. If her eyes could have burned him, he'd be flaming like a marshmallow dropped into a campfire. Only, he wasn't as gooey on the inside.

Feeling that he'd put in a good day's work, Ethelred decided it was time for tea at his favorite café in Brussels. Yes, being a demon was much like American Express—membership did indeed have its privileges.

He settled into his chair with his tea and was jostled by the appearance of one Luminista Grey. She popped into the chair opposite him like she was a witch born to it. She was talking, but he didn't care much for what she had to say. Although, he didn't mind watching her various bits jiggle about as she expressed herself.

"Did you hear me?" Luminista demanded.

"Everyone heard you, wench. Do be still while I have my breakfast tea." How had she found him? He was minding his own business in his favorite café in Brussels— nowhere near the Appalachian cabin where he'd left her and Emilian. How had she even gotten there? Although, it was the perfect opportunity to set the first of his plans in motion.

"You're not having breakfast tea. You're spying."

"Pardon me?"

"Cut the crap," Luminista clarified. "You're reading tea leaves. And with your demon power, you're watching *poor little Tally.*" She snorted.

"So what if I am?" he said, just to be contrary. "She's been cleaning Cupid's love gun all morning. She's rather good at it, actually, so it's quite a show."

"I know what you're thinking and I won't have it."

Had he heard her correctly? Perhaps he had brimstone in his ears.

"Don't act like you didn't hear me. You're the only thing that's keeping my brother from losing his humanity. You need to rearrange your parole schedule or whatever."

"Yes, Princess. Because the world revolves around you." Ethelred did enjoy needling her. He hadn't bothered to tell her that he had, indeed, rearranged not only his schedule, but *everything.*

"Did you forget the part where the world stops revolving if my brother—"

Ethelred flicked his thumb and his fingers together like little chattery mouths. "Don't you know any other songs?"

"Okay, how about this one? You're *my* demon. Apocalypse Barbie already has an angel. She can't have you, too."

"Hmm. And your brother is Apocalypse Ken. Maybe we should set them up? That could be fun." It really could. It might even solve the cursed end of the world problem.

"No. I don't want her near anything that belongs to me."

"Jealous much?" Ethelred arched a brow. He was enjoying this little creature. She was petulant, selfish, demanding, but her insides were soft and melty. Like M&Ms. She was desperate to save her brother, and desperate to be something apart from him as well. There was really so much raw material to work with.

"No." Her plump bottom lip seemed to swell further with her pout.

"Really, you have nothing to be jealous of. She had it worse than Emilian. He gets to forget what he does when he's a beast. Tally has to remember those she hurt, killed. Emilian grew up knowing his change would come. His mother's rage. He never expected her love. A man Tally loved turned her into a portal for some of the darkest magick known to the universe."

"Do I care? No."

"Your brother did almost rip her apart."

"Whatever. He's done that to me before, too. She needs to grow a pair."

"Easy for you to judge when you haven't been in her shoes."

"Why are you defending her?" Luminista growled.

"How many times must I say it? I'm the Devil's Advocate."

"Fine. Advocate."

He shrugged, finding he had nothing else to say now that she wanted to hear it.

"Okay, then who was the guy with the pink wings? I really liked those guns."

Ethelred found himself unreasonably irritated. "He belongs to Tally."

"Oh, really? Well, if she gets what belongs to me . . ." Luminista smirked, as if all of her machinations had just manifested in one big trophy.

"I don't belong to you, you tiresome slag." He sipped his tea. "That guy was Cupid. Would you like to know how he got the job?"

"I suppose you're going to tell me, whether I want you to or not."

"Why yes, yes I am." He was pleased. "You're learning. The little witch became a lamia. He and his brothers—"

"He has brothers?"

"He's one of three. Triplets."

"Dear Goddess, save me. There's more than one of him?"

"*Anyway,* as I was saying," *Yes, back to me.* "Drusilla Tallow increased the ranks of both Heaven and Hell by leaps and bounds. She's had power unlike anything you shall ever know." He couldn't resist a little dig at her. She deserved to suffer for making him feel things for her. It was her fault, after all. He'd told her what the consequences would be if she didn't take her proposition back, but no. So she'd signed up for this gig with full disclosure.

"I have lots of power, demon." She wiggled into his lap, knocking over his tea.

It occurred to him that she was just like a damned cat, demanding his attention. She wasn't the least bit sorry to deprive him of his morning ritual. To his further irritation, he found it endearing.

"Thankfully, I'm immune." He managed a bored tone.

"Liar," Luminista said as she wiggled her ass against his erection.

"Conceited, aren't you? How do you know I wasn't thinking about your brother?"

"Because you love *me*."

"Loving you doesn't necessarily mean I'm attracted to you."

She braced her hands on his shoulders, her stardust brows drawn together and genuine confusion marring her lovely face. "You're not?"

"No. Not a single bit." *Liar, liar, pointy little tail on fire.* "And I am not just a demon. I'm a Crown Prince of Hell."

"You should get used to me because we're moving in with you."

"You most certainly are *not*."

"We are." She stomped her foot. "Otherwise, how are you going to keep my brother from devouring the world until we find a cure?"

He had to struggle not to laugh. It was so easy to get her to do what he wanted. All he had to do was push her hard in one direction to send her barreling the opposite way with all the force of a freight train.

"Well, at the vote this morning, the Powers That Be wanted to smite you and your brother. Erase your names and souls from the Book of Life. That would fix the problem."

Luminista froze, her eyes wide and shadowed. "Erased? So, I would just end? No Heaven or Hell, just nothing?"

The indigestion was back—acid crawling up his windpipe from his gut. Ethelred wrinkled his nose. "No, we'll find another solution. I already told them I'd keep you close. For now."

She collapsed against him, her head on his shoulder, her breath tickling the side of his neck as she clung to him like a baby koala.

"Stop that."

"No. I'm afraid. If you love me, it's your job to comfort me."

"I don't love you. I don't even like you."

"Shut up and reassure me, demon," she snapped.

"I can't very well shut up *and* reassure you at the same time. So which is it to be?"

The baby koala made a sound like it was choking. Or having an allergy attack. Luminista was crying. The wretched beast was actually crying.

For fuck's sake.

Ethelred let his arms go around her slowly and he stroked a hand down her spine. He couldn't help noticing she smelled like sugar cookie tea. She sobbed harder.

He guessed he was doing the comfort thing wrong. Demons were no good at this love stuff.

"You won't let them erase me?" she hiccupped.

"No, I won't."

The part of this whole exchange that bothered Ethelred the most was that he knew he meant it.

CHAPTER THIRTEEN
Going To See a Woman About a Clam

It had been one hell of a morning, to say the least.

First the stampede of people through Falcon's bedroom, then fantastic sex, and a field trip with Ethelred. She needed a nap. There had been a lot to process.

Evil was not really evil, and a werewolf was going to be living in her house. Falcon was just being Falcon, and Tristan was in love with her? The world was coming apart at the seams.

Tally didn't believe Tristan was really in love with her. She was thankful he'd forgiven her—it meant a lot—but his confession of love wasn't worth the air he'd used to speak it. Still, she couldn't stop pushing it around in her head like yesterday's leftovers. Why now? She'd tried to kill him. What was he thinking? She was sure he only thought himself in love with her because she was with Falcon.

Well, as "with" any warlock a witch could be when he didn't believe in love.

Not that the love part mattered. He'd defended her against evil, made her laugh, and fucked like an Olympic champion gigolo—after they'd both gotten over the initial fear of the great and terrible evil. He'd said it was because he wanted her so much, but Tally had a hard time believing that.

She stretched languidly, her body pleasantly exhausted from Falcon's attentions, and promptly fell asleep.

Tally found herself standing with a sheet wrapped around her, still naked. She wondered why she wasn't somewhere more pleasant, like flying or floating among a million stars. Or clothed. It was her dream, yet she had absolutely no say in the matter. No, she was still in the same old place. Naked. But without Falcon.

She struggled to wake up. She knew she wasn't going to like this dream.

"Tally!" Merlin's voice thundered through her dream-scape.

She screamed and in an attempt to clutch the sheet more tightly around her, dropped it. To add insult to grievous injury—or perhaps that would be injury to insult because in her mad scramble to reposition her sheet it became tangled around her ankles—Tally was shoved facedown on the bed like an ungrateful and unworthy supplicant.

If tripping wasn't bad enough, she was naked. It wouldn't have been so bad if she was freshly scrubbed from the shower naked, but no. She was post coital perversion naked. To Tally, it seemed to defy the laws of physics that while she had a reasonable behind for the sheet to gravitate to, the damn thing had a magnetic attraction to her ankles.

Yes, this was the pinnacle of misery. One would think she'd be grateful she hadn't landed on the floor. Not Tally. The bed made her pose that much more obscene. She was facedown, ass up, with thighs spread.

"Wow. I only got to steal a glimpse at Middy when she was in the changing room. This is much better," he chortled.

"You are a dirty old man, Merlin." Tally squirmed to turn over on the bed while she clamped her legs together to avoid showing off any more than she already had. Merlin was kind enough to stand and gawk without so much as even an offer to look away, let alone come to her aid.

"I've never denied it. Will you hurry up? It's a lovely landscape, but I'm here to talk business."

"You could help me, you know."

"I could, but it wouldn't be as much fun. I already repealed the Shall Not. Now you want me to help you cover your ass, too?"

"The whole C-Y-A thing is subjective, don't you think?"

"You're a smart one, still bantering when your hind parts are in the air. Most women feel vulnerable in such a position."

"Seriously, you're asking how I'm feeling? Stop trying to shrink my head, or worse, hit on me," Tally grumbled.

"I'm on a strict diet of Nimue, but she knows I browse the menu."

"Ew. Don't tell me about old people sex." Tally finally righted herself and sat up on the bed, sheet in place. "You don't look old at all."

"Finally!" he exclaimed.

"I'm still not sleeping with you though, or displaying my parts," Tally said primly.

"I've already seen the core of your parts, my dear. I could see all the way to your back teeth from my vantage on that last pose."

She gasped. "What do you want?"

"Oh. Right. First of all, you've got early release from parole for good behavior. I've never seen anyone learn their lessons so quickly. And it was obvious you weren't just 'spewing the party line' as they say."

His verbiage was awfully familiar. It sounded much like her conversation with Falcon before they'd . . . Had Merlin been listening? The very idea made her feel dirty—in a bad way.

"As *they* say, huh? Okay, great, but I have the feeling you're here for something else."

"Yeah, that. You're going to break the gypsy's curse."

"Excuse me?"

"Because you're going to take it from him," Merlin added with a much too innocent smile.

"How about when shit sticks to the moon?" Tally replied sweetly.

"Do you want Falcon to die?"

"He's Cupid. He can't die."

"He will lose his job if he doesn't believe in love. And that means he's going to die. I've seen what's coming. The choice, ultimately, is yours."

"What does that have to do with me breaking the gypsy's curse?" Merlin just shrugged, unwilling or unable to answer. "Will I die if I take on the curse?" Tally asked pointedly.

"I can't tell you." He didn't look at all sorry about it, either.

"You're an asshole."

"What?"

"You. Are. An. Asshole. You come down here and give out little snippets of information, but then when we ask the important questions, you're all Mr. Classified. It's crap."

"Look, I wasn't even supposed to tell you that much."

"And yet you did. You dole out these pieces of information for your own ends and half the time, it seems like those ends are entertainment purposes."

"Hmm. It looks like when you do something, you do it in a big way." Merlin laughed.

"What's that supposed to mean?"

"Well, you were never a mousy little thing like Middy, but you didn't always say what was on your mind, either. Now, you open your mouth and out comes word vomit."

"You know I hate word vomit. Stay out of my head. Is there no privacy?"

"Not really. I had to be sure you were actually learning your lessons."

"Who says you get to decide if I've learned them or not?"

"Exactly."

"Wait, what?" Tally blinked like a confused owl.

"Get dressed."

"You're the one who has me naked."

"I do, don't I?" Merlin eyed her lasciviously.

"Have I mentioned you're a dick?" Tally sighed.

"No, but you did say I was an asshole. Just don't call me a pussy and we're good." Merlin winked at her.

"Are you ever serious?"

"Are you ever *not* naked?"

"I don't know how Nimue stands you," Tally huffed.

"She's worse. She always gets the last word." Merlin looked her up and down and obviously didn't like what he saw. "Are you going to get dressed?

"Are you going to turn around?" she tossed back.

"I've already seen it. Why bother?"

"I thought men from your time were supposed be all about Round Table chivalry?"

"Oh, no, my dear. Arthur meant well, but most knights, even those of the Round Table were whoremongering louts. But louts though they all were, Arthur was a nice guy," Merlin supplied.

Tally fussed with the sheet, hoping Merlin would get a clue she wasn't moving until he turned around. "And look what happened to him. I guess nice guys really do finish last."

"Don't they? Look at me. Nimue locked me in a tree stump for a hundred years."

"I'm sure you deserved it. Further, you are not a *nice guy*."

"How am I not nice? I gave you to Falcon for parole, I repealed the Shall Not, I—" he began.

"For starters? You could give me my magick back."

"I didn't take it away."

She sighed again. "You could let me use it."

"I did say you were off parole."

"Oh. Now I feel stupid." Tally blushed.

"That's because you were too busy trying to be right instead of listening to what I'm telling you."

"Are you going to turn around or what?"

"I could incinerate that sheet," he stated.

"I could tell Nimue."

"You drive a hard bargain. What's with you and Falcon both holding that woman over my head?"

"You need to think about your behavior instead of trying to be right," Tally threw his own words back at him.

"I am right. It's just you're still talking."

"Shut up."

"Get dressed."

"Turn around."

"Fine. Sweet Me, but you're difficult. Five minutes, woman. And no primping with your hair. Wait, why are we even arguing? You have your magick back. Charm yourself gorgeous and let's go."

"Where are we going?"

"To see a woman about a clam."

"I don't like how this sounds."

"Too bad!" Merlin said gleefully. "I wonder if Caspian will like this one any better? It worked for Dred; we'll see how it works on the fairer sex." Merlin snickered.

"Wait, what?" Who was Caspian and what did he have to do with Dred?

Merlin had exited her dream, but he was still near. What bothered Tally was that while she was skipping along the primrose path, literally, she could still hear Merlin talking to her sleeping body. That didn't sit right with her at all. It shouldn't be so easy for him to put someone to sleep, immersed in some shiny, happy Hell of his design—and it had to be his, because there was no way that this tripe lived in *her* head.

There were flowers. Lots of flowers. She hated flowers. They made her sneeze. Tally wasn't one of those cute little witches who sneezed with a delicate little nose twitch like some cuddly forest animal's. When she sneezed, it was a call out to sea to warn captains of the fog. Or a short burst from a tornado siren. And no matter how hard she tried, she spit like a camel every time she sneezed.

Tally kept waiting for her eyes to water, for her nose to itch, and the back of her throat to feel like someone was gagging her with a feather duster.

Nothing.

She had to admit the flowers were kind of pretty when they weren't out to get her. They were all pink. Tally had developed a recent affinity for pink.

That was until she saw the obscenely pink thing waiting for her in the clearing.

Merlin was one sick fuck. That's all there was to say.

Tally didn't know which bothered her more—the fact that it was shaved with a little heart design vajazzled with tiny cubic zirconia, or that she knew it was going to talk. She was horrified by both. She'd never get vajazzled, so this couldn't be her snatch.

She wanted to hold her breath. She didn't want to be this close to her snatch, seeing as she'd had sex not too long ago. In small doses, it didn't bother her, but this was a five-foot-three-inch pussy with feet. Would it have bad breath?

Tally supposed she shouldn't worry about its breath, but what it had to say to her. Obviously, it was important, or Merlin wouldn't have done this. Unless he was really bored—Tally wasn't going to discount the possibility.

"Hi, sweetie," it cooed.

Oh, this was so not happening. Nope. Nuh-uh. Especially when the lips moved as it talked. She was going to have nightmares about her nightmares until . . . well, forever. After she was dead, Tally was sure this very moment would still be emblazoned in her brain like a bad tattoo.

"You're not going to freak out, are you? We haven't got much time and this is important."

Why did everyone she met ask her if she was going to freak out? Was she a freaking-out sort? Tally didn't think she was, even though these situations certainly warranted a minor case of freaking right the hell out.

"Nope, I think I'm good. I'll freak out later."

"Excellent."

Why did it have a Southern accent? The vajazzled heart changed shape until it spelled out Falcon's name. Tally's stomach flopped over on itself and she raised an eyebrow.

"It's that simple. You love him."

"No, I don't," she squeaked.

"I thought you said you weren't going to freak out?"

"I'm not freaking out. You're mistaken about that, too," Tally reaffirmed.

"No, sweets. I'm not. We love him."

"You love him. He's a great fuck," Tally agreed.

"No, no." It sighed and Tally held her breath, just in case. "We. Love. Him. Figure it out, before we lose him."

"He doesn't want to be loved."

"He does. He doesn't know it yet. It's up to us to show him. After we save him, of course, but I can't talk about that."

"Again with the cryptic crap. I've had enough of this. . . ." Tally trailed off when she saw the thing opening its mouth and stretching a little too wide for Tally's comfort. No wonder males had so many issues with the vagina. They thought they were going to be eaten whole.

"Look, Ma! No great and terrible evil!"

"I don't need to look, really," Tally reassured it.

"No, you do. You're still worried we're going to chomp Falcon up into bitty, digestible pieces. Come on. Have a look. We haven't been friends since this thing happened. I miss you."

"What?" Tally choked.

"Touching me is healthy. We like it. Falcon, as talented as he is, won't be around to massage me all the time. We're in our prime. What happened with Vargill isn't my fault. You have to stop blaming me and yourself. You've learned the lessons, right? So, come say hello."

"I don't wanna."

"You're not getting out of here until you do and my time is almost up. There's only one other body part who's interested in talking and I don't think you want to hear what he has to say."

"He?"

"He's mad at you and Tristan for a certain experimental phase. . . ."

"Fine." Tally took a step closer to the walking vagina and peered inside. It was right. No teeth. "Okay."

"Now, touch me."

"I can't."

"Why not?" It sounded bereft.

"Look, you're nice and everything, but I'm not into snatch."

"I appreciate your honesty, but you have to hit your button if you want to go home."

"My button?"

"You know the button? The man in the boat? The bud? Hard pleasure nubbin? Merlin's Bribe for Childbirth? Nature's Rubik's Cube? I got that last one from *Robot Chicken.* Wait, no, I think it was *Family Guy.*"

"Okay, that's enough. I don't need to hear you're having your own thoughts while we watch reruns on Hulu."

"Look, I'm not really me. I'm you. A part of you that you don't want to face and understandably so. Push the bean just to show what you've learned and you can get the hell out of here."

Tally reached out a tentative hand and poked at the warm flesh. It didn't feel so very foreign. In fact, it was kind of nice. When she poked it, she felt it right where she would if she was touching it on herself.

"There you go, honey. I'll see you at home," it said.

And Tally woke up in her bed, with her fingers shoved inside her wet, clenching slit to the second knuckle.

She didn't really *need* another orgasm, but it felt so good. Not only because of the physical pleasure it brought her, but because she was starting to feel at home in her own skin again.

Maybe, just maybe, Merlin knew what he was doing after all.

CHAPTER FOURTEEN
Birds of a Feather

Something about Tally was different. Falcon couldn't put his finger on it, but it bothered him. She'd hummed in the shower and hadn't even cursed his closet gnome when it wouldn't give her a pair of socks. She seemed *happy*.

He did realize that on the surface that sounded like ten kinds of shitty. Falcon wanted her to be happy, but the way things were headed, the world was going to end swallowed by a wolf. Maybe it was the kind of manic joy that came with just saying "fuck it"?

Falcon wandered downstairs to warn his mother and brothers that Tally had spent the night—and would be spending the night for the foreseeable future.

He saw his mother, Stardust, fussing over some potion or another on the stove. The house smelled like homemade chocolate chip cookies, still gooey from the oven. His mother was cruel that way. Not intentionally, of course. She knew how her boys loved homemade cookies. It was just the ones that came out of her oven never tasted like cookies. Sometimes sawdust or ferret bedding, but never cookies. Potions she could do, but cooking—he was sure there was actually a law against the way she did it.

"Just where the bloody hell have you been, boy-o?" Raven demanded as Falcon walked in and dropped a kiss on his mother's forehead.

"You're not British," Hawk corrected him.

"No, but I like to say 'bollocks' and 'quim.' " Falcon imagined Raven could feel the ghost of his mother's hand connecting with the back of his head from the look she fired his way. "And that I love me mum," he added.

Stardust Cherrywood smiled back at her son and went on about the business of whatever witchery she was brewing on the stove.

Raven took the opportunity to add, "And Dred's black book says it will get me laid. The thing talks. Can you believe that?"

"I'd believe just about anything when it comes to Dred." Hawk shrugged.

"You didn't answer the question." Raven smirked. "And tell us about the Amazons."

"Better than that, Raven. I got you a date with one."

"You're serious?"

"No," Falcon snorted. "You couldn't handle the Valkyries."

"You said they canceled?"

Falcon smirked and it bloomed into a sly grin. Raven punched him and Falcon blocked, until Hawk got behind him.

"Total dick move, Hawk. Dick. Move."

"Take your lumps," Hawk fired back.

"Okay. I'll take them, but I'll keep the Amazons' Witch-Berry numbers."

"Maybe I was a bit hasty," Hawk conceded and released him.

Falcon slapped down two business cards and animated warrior women danced across them.

"Do we get the lust potion you dip your arrows in, too?" Raven asked excitedly.

"Hell no. That would be like slipping them roofies. What's wrong with you? You're lucky Mom didn't hear you or she'd kick your ass. Or worse, make you eat whatever that is trying to crawl out of the Crock-Pot." Falcon shook his head and then ducked, just as a wooden spoon sailed past his head.

"Sorry, Mom. I have to be honest. It's an angel thing." Falcon supposed it was beyond ironic that he was lying. About the angel thing, not about her cooking.

Stardust's scowl warmed to a smile. She motioned for Falcon to come back over to her and he did, even though he knew what was to follow. He presented his face and she pinched his cheeks and cooed to him about how proud she was of his Crown Prince of Heaven status.

Then he braced himself for the slap. He always got the slap for dying. It always hurt like hell, too. The Trifecta had decided at a very young age that their mother had needles in her hands. She was like a porcupine and could summon them at will to slap the ever-loving hell out of them when they'd been particularly bad.

He smiled at his mother before she slapped him. Falcon could understand her dismay. If he hadn't taken the Cupid job, he'd have stayed dead. It would break her heart in a million pieces to lose any of her children.

Instead of slapping him, she just patted his cheek. "You're a good boy, Falcon. Not like those other two. How's Drusilla?"

How to answer that one? Hot and tasty?

"She's good. You can ask her yourself. We had a bit of a problem with the house and we stayed over."

"You'll take good care of our Tally," Stardust said with a warm smile. Her warm, dark eyes sparkled with mischief.

And how did he know it was mischief? Because he'd seen it mirrored on his brothers' faces before they'd all stomped directly in exceedingly deep piles of shit.

"Mama—" he began. He always called her "Mama" when he was trying to get his way. It usually worked.

"Well, I'd just hoped that one of you would marry her. I

love that girl like my own child and I want her to be a part of the family."

"That doesn't explain the sparkle in your eyes, woman," Falcon teased.

"Now that my son is Cupid, I'd think he could indulge his aging mother with an arrow to one of your brothers."

"Like hell," Raven growled.

"Mom, the witch has a great and terrible evil in—" Hawk started.

"She does not!" Falcon's wings exploded out of his back and he looked every inch an avenging angel ready to smite his hapless brothers.

"Whoa! You're a little touchy there, Falcon," Hawk said.

"Oh, my Goddess! You fucked her?" Raven's mouth fell open.

Stardust took the opportunity to hex a bar of soap into his mouth. "You watch your mouth. Especially about our Tally." She turned to Falcon. "If you're engaging in relations with that witch, you'd better treat her well, Falcon. I don't care how big your wings are, I'll still take a wooden spoon to your butt."

"Mom, it's a Shall Not." *Liar.*

"Oh," she said as if she understood. "Well, what about shooting one of your brothers for her?"

"I'm not shooting my brothers." Hell no, he wouldn't shoot either one of them. They were on their own. Not to mention, the idea of Tally with either one of them pissed him off like a bear with his head stuck in a beehive with no honey.

"Well, thank Merlin for that," Hawk said and Raven nodded along, the soap still in his mouth.

"You should know, Hawk—" Falcon squinted at him. "I can see your aura. It's a little pink."

"*Your* wings!" he shot back.

"Yes, dumbass. I'm aware of my wings. I'm telling you

though—your aura is pink already. That means you're in love. You'll save yourself a lot of trouble if you just admit it."

"Look, just because my girlfriend's pregnant doesn't mean I'm in love." Hawk froze and his head turned toward his mother with all the recalcitrance of a rusty hinge.

Stardust Cherrywood turned a shade of red best reserved for candy apples, nail polish, and fast cars. "She's what?" Her eyebrows shot up into her still-dark hair like rummaging rodents.

Raven snickered around his soap.

"If you can still talk, that bar isn't big enough." Stardust shot him a look that would've been more at home on a vengeful goddess.

"I wanted to tell you, but I knew you'd be a little upset," Hawk ventured, his hands out in front of him in supplication.

"Who is this girl and how far along is she?"

"She's due in a month. It's a boy. We named him Orion."

"When's the wedding." It wasn't a question, not really.

"Neither of us wants to get married."

"After I talk to her family, she will." Stardust nodded as if that would make it so.

"She's not a witch. She's mortal."

"*Uno che va in culo a sua madre!*" Stardust gripped the counter for support.

Falcon had to stymie a snicker. She'd basically said "motherfucker." Since Hawk's woman was pregnant, he found it to be an ironic word choice. Hawk looked for a moment like he was considering how fast he could get out of there and whether it would worth the curses she was sure to fling at his head when he got back.

Tally's laughter echoed from the stairs and she wandered into the kitchen. "Mama Stardust, what did they do now?"

Stardust continued on in a rush of heated Italian, but

Tally just put an arm around her shoulders and stirred the bubbling brew on the stove. She'd always been good at soothing his mother.

Stardust sighed and explained what had happened.

Tally just smiled that secret smile she'd been wearing since they woke up. "I think Merlin may actually know what he's doing. It will all work out. I'm sure of it."

"Which of my boys do you want? I will give you one. You will marry him and give me fat grandbabies."

Tally didn't look at all like the deer in headlights he felt like. She simply kept smiling. "You know, I've always been particularly attached to Falcon. He taught me to ride my first broom, you know. I think I'll take him." She winked at him.

Stardust clapped her hands together. "Good! We'll plan the wedding today."

If Falcon had been a lesser warlock, he might have pissed himself.

But Tally managed his mother in a way no one else could. She kissed Stardust's cheek dutifully. "Thank you, Mama Stardust. But we have to wait for Falcon to shoot himself with one of his love bullets before we can do that."

His mother's eyes narrowed with a predatory gleam. "Is that all? *I* will shoot him."

Tally laughed again, the sound light and musical to his ears. He liked her laughter. "No, no. I was teasing. You always told me things will happen in their own time. And they will. Both for me and for Falcon, even for Hawk and Raven." Stardust was still making a face. "Just like they did for Middy."

"Okay." She seemed resigned. "But, it wouldn't hurt to have it all planned, would it?"

"Tally is going to work with me today. No time," Falcon interjected.

"We've got to go to work, too, Mom." Hawk grabbed

Raven by the collar of his shirt and yanked him out the back door. They forgot their brooms, but Falcon knew they wouldn't be back for them any time soon.

Stardust kissed both him and Tally on the cheek. "You be careful. Spread some love. All the worlds can always use more."

He grabbed Tally and flashed them to a cloud, where he charmed a picnic to spread itself out before them. "It can't hurt to have lunch before we put our noses to the grindstone, right?"

Tally giggled, genuine joy on her face. "A picnic on a cloud? I thought they were all mist? This feels like one of those bouncy houses Middy and I loved as kids." She bounced up and down to demonstrate.

"One of the perks of being Cupid. I'm supposed to hang out in cloud cover and shoot the unsuspecting."

He wondered if he should bring up her discussion with his mother or if she would. She'd said she didn't want any kind of a relationship. They'd had the discussion, but the way she was talking with his mother it was like she expected something to suddenly change.

But she didn't say anything. She kept popping grapes in her mouth and leaned back on the cloud, seemingly content to watch the world below drift by.

"Oh!" she squealed and popped up onto her knees. "Give me your love gun."

"I, uh, just gave it to you again this morning."

"Warlocks." She shook her head. "Give me the gun or the bow and arrow. Hurry up!"

For one horrifying moment, Falcon thought she meant to shoot him. Until she jerked the gun out of his hand and aimed it at a young girl who was sitting on a bench in a park down below. She was crying, sobbing like her heart was broken.

Tally aimed and fired.

Falcon could suddenly see everything about this girl, the path of her life, and whom she would love. Whom she was meant to be with. As soon as Tally's bullet hit her, it splintered in half. Those branches that had grown from the tree of her heart withered and died; new branches erupted and bloomed. The new leaves were brighter, more vibrant than the old ones representing the man she was supposed to be with, the one who'd made her cry. His branches withered, died, and the soil of his heart went fallow.

Together, they would have both bloomed, but she was obviously better off without him. And he ended up with no one.

"There! All fixed."

"Tally, you can't just shoot people randomly."

"It wasn't random. I knew she'd be happier."

"How did you know that?"

She shrugged. "I just did. It was like she was a seed. Her love was the tree she'd grow into."

Tally had seen that girl's path with *his* magick! "If you saw that, then you saw what happened to the other boy she was supposed to love."

"The other boy she was supposed to love was unworthy. Why should she have to suffer so he can bloom? Her leaves and branches were stronger, brighter, and her life will be better without him. His blooms were small and sickly anyway."

Falcon felt like they were talking about him and Tally rather than the girl Tally had shot. "Who are we to decide that?"

"First, it's your freaking job. Second, we're not. Not really. Nature does. Survival of the fittest, right? Those sad little bursts wouldn't survive the first freeze. The first bit of trouble between them and they'd wither and die."

"Just because a love hasn't yet bloomed into what it could be doesn't mean it wouldn't ever."

She sighed. "Right, but again, why should that girl who loves with her whole heart have to suffer until he decides she's good enough?"

Oh, they definitely weren't talking about those other people anymore.

"If she loves him, wouldn't that be worth it?"

"No. Not for one second. He will never love her the way she loves him. So, I saved her a lot of pain. If he never loves, that's his loss. His failing. It shouldn't be hers when she was so obviously made to love."

"I don't agree."

"That's why you're a shitty Cupid."

"I wouldn't even be Cupid if—" He snapped his mouth shut and leaned back on the cloud.

"It's okay, Falcon. You can say it. It's the truth. I didn't hesitate to tell you that you're a shitty Cupid and you shouldn't hesitate to tell me that you blame me for putting you in this position. Because I did. My actions brought you here. I own that. But that doesn't mean you shouldn't do the best with that you have."

"I'm supposed to be the good guy, Tally. I know it wasn't your fault. I shouldn't have said that."

"But it was my fault. I made my own choices. And you almost died."

Falcon realized that now was the time to tell her that he forgave her. She shouldn't have had to ask for his forgiveness the way she had with Tristan. His own words screamed back in his ears. *I'm supposed to be the good guy.* But Falcon wasn't. He was selfish and cowardly. He wasn't the good guy at all.

"Tally, I already said I don't blame you. I was just being more of what I'm good at. Shitty."

"You always were the one to try and shoulder everything when Middy and I were growing up. For your mom, your brothers . . . That's what you're good at."

"I know you didn't ask me for it like you did Tristan, but you shouldn't have to ask. You should already know that I do forgive you. My mother forgives you. My brothers forgive you. And Middy said there was nothing to even forgive you for."

Tally's eyes widened as he spoke; then she closed them, her hands clasped together and her knuckles white from her grip.

"Thank you," she whispered. Tally sat that way for a long moment and when she opened her eyes, she seemed to be more herself. Until she spoke. "For your own sake, I hope you find a way to believe in love. You don't have to love me, but if your magick fails and you lose your position as Cupid, you're going to die."

"Tally, I care about you." He wanted to say more, but he didn't know what.

"I know. I care about you, too. But I meant what I said. It's not about me. Or even us."

"No, it's about the world." Falcon knew that. He also knew that if his magick failed, the power of his bullets and arrows would fail. Ethelred would no longer be in love with Luminista. The new Cupid could shoot Ethelred again, so he would fall in love with the male twin. And love would break the curse on Emilian Grey. "And you were absolutely right to tell me that I have to do the best with what I have." In fact, those words had made the decision for him.

His death seemed a small price to pay to set so much else right. But he didn't want Tally to feel any guilt. She had enough to deal with.

"And you can apply that to everything else, too. You are not your father, Falcon. You're you. He left. But you don't run away from responsibility."

Goddess, how could she still be painting him in such glowing colors? He'd not treated her any better than any of the other assholes in her life. He'd still just been trying to get between her thighs and she'd let him. With no regrets, no recrimination.

Falcon Cherrywood realized then, at that moment, he was an asshole.

But it was a double punch because Tally loved him. The knowledge hit him hard. She *loved* him. Just the way he was. She didn't want anything more from him than what he said he could give.

He was the guy with the sickly blooms.

She would bloom so much brighter, be so much happier without him.

Falcon waited a moment, holding on to the realization like a child would a blanket. He let it wrap around him. Just for those few seconds out of time. "What's she doing now?" he asked, fighting to keep his expression neutral.

Tally peered over the edge of the cloud and when he was sure her attention was fully engaged, he pulled out his love gun and he shot her.

The next time she saw the Angel of Death, all of those feelings she'd had for him when she'd graduated from the Academy would well to the surface with the exquisite intensity of first love. She'd forget anything she felt for Falcon but sisterly affection.

He knew it was the right thing to do, but it left him with a hole inside him—dark and cavernous.

"She's gone now. The cloud was moving too fast." Tally smiled up at him. "So, that was enough work for one day, I think."

"Yeah? You'd be a bad Cupid, too." Speaking of bad Cupid, he was going to shoot the ever-loving hell out of Tristan, too. Just to make sure that when he'd said he loved Tally, he'd meant it.

"Probably. I like this cloud, though. I think we should break it in." She flashed him a wicked smile.

Falcon almost went to her, fell on his knees and buried his face in her hair, crushing her lips to his so she'd know she belonged to him. But he wasn't going to be selfish anymore. He had to let her go.

So he was going to tell her the truth.

"Tally," he began, his voice lower, more raspy than before.

"Oh. I see. Okay." Invisible armor snapped into place—her shoulders squared, her chin lifted in defiance, her body language tilted away from him. If he hadn't seen her bottom lip quiver for that single second, he never would have known how much he'd hurt her.

"I have to explain."

"You don't need to do that. I always knew this was short-term."

"It's important to me that you hear what I have to say. You're going to need to choose another Heavenly parole officer."

"Yeah, whatever. Just take me back to the beach house."

"No, damn it. Listen." Her lashes fluttered and she drew her gaze slowly up to meet his. "I am going to die, Tally. I don't believe in love and I can't force it. I don't *want* to believe in it. There is nothing that can change that. All of my magick dies with me. Except for the bullet I just shot you with. You're going to be happy with Tristan. I promised you that you wouldn't fail, and you won't."

Her mouth fell open in horror, but then promptly snapped shut. "You're an asshole, Falcon Cherrywood. A number-one, first-class asshole. This job is fucking perfect for you. I'm not angry because you don't want to love me, let's be clear on that. I'm pissed that you would manipulate my feelings for someone I told you I didn't really love and didn't want to love. It would be just like if I stole your gun and shot you so you'd love me."

She grabbed the bottle of wine and disappeared.

"That anger is what I'm counting on," he said to the empty space where she'd been. Then it occurred to him she'd teleported. That definitely violated the no magick rule. Her ass was really going to be in a sling. Shit. He used his magick to locate her and teleported after.

CHAPTER FIFTEEN

Fly, My Pretty, Fly

Tally materialized in the front room of the beach house, much to everyone's surprise. Ethelred and Luminista were playing Twister, and there were boxes of board games spread around the living room. A teapot and two proper cups were on the end table, one with a lipstick print.

"Thought you couldn't be here because you're scared of my brother?" Luminista sneered as she untangled herself from Ethelred.

"Don't fuck with me today, little girl." Tally turned her attention to the demon. "Quick, can you ward the place against angels?"

"I can, but the question is, will I?" A grin bloomed like something rancid on his face.

"Look, I can ward the place against both of you. But I don't know how to do just one. So, your choice."

Ethelred looked disappointed, but waved his hand and dark sigils burned themselves over all the doorways and windows. "You do know that just gave me complete control over you, don't you? This is now my domain."

Tally's magick crackled around her fingers in response to the threat.

"Oh, this is going to be so much fun!" Ethelred clapped. The front door exploded inward with such force, it was blown off the hinges. "Why can't I come in?" Falcon demanded. "What have you done?" he said to Ethelred.

"Only what our parolee asked of me. Seems like she doesn't want to see you."

"Tally," Falcon began.

Morrigan, but she couldn't even look at him. It hurt too much. Part of her screamed that if he was going to die, she should take what time she could get with him. He'd realized how she felt about him and he'd pushed her away as hard and fast as he could. It wasn't enough that she accepted he didn't love her; he didn't want her love, either.

"Go."

"You teleported. Your magick . . ."

"So what, Falcon? I used it. I chose to use it. I violated my parole. Your job is done. Do what you want as long as it's away from here." She knew she should have told him Merlin had released her for good behavior, but she decided she didn't owe Falcon any explanations.

He nodded slowly, didn't speak, but turned and flew away.

It was as if his presence had been a prop, holding her up. Tally's legs were suddenly boneless and Ethelred guided her to sit on the couch.

"Pour Tally a cup of tea, Lumi."

"Don't call me that. And I certainly will do no such thing as—" Luminista broke off and her eyes narrowed. "Fine."

"Don't put anything but sugar and milk in it, either."

The gypsy girl growled in displeasure.

Ethelred sat down beside her and put his arm around her shoulders. "There, there. Tell me what happened."

Tally looked at Ethelred like he'd grown another head. Why was he being so . . .

"What? Am I doing it wrong again? Lumi says this is comforting."

"It is." Tally nodded slowly. "But it's you."

"Yes, yes. Whatever. Are you going to tell us all about your big drama or not? We were playing Twister and I was winning."

"You liar. I was winning!" Luminista cried.

Ethelred smirked. "You were winning the game, but I was *winning*."

"I thought you said you weren't into girls just now?"

The demon shrugged. "Stupid Cupid went a-meddling. What can I do, but obey?"

"Really?" She rolled her eyes. "He is such a bastard." Even saying that made her want to cry. He wasn't a bastard. He'd said what he wanted from the beginning. Warned her. And she'd skipped along the primrose path, like she always did, only to come to the same end. She should've known better. She really should have.

Luminista was on the other side of her. "He shot you, didn't he? To make you love someone else?"

"How did you know?" Tally demanded.

"Some things are universal. I guess I don't need to hate you anymore. But Ethelred is mine, okay?"

"Woman, what have I told you about staking your claim? I'm a demon. I'm not yours. In fact, I'm more determined than ever to seduce Falcon. And this one. Just because."

"Not by yourself, you're not."

Ethelred perked up, his attention now firmly on Luminista. "Oh, really?"

"Can you two go upstairs to play your sex games? I'm kind of having a meltdown right now."

"No, this is the perfect time to play sex games. You're at your most vulnerable," Ethelred supplied happily.

Tally narrowed her eyes and power crackled around her fingers again.

"That's so cool, you have to teach me how to do that," Luminista squealed.

"About that, you know you're not supposed to be using your power. I mean, I'm all for Team Hell, but you know I like to come by my wins honestly. Mostly."

"Oh, I'm not on parole anymore. Merlin let me off for good behavior, lessons learned, and all that. I came here because I didn't have anywhere else to go."

"I know what that's like, too." Luminista nodded.

Ethelred perked up again. "And this is where we make our exit, Lumi, darkling."

"Stop calling me that."

Ethelred dragged her from the couch and up the stairs. Tally wondered what the big hurry was until she saw Emilian Grey emerge from the garage. He froze, with his hand on the doorframe.

She hadn't even stopped to think he'd be here.

The heavy silver collar around his neck did little to reassure her, especially as his eyes began to change to an awful uric hue. He closed his eyes, his chest rising and falling rapidly with the deep breaths he forced into his body.

"I thought you weren't going to be here," he said.

"Me, too."

They were both silent for a long moment. His eyes were still closed. "Can we talk, if I stay over here?" he asked her.

He held the world's destruction inside him. Poor bastard. Tally knew exactly how he felt. "No."

"I understand."

"No, you don't have to stay over there. When you have control of yourself, you can come sit next to me."

His eyes opened and the uric color was still there. The animalistic hunger in them made her want to rear back, to run and keep running until she was sure he'd never catch her. But she held her ground. "You stink of fear." The voice wasn't Emilian's.

"You would be the one stinking of fear if you'd met me

a few months ago. I want to talk to Emilian. What you and I have to say to each other will keep until later." Later as in never.

Emilian's eyes changed back to a strange silver with yellow rings around the iris, and it occurred to her that even though he was the apocalypse, he was very beautiful.

The gypsy prince breathed for a few more moments, just inhaling and exhaling, as if that in itself were a victory for him. Then he made his way over to her. Each step was careful and measured until he sat down next to her.

Tally would admit that she was afraid. Fear ran thicker than blood in her veins.

"How did you do that?" he asked.

"Do what?"

"You quieted the beast. He obeyed you. He's *afraid* of you. Are you a Crown Princess of Hell?"

"No, but I'm pretty sure I'm headed to that sunny locale in a handbasket as we speak." She gave him a weak smile. "Afraid of *me*? I highly doubt that. I'm just a witch."

"That's why I changed back to myself at the cabin. He was afraid."

They were both quiet again, the silence awkward and gravid with something Tally couldn't name.

"I know sorry isn't adequate, but I am. Fuck, but I'm sorry."

Tally pushed her small hand into his and he looked up at her, eyes wide with disbelief. "It's okay, Emilian. Sorry *is* enough."

He patted her hand, but tried to pull away. "Not when I'm going to be the end of all things."

She refused to let go of him. "Sometimes, sorry is all we have. These dark things, they get inside us and they feed on guilt and pain. We keep feeding them because we don't know what else to do."

"How do you know? I can't forgive myself for what I

know I'm going to do. Because I know what's going to happen. I should be able to stop it."

"I do know, Emilian. I do." Tally nodded. "To people in the magickal world, I'm the story they tell their children to get them to mind. Like the boogeyman. If people see me on the street, they cross to the other side to avoid me. They spit on the ground where I've walked in case it's cursed. What's your body count?"

"What?"

"How many people has your beast killed?" she asked softly.

"None. But he's going to kill—"

"Then you have nothing to be sorry for yet. The evil that was inside me has a body count, Emilian. And if not for the sacrifice of good people, it could have been the whole world. I could have been the apocalypse for both the mortal and the magickal world. I have to live with that. So when I say that I understand the burden you carry, I do."

The gypsy prince seemed to dissolve in front of her, melting against her as he buried his face in her neck like a small boy who'd skinned his knee.

Tally carded her fingers through his hair in a soothing motion. "It's okay, Emilian. You're not alone." He shuddered against her with a dry sound of absolute wretchedness. There was pain in that sound such as few people would ever know. Such as no one should have to know. "You're not alone," she said again.

Merlin's words came back to her about breaking the curse. The Wheel of Life turned to a rhythm that was more complex than any consciousness could comprehend. Tally had been given lessons to learn and everything had happened in order to teach her those lessons. It wasn't a tapestry of fate, but more like a flower. Each bloom had many petals that touched other blossoms and caused them to bloom, the petals being the lessons each life had to learn.

The concept was almost too profound to process, but suddenly her narrow vision of life, herself, and the world expanded. She could see the whole Wheel, and it was beautiful.

She knew what she had to do and she needed Ethelred's help to do it.

Even knowing what she did now, she was still afraid. Tally could see that she would, in fact, save the world. Which was only fitting, because she'd almost destroyed it. This was why Merlin had let her off parole. Because parole wasn't really what it was about. This moment, now, this was her second chance.

While she could see that she would succeed in saving everyone else, the Powers That Be had chosen not to show her if she could save herself.

But Tally guessed that was kind of the point.

CHAPTER SIXTEEN

One Bourbon, One Scotch, One Beer

What the actual fuck?

This was not what Falcon had intended when he'd shot Tally, he decided as he watched the scene unfold from the window. She'd gone from bad to worse. She was supposed to call Tristan, and the Angel of Death was supposed to come and save her. When she saw Tristan, Falcon's bullet would activate and she'd forget all about him.

It was perverse of him, but he had to see it happen to make sure Tally was taken care of. He didn't want to leave her alone until he was certain.

But it looked as if she didn't need him to take care of that for her. Watching Ethelred put his arm around her and seeing Tally accept that touch sparked something dangerous in Falcon's gut.

He'd been ready to charge in, magick blazing, when Emilian entered, but Tally had that handled, too. She held the end of the world in her arms and she petted his hair, comforted *him*. Tally didn't need Falcon for anything he could give her.

A wish erupted into the forefront of his mind, something he had never let himself want. It burned its way through all of his walls and fortifications. A yearning for something he knew he could never have. A future. A forever home with a forever mate. Triplet girls who looked just like their mother, who were as he'd described her: tiny, golden balls of pixie mayhem. Sudden images of that future assaulted him, each like a knife that sliced into the core of him.

He saw his mother bouncing those girls on her knees, birthday parties, and private evenings spent wandering the beaches of Captiva Island, shelling, watching the odyssey of the baby turtles returning to sea. He saw him and Tally making love in moonlit grottos among the mangroves.

And he wanted that with her more than he wanted his next breath.

Even if he could be sure the wanderlust wouldn't take him, death would. It was the only way to ensure the gypsy curse would be broken. He'd trade his life for five more minutes with Tally, but not the whole world. Not her life. Tristan would make her happy.

He needed a drink. Or four. He could at least go out with a bottle of good bourbon in his hand.

Falcon teleported to The Banshee's Bawl, a favored bar on the magickal side of St. Louis. He barely made it. He blinked in and out like a cell phone with a bad signal. His body was like static, flickering through beams of light. His magick was already failing. Merlin had said it would happen fast, but Falcon had thought he'd have just a bit more time.

He wandered into the bar. It was fairly empty, populated by just a few witches and warlocks looking for a hookup or to buy unsavory magicks. He was simultaneously pleased and irritated to see the Angel of Death, Tristan Belledare, sitting in a darkened corner.

He made his way over to Tristan's table and sat down. Falcon entertained the idea of just shooting him from afar, but he didn't trust his aim this late in the game.

"Not a good time, man," Tristan growled.

"Not for either of us, buddy."

"I'm in the middle of something."

"Yeah, me, too, and I have to get it done before I die. Which is going to be any minute now."

"What?" Tristan demanded as he pushed a bottle of whiskey closer. "Take a drink and start talking."

"Were you serious when you told Tally you loved her?"

Tristan looked like a kid in the last round of a spelling bee who'd just been asked to spell "hippopotomonstrosesquipedaliophobia."

"Is that a no?" Falcon pulled his gun and cocked it under the table.

"What is wrong with you? Do they have a name for it?" Tristan demanded.

"Yes. It's called handling my business. We both know I wasn't meant to be Cupid. Either I believe in love, or I die. So—"

"I don't know how to break it to you, but you're not on my list to reap today. Or for the foreseeable future."

"Then that's bad fucking news."

"Are you in such a hurry to die?"

"No. I'm in a hurry to save the world. I stabbed Ethelred with a love arrow because he pissed me off."

Tristan laughed. "I would have liked to have seen his face."

"Pay attention."

"Right, sorry. Go on." The Angel of Death took another gulp of whiskey.

"I fucked with Merlin's Grand Plan with this gypsy curse thing. I can't let the Powers That Be wipe two souls out of existence for my mistake. If I don't believe in love, I lose my job. Then I'll die as I was meant to the day of your funeral when the lamia knocked me off my broom. And the magick that enchanted Ethelred will fade so Merlin's Grand Plan can be shoved back on track."

"So you think you can give me Tally giftwrapped?" The Angel of Death rolled his eyes. "Why am I the only one who understands it doesn't work that way? Dred tried to give me Middy, too, when he found out she was going to die."

"He tried to do what with my sister?"

"Shut up and listen to me, idiot. You cannot give one person to another. People love where they love."

"Unless you're Cupid."

"And you want to shoot me to ensure that I will love Tally forever?" Tristan made a big show of pretending to think it over. "Yeah, that's all well and good, but did you forget that Tally is in love with you?"

"I already shot her."

"You *what*?" Tristan palmed his forehead and then looked skyward. "If I ever meet a witch who has the misfortune to love me, I swear I won't be this stupid." He sighed. "Did you forget the part where I told you that you're not on the schedule to be reaped? A Crown Prince of Heaven such as yourself requires a personal appearance on my part. You're not going to die today. Then there's the part where I told Tally I was in love with her still just to piss you off. The apology I meant."

Just then, a woman emerged from the bathroom and headed for their table. She was, in a word, beautiful. Tall, with a curvy shape, long curly black hair, and skin he couldn't quite describe—but the color made him think of long days spent under an island sun.

"Falcon, this is Ghislaine. *My* assignment," Tristan explained.

A wicked gleam came into the woman's large, amber eyes and she smirked. "Seems Ethelred left quite a bit out of Michael Grigorovich's contract. He has relatives in the mortal world hunting for Emilian and a way to access all the power he amassed before he died. Bad men who have already taken over the Grigorovich crime family."

"Are you related to Emilian, too?" It seemed the best-laid plans of gods and men always ran amok. There was a reason it rhymed with fuck. Because they were all fucked facedown.

"No. I have a particular gift that the Grigorovich family wants." She looked at Tristan, who motioned for her to continue. "I can raise an army of the dead. I'm a Zombie Master. Apparently, The Powers That Be don't like what I've been doing with my gifts. Death here is supposed to keep me on a short leash."

"We're always on the brink of extinction, or apocalypse. If it's not one damn thing, it's another."

"Exactly!" Tristan snapped to attention. "So even if you do make this stupid and unnecessary sacrifice, someone else is going to come along and shit all over it anyway. Why bother?"

"I guess my number's just up. Better souls have gone before me, and my life is all I have to give." He shrugged, embarrassed at being laid so bare in front of anyone, especially Tristan and this woman he'd just met.

The Zombie Master looked at him, a soft expression on her face. "Are you sure about that?"

"And that's why I'm a Crown Prince of Hell," Tristan snorted. "You wouldn't catch me hanging my ass out in the breeze for people who aren't smart enough to appreciate the sacrifices that have already been made for them. I say we let Darwinism have its wicked way with the populace and call it a day."

"You still didn't answer my question, Belledare. About Tally."

"I did, but you weren't listening. So I'll repeat myself. Just this once. I'll get crayons and puppets so you understand. Tally doesn't love me. But I give you my word as a Crown Prince of Hell, if you die, I'll look after her."

"Not good enough."

"That's just how it has to be. Because if you shoot me with that thing, I'm going to shove it up your ass."

"I'd trade that to know she's okay. That works for me." Falcon nodded seriously.

"Look, here's why you're not going to die today. You already love her. You don't have to admit that you do, or that you believe in love, because I already know it." Ghislaine turned to look at Tristan as he spoke. "What? It's not like I suddenly grew a vagina because I see what's in front of my face. I had to have this same talk with the guy who married his sister. If all warlocks are this dense, I'm surprised the species has survived at all. And I am sick to death of playing Cupid. That's his job!" He motioned to Falcon. "I'm the Angel of Mother-Fucking-Death. I should be reaping souls, not doing the pansy dance."

"No." Falcon shook his head, horrified. "I can't love her. I can't. Otherwise, there's no way to fix what I've done."

"Like I said," Tristan replied. "Puppets and crayons." He looked around the bar for a moment before motioning a blond witch over to their table.

She sat down next to Falcon, practically in his lap. She'd exposed her many charms with a pink gingham shirt unbuttoned to maximize her cleavage and tied off to expose her navel. She had a metal post through her belly button that had a star on the top and glittering things dangling from it that Falcon assumed were supposed to look like the tail of a comet or a shooting star, whatever. Perhaps it was supposed to draw attention to the way her very short shorts hung on her hips and her long, tanned legs.

But Falcon wasn't interested. "So?"

"So?" Tristan parroted. "Look at her. You're not even interested."

"Or maybe," the blonde began, "he's into this instead." In

place of the blonde bombshell sitting next to him was the demon Ethelred.

And before Falcon could react, Ethelred grabbed the gun and shot Cupid with his own love bullet. The demon grinned. "It's a gift from Tally."

"She's going straight to Hell." Tristan laughed. The bastard actually laughed.

"She is." Ethelred grinned. "But not for this. She says love *yourself*. And I say, payback's a bitch."

"Oh, you think that shit's funny? My arrow can't be undone if I live. You're stuck with Luminista."

"That's fine. I've been under so long, it doesn't matter now." He cackled some more. "And the best part is, Angel boy, you lose. I get Tally, too!"

CHAPTER SEVENTEEN

The Road to Hell Is Paved with Good Intentions

Ethelred had turned a rather interesting shade of purple upon his return from his errand. Tally had never seen anyone laugh so hard. Ever. Not the first time Middy cursed the cat litter to chase her brothers, not when Dred had turned Middy's braids into snakes in third grade, not even when Tally herself had cursed her tutor to spit up a Scrabble tile of the letter "y" every time she said "caysh" instead of "cash."

It was that sort of mischievous glee that only the very young or the very wicked could experience. If he'd needed to breathe, Tally would've been calling the paramedics.

He gasped, finally taking air. "It was priceless, witch. The look on his face."

"Really, it's not that funny." She put her hand on her hip.

"I don't see why you didn't want him to love *you*. Why himself?" Luminista asked.

"Because a person can't truly love someone else until they love themselves." Tally had always known that, but it wasn't something she'd ever truly felt about herself. She didn't know if she felt it now, but she wanted to. Although what she had to do next might make that impossible.

"Oh. I should be fine then. Because I love the hell out of me." Luminista grinned.

"Morrigan!" Tally swore. "You two really are perfect for each other."

"I know, aren't we just?" Luminista sighed and Ethelred rolled his eyes.

"Okay, on to the rest of my plan." Tally exhaled heavily. She'd talked to Ethelred about it briefly before sending him after Falcon.

Ethelred suddenly straightened and all joviality was gone. He reminded her of the day she'd first met him. "Are you sure this is what you want?"

"No." She gave a shaky laugh. "But it's what I have to do. I am the only one who can fix this."

"Hero complex, much?" Luminista snorted.

"No, I am the only one who *should* fix this. If Falcon dies because he can't believe in love, or doesn't want to believe in love, that's still my fault. I knocked him from his broom. His first death is all me."

"But so was Tristan's, Midnight's, and even Dred's. And look where they ended up? They're better off," Ethelred replied.

"Still playing Devil's Advocate?" Tally asked.

"Always, little witch." He gave her a genuine smile this time. "There's no going back, you know."

"I know."

"And frankly, I'm a little pissed. Do you know how long it took me to become a Crown Prince?"

"I'm sure I'll fuck it up and get demoted to Infernal Shit Shoveler," Tally replied.

"I'll have to get the Big Boss in on this contract." Ethelred looked thoughtful for a moment. "You know, for all the grief I gave you, Tally, I never expected you to choose Hell."

"I didn't, either. Hell is relative though, isn't it?"

"I usually say that it is, but in this case, no, Tally, it's not.

If this goes badly, you'll be sent back to the Abyss with the lamia *and* Emilian's curse. You'll be a Crown Princess of Hell. Immortal. So you'll have an eternity of pain."

"Great pep talk." Tally nodded, trying to keep the tears from falling.

"I've always told you the truth, Tally," Ethelred said solemnly.

"I'm ready to sign." Her voice shook, but there was no going back. As a Crown Princess of Hell, it was possible she'd have the power to summon the lamia and control it. With that magick, she could take the curse from Emilian Grey and save everyone. In essence, she was hoping that the lamia would devour the beast.

She knew the most likely outcome was the scenario that Ethelred predicted, and she was terrified. But Falcon, Midnight, and all the people she loved would be safe. Even if there was no other possible outcome than eternity in the Abyss, Tally knew she'd do it anyway.

Strangling fear bubbled inside her and the dark places in her memory spilled over into her consciousness. It was endless darkness, despair, and a gnawing in her gut that could never be satisfied—a hunger never sated, though blood and flesh were its tribute. It was the great and terrible evil, the lamia, reaching back for her through the Abyss.

She'd been wrong. Her body was still the portal. It seemed the lamia had known, felt her reaching, and had waited for the right moment to pounce.

"Ethelred," she gasped. "I don't think I can wait to make the deal." Tremors shook her body. "You need to leave now."

"Tally—" A panicked expression bent his features.

"If you want Luminista safe, get her out of here. I can't stop this."

One thing she could count on with Ethelred was the lack of nobility. He didn't need to be told twice. "I'll see you on the flip, Drusilla." He grabbed Luminista and disappeared.

Tally pushed down the fear, the memories of pain, and fought for control. She had to try to communicate with the lamia before it obliterated her will.

She reached out past the veils of dimensions, past all she knew to touch the cold, reptilian mind of the thing that had possessed her. Tally found just as the tendrils of her subconscious curled into the awareness she sought, an impossible wall blocked her. It was tall and vast, infinite.

The lamia was protecting itself from her!

Maybe the creature wasn't at all what it seemed.

Tally tried again to quell her fear and reached with more confidence. A splitting pain throbbed in her forehead and Tally saw a black box in the corner of her mind spring open. It was the memories of when the lamia had been inside her. She'd locked those away; she never wanted to feel those things again.

They were missiles, hitting her again and again. She felt sick, the bloodlust raising bile in her throat and rage that burned through her like a lava flow. Tally felt the anger as if it were her own. She knew she had to let go and allow it to fill her, but she had to channel it against the beast.

Tally schooled her breathing and centered her awareness. The memories still crashed into her, but she was able to absorb them without being shackled by them. The brick wall was in front of her again and she felt a flash of fear as the bricks began to crumble to dust, one by one.

Tally fought to control her fear, but the crumbling of the bricks stopped. A face looked back at her from behind the wall. It was her own face, but it was something else, too.

"Why are you doing this, witch?" a low, gravelly, yet distinctly feminine voice asked her.

"I have to save him. Them."

"You bring me to your dimension for righteous destruction?"

"I don't know how righteous it is. I'm using outlaw magick to invoke the greatest evil we've ever known because it's the only thing that will stop what's happening."

"Where is your Hand of Glory?" The creature referred to some of the darkest magick known to her kind, one of the only things that should have been able to summon a lamia.

"I don't have one." Tally wondered if perhaps it had been extremely naïve on her part to tell the creature the truth.

"Very interesting." Her likeness sniffed the air. "There is no lie on you. You are the same vessel as before and yet, you are not. Your need tastes different."

"It is." Tally nodded and reached out trembling fingers to pull another brick from the barrier.

"Do you fear me?"

"Oh, yes," Tally answered honestly.

"You've done penance for the atrocities we've committed?"

"Merlin says I've atoned. But I'm shitting all over my Second Chance by summoning you."

"I can see him in your mind, Drusilla Tallow, this creature you wish me to devour. He tastes like ashes." The lamia licked its lips.

"He will destroy my world. I was hoping to invoke you first, to make a deal. I want to save the vessels." She pulled another brick away.

"What do you have that I want, witch?"

"I don't know."

"What if you free me and I don't honor our deal?"

"You will. Before I pull these last bricks from your prison, our deal will be sealed with blood in the demon way."

"I have a condition. You must let me stay with you."

Tally paused. Stay with her? She was supposed to have a pet lamia? What was she supposed to do, walk it and feed it? This was insanity. Complete insanity.

"I've tasted your world and I want to stay."

"You'd be caged," Tally said.

"I've been here a long time. Alone. Your loneliness called to me, and it fed me, more than the flesh sacrificed to me. It's been an age since I've been invoked to punish the wicked, since I flew free over the Aegean."

Tally couldn't say damn the consequences. This creature could still do as much damage as the beast inside Emilian.

"You hesitate and rightfully so. But think on it, witch. No one could open the portal inside of you. No one could use you in a way you wouldn't allow. My strength and my power, all at your disposal."

"What about your hungers? I don't want to hurt innocents."

"I will serve your Heaven."

"That's not an answer. You will serve Heaven, but will I suffer the hunger? Will I have to be strong enough to fight it? I'm not that strong."

"I can't answer that. I can consume this beast, but it will become a part of you, too."

There wasn't a choice. If she couldn't bear the hunger, then she could ask Merlin to smite her. It would be worth it. The people she loved would be safe and Tally would know she'd truly atoned for what she'd done.

"It's a deal?" Tally asked.

"Yes, witch."

The creature bit its human-looking digit and presented it to Tally, its flesh producing steady droplets of blood. Tally had nothing with which to cut herself, but she was in a surreal, dream plane. She concentrated on the tip of her finger and the blood began to flow—her skin had opened up to do her will.

Tally pressed her finger against the creature's and the wall became dust. Tally screamed as she felt an unbearable pressure on her chest. The pressure merged into pain—a thousand claws tearing into her skin, something pushing through the real of her into the ethereal.

It burned so hot it was cold and terror rose up in her, strangling the air from her lungs and rational thought from her mind. She was sinking into the darkness, slipping away into the cage, to the black box where she'd kept all the horrors Martin and Barista had inflicted on her.

Falcon! His name was a prayer on her lips and she was snapped back into awareness of her own body.

Tally felt strong and solid, powerful. It was a good feeling, a rush. She was high on the strength coursing through her. She felt invincible and she was hungry. She closed her eyes and took a deep breath, but all she craved was pizza.

She wondered if that would change when she took the curse from Emilian Grey. If she would become the beast inside him.

It didn't matter, she told herself. No sacrifice was too great for Falcon's life. Even if she lived through this, she'd have to say good-bye to him. It also meant she could never tell him she loved him. Her decision made, she felt a certain sad peace. This whole redemption thing wasn't all it was cracked up to be, but it was so much more, too. A lot like love.

Then she heard a sound that chilled her to her bones: the long, slow scrape of claws against the thin wood of the walls.

The beast had come.

CHAPTER EIGHTEEN

Love Gun Misfire

S hot with his own damn bullet. How humiliating.

Then again, he supposed that didn't matter if the world was going to end.

The easy thing to do would be to sit in The Banshee's Bawl and drink until it was over. But that wasn't what he wanted.

It surprised him to realize what he did want.

Just Tally.

For five minutes or five million years—whatever she or Fate would give him.

He loved her.

He loved the way her hair curled around his finger, the way her nose crinkled when he said something she didn't like, her smile, and most of all, he loved her heart. It was big enough to love him even after everything she'd been through, and knowing he wouldn't love her back. Not in the way she needed.

She was so strong, so brave. And she deserved so much better than anything he could ever give her.

Tally had told him to love himself, but he'd done enough of that. Seducing her in the pergola, insisting on being her parole officer when Merlin was happy to reassign him, working everything to his angle to get what he wanted.

No, he couldn't love himself because his actions had hurt her. Just as he'd known they would.

There wasn't enough bourbon in the world to wash away his sins.

Some fucking Angel of Love he'd turned out to be.

Why couldn't she have just let him die, not believing in love? That would have fixed everything.

Suddenly, Ethelred's words slammed into him. *I get Tally, too.* She'd chosen Hell. Falcon had failed her in so many ways. Had she traded her soul for that bullet? No, she wouldn't be so shortsighted. She wouldn't have traded herself for anything less than the world. She'd almost destroyed it, so she'd believe she was the one who should save it.

Which would explain why Tristan had said Falcon wasn't on the docket to be reaped.

He wouldn't let her be damned.

Falcon didn't quite have a plan, but that didn't matter. His sister had told him love saved Tally the first time and he knew it would again. Even Merlin had told him that true love was the most powerful magick of all.

And he loved Tally. He'd die for her, but he realized that, most important, he'd live for her, too.

He put the glass of bourbon down, dropped some money on the table, and left.

The more love there was in the world, the more powerful he'd become. He knew in his gut he'd need all the power he could get to fix what he'd fucked up, but what filled him with a joy such as he'd never known was that he *could* fix it. He had faith in himself. In Love, with the capital "L." Maybe he could even love himself just a little bit.

He realized now that being selfish wasn't loving himself. It was like shoving a piece of candy in a crying kid's mouth. It didn't address what he really needed; it was only a stopgap. The things he really needed couldn't be accomplished through any kind of instant gratification. They were dreams, goals, a lifetime of accomplishments built on the kind of foundation he had with Tally.

He got out his love gun and took to the skies, searching for people to shoot. Falcon knew he could only water the seeds and fertilize what was already there. Love out of nothing at all was meant for dark magick and Air Supply songs.

After the first bullet, Falcon began enjoying his job. He could see the paths of people's lives just as he had that day on the cloud with Tally. He pruned what was unnecessary, dead or broken, and was surprised to see new buds growing everywhere. Within minutes, he didn't even have to shoot the gun anymore—he could bring blooms with a thought.

He was riding high, until he saw a man he hadn't laid eyes on since he was ten.

Orion Cherrywood. His father.

The bastard was sitting on a park bench with a mortal woman half his age—and his heart was black and dead—except for one, tiny green shoot that struggled through the stony soil of his soul. Falcon could see that shoot could become as strong, tall, and powerful as a redwood.

The new feelings in Falcon's own heart began to wilt, to shy away from the pain that awaited him there. He should have known that Fate would have another obstacle for him to overcome—this thing that had been at the core of all of his hurts. Falcon had yet to slay any dragons, and by Merlin, he was going to get that damned shining armor to fit if it killed him. Tally deserved nothing less.

He dropped down to the mortal world and hid his wings, his gun, and his red leather pants and manifested some street clothes. He wandered down the path that would lead him to that bench and suddenly realized he had no idea of what he was going to say.

Or if he should say anything at all. Falcon could always shoot his father and Orion would never know he'd been there.

"Falcon!" Orion's voice was a half whisper, his dark eyes wide.

No choice now. He supposed he could still shoot him and disappear; it would serve the bastard right. He'd think Falcon had come to kill him, and the pain of love blooming in his chest after all this time would certainly feel like a real bullet.

"Are you sure?" Falcon couldn't resist asking. After all, it had been years.

"I know my own sons." Orion suddenly looked old. Not in any measurable way, like lines around his eyes and mouth, or sagging skin. He was a warlock. But it was in the shadows in the depths of his eyes.

"How's your mother?" Orion asked.

Again, all of the old venom roiled up inside him. He wanted to say that if Orion gave a shit, he could have asked her himself. He could have at least let his family know where he was. But instead, Falcon said, "She's been taking a cooking class with Roderick Snow."

"How's Barista feel about that?" Orion smiled, but the expression didn't reach his eyes. It was sad.

"That's a long story I don't think we have time for." Barista was dead. She'd been Martin Vargill's partner in crime and had tried to kill, well, everyone. "Who's your friend?"

Orion looked embarrassed for a moment. "This is my therapist, Carolyn. Carolyn, this is my son, Falcon."

The woman beamed at him. "Then this is my cue. It was nice to meet you, Falcon. I hope you listen to what your father has to say."

Therapist? What the hell?

The woman got up and placed a comforting hand on his father's shoulder and walked down toward the small fountain in the center of the park.

For a moment, Orion didn't seem to want to look at him and Falcon remembered he had his own atoning to do, so he swallowed hard and said, "She seemed to think you had something to say."

"I don't know where to start."

How would he know where to start with Tally? "How about with Love?"

Orion seemed to take that as an invitation and popped to his feet to yank Falcon against him in a tight hug. "Thank Merlin, boy! I never thought I'd see you again or you'd want to see me. I'm so sorry. I never stopped loving you boys, Midnight . . . or your mother."

Falcon stood frozen by the sudden onslaught of conflicting emotions and sensations. His arms slowly melted around his father, but this time he couldn't stop the question he had to know the answer to.

"Why did you leave? Why weren't we enough?"

"It's me who wasn't enough."

All of Falcon's previous insecurities slammed back through him. He knew he shared his father's faults. He was still his father's son.

"That doesn't mean it was okay to leave us."

"I had to, Falcon." He broke away from him and looked into his eyes. "I was addicted to dark magick and no matter what I tried, I couldn't get clean. When some of the people I owed money to started coming around the house, your mother told me to choose between my family and the magick. I chose the magick." He was silent for a long moment and Falcon didn't know what to say. "I've regretted it every day of my life."

"Are you clean now?"

"Five years. I'm almost completely magick free. I use a glamour to make living in the mortal world easier, but that's it."

"Let me see."

"I—"

"Let me see the rest of the price you paid for the dark magick. No one else will see you." Falcon used his magick to insulate them from the rest of the world.

Orion dropped his glamour and Falcon had to fight not to flinch. His father's formerly handsome face was a wreck. The left side had been burned and scarred almost beyond recognition. His left eye was nothing but a burned-out socket. There was a crisscross network of thin white scars on the right side of his face that traveled down his neck. His left arm had been burned as well, as if a fountain of fire had flowed down the flesh. The hand was mangled, too, missing the pinky and ring finger. Common things sacrificed in the pursuit of dark magick. The loss of his ring finger must be recent, because the scar was still a bright pink.

"I thought you were clean."

Orion snapped the glamour back into place. "I am. Before Midnight was born, I traded a piece of her magick to a dark warlock for a crystal skull. I've since returned it." He sighed. "I wish I could renounce all my magick. I've thought about it, but I can't live in either world looking as I do. Though, it's nothing less than what I deserve."

"Midnight got married," Falcon blurted.

"I know. She's been to see me."

"Why didn't she tell me?"

"Probably because it was just yesterday. She said I should come home, Falcon."

"That would be like asking a dope fiend to live in Colombia."

"I know better."

Falcon couldn't get the sight of what his father's addiction had done to him out of his brain. "But maybe you should see Mom."

"I don't think she wants to see me."

"She loves you. Always has. Always will."

"How do you know that?"

"I'm Cupid." Falcon shrugged, and then sighed. He knew what he had to do. "I'm going to give you the same gift my woman gave to me."

"It's not the clap, is it?" Orion raised a brow.

Falcon laughed. "No, but it's more uncomfortable. At first. Love yourself, Orion."

"I don't understand."

"You will." Suddenly, Falcon wanted to puke and he had the sense that Tally needed him. Terror knifed through him. "I have to go."

"Can I see you again?"

"If the world doesn't end."

CHAPTER NINETEEN

Not by the Hair of My Chinny-Chin-Chin

"Little witch, little witch, let me in." A deep growl sounded from behind the door. The voice had once been Emilian's, but now it sounded like a layered track, as if there were three voices speaking the same words, but a millisecond off from each other.

Tally wouldn't lie to herself and pretend she wasn't afraid. She was terrified and it seeped from her every pore. She was sure the wolf could smell the fear on her like a sweet perfume.

There was a cold, distant part of her mind now and it told her this was what she wanted. If the beast thought she was afraid, he'd feel powerful and in control. She was afraid of that, too, the voice in her head, so alien, but achingly familiar. It was hungry and reptilian, but it burned.

Tally wanted to hide under the bed and cover her eyes the way she'd done when she was a child and she'd feared the monster in the closet. The urge to flee brought another memory of Falcon. She and Middy had been hiding under Middy's bed, having scared themselves stupid with a marathon of horror movies, and then they'd read Stephen King stories aloud to each other. "The Boogeyman" had scared the bemerlin out of both of them and Middy's closet gnome had creaked the closet door open, sending the girls into a shrieking frenzy. He'd later tried to sue for damages, citing their screaming for his hearing loss. Of course, if he'd been doing his job instead of eavesdropping on two little witches . . . Falcon had come to their rescue and ousted the gnome and made him admit what he'd done.

He also explained to them he was much scarier than any boogeyman. He'd promised the dark was more afraid of him than Middy or Tally were of it. They'd believed each and every word.

Now it was Tally's turn to make the dark things quake in fear of her.

She took a deep breath and opened the door, rather than waiting for him to kick it in. "It took you long enough," Tally spat.

Tally was surprised to see the beast still wore Emilian's skin. It was caught in mid-transformation. It had the form of Emilian's body, but was covered in a fine pelt; its face had an elongated snout, fissures in the flesh, and slavering jaws full of snapping teeth. Its hands were claws, but the rest of its body pulsed with power, hovering at the edge of transition.

Tally turned her back on the predator to allow him to enter behind her. She sat down in one of the chairs in the living room and motioned for him to do the same.

She reclined in the chair as if she hadn't a care in the world and the fear ebbed like low tide. Tally found she was hungry and the burn wasn't only in her stomach, but throbbed down through her mound. The lamia found this beast attractive, and wanted to devour him whole.

Perhaps she'd let her. The idea of surrendering control to the thing inside her gave her a languorous rush. It would be so easy and it would feel so good.

The beast sniffed the air around her warily and his eyes narrowed. "Clever girl, using the fear to draw me in. You fairly reek of it, but there's something else, too."

Tally crossed her legs, giving him a view of her upper thigh. "What would that be?"

His eyes were instantly drawn to her skin and he licked his lips. He could be controlled by his cock, the lamia whispered to her. Tally knew very well what kind of weapon she had at her disposal by using her body, but she didn't want to use sex as a weapon. The only hands she wanted on her flesh were Falcon's. The only man she wanted inside her never would be again.

"Such ample charms you have. All the better to eat me with, I'd think," the animal growled.

"You've taken this wolf thing to heart. You keep quoting an overused fairy tale." Tally cocked her head to the side as she studied him. "Is that supposed to be scary?"

"No more so than you flashing your body when I know what you carry can consume me."

She raised her leg on the side of the chair, exposing herself farther. "Maybe I've just got a thing for dark and brutal."

Tally couldn't believe the words coming out of her mouth; they weren't hers. This wasn't what she wanted, but it was what the lamia wanted. It whispered to her in soft, dulcet tones. It told her to trust, to believe. That this was the path to redemption and victory.

"You can't control me with sex. None of my previous lovers could," the beast growled.

"This isn't what you came for? To see if *you* could control *me* with sex? To make me so grateful any man would want me that I'd do anything for you?" Tally replied in a sultry tone. "Perhaps you're afraid," she said as she got up from the chair and advanced on him, splaying her hand on his chest. "Tell me true, are you afraid?"

His claws grew into talons and the lamia was aroused by the pain of them piercing her flesh. She laughed, daring him to do more. The last of Emilian melted away, and it was the beast who would devour the world that stood before her now.

"I am afraid of nothing, whore."

Whore. The insult ripped into the human part of her, tore at her defenses. Once, she would have felt hot, salty tears threaten, but the creature inside her forbade them. It whispered she could cry later when they were alone, when this bastard was nothing. She felt like a whore; that's why it hurt. She had no doubt this body would do what it must to this beast. She would destroy him and then feast on his bones. The Tally part of her didn't want to do it. She wanted her flesh to be sacred, for Falcon. For all the good it would do him if he were dead, the lamia sneered at her thoughts.

"So many before me were unworthy, weren't they? Not me. I am a punisher of men, a destroyer of the unworthy."

I'll do it. It won't be you. You can tell your mate it wasn't you. Let go. Let me out, the lamia entreated.

She could float in the silent peace of oblivion while the lamia used her body and saved the world. Tally herself could still be sacred, could still be pure for Falcon.

But that wasn't the nature of sacrifice or redemption.

Tally felt a clarity she'd never known and a strength that was solely hers. She smiled up into the face of evil. "Be with me. We'll end this world together."

Its talons closed around her throat.

"I can't die," Tally said and smiled as her airway closed.

The human part of her was so far away now. It struggled, and it felt fear as her lungs fought for oxygen, but the lamia was calm; it forced her to be calm and to endure. The beast braced her against the table and just as he was going to enter her, he snapped a titanium cuff around her wrist.

"Call it protection from sexually transmitted death."

The air around the cuff sizzled with power and the lamia inside her howled. It had been chained by magick, caged.

The door hadn't been locked, so it wasn't much of an entrance, but an avenging angel filled the doorway, his armored wings spread and their true glory illuminated by the sun reflected off each crystalline plate.

His guns were still strapped to his hips and thighs, but he held a sword and it burst into flame. Falcon's body moved with deadly grace as he brandished the sword, his muscle and bone following a single sharp line. He was beautiful in the magnificence of his fury.

She wondered how much he'd heard and if he'd ever forgive her. The pain on his face, the hard lines around the grim slash of his mouth, the stony vengeance in his eyes— no, he'd never forgive her.

The lamia whispered that his emotion would make him careless, sloppy. He'd fight and he'd lose. Better to cut him with her words than to let them fight. The pain was in her veins now instead of her blood. Her intent to wound him cut her before she even spoke.

"A little late to the party, lover?" She licked her lips.

"A hot little piece of destruction you've got here," the beast said.

Tally saw pieces of Falcon shatter. She wanted to cry out, to tell him she loved him, no matter what this looked like. Her heart swelled and cracked; despair threatened to drown her.

"Tally, what are you doing?" he asked.

As if she could give him another answer, as if she could explain away the words of invitation she'd issued to the beast.

"I'm *hungry*." She prayed he'd understand everything with those words, prayed he'd walk away. Tally needed him to hate her just then. But later, she hoped he'd realize what she'd done and forgive her.

"I thought we agreed the dog wasn't allowed in the house." Under any other circumstances, his wit would have been funny. Now, it broke her heart.

"Instead, Cupid has to stay outside and play with his love

guns all by himself." The beast bared its teeth and threw a bag of powder at the door. It exploded and the blast sent Falcon flying from the entrance.

The places on his skin where the powder touched him sizzled and burned. His blood turned to ash when it dripped near the ward Ethelred had wrought. Falcon would burn should he try to cross the threshold.

"The dust of a woman's bones who was killed by someone she loved. It's easier to find than you'd think." The beast wore Emilian's face again and winked at Tally.

Tally had to bite the inside of her cheek to keep from crying out. "I'm already bored," she said and turned her head away so she wouldn't have to see Falcon's suffering.

Falcon seethed, his chest rising and falling with simple rage. He pulled his wings around his body and tried to push through the barrier. His beautiful wings caught fire as soon as they touched the boundary of the warding.

"Come to me, Tally," he said, as the tips of his wings burned.

Oh, sweet Merlin, he was still trying to save her. He would die to do it, just as Merlin had said he would. She had to get Emilian out of there.

"So, what's the deal, Princeling?" She adopted Ethelred's pet name for him with a sneer.

Falcon stepped back from the door as she spoke, a low sound like a growl issuing from deep in his chest. Tally could see he was debating how long it would take to push through the barrier and how much of his flesh would burn.

"Your love is going to burn," the beast said with a curious excitement.

"I don't care what he does," she said and leaned back on the table.

Please, she prayed. *Please let me save him.*

"You really don't care, do you? Perhaps we'll play some more." The beast grabbed her by the throat again.

She submitted to his grasp and looked at Falcon one last time. Tally prayed he could see the truth in her eyes, could see she didn't mean any of what she said. It was a double-edged sword. She wanted Falcon to know it was a lie, but she had to be pretty damn convincing if she wanted Emilian to believe her. She was damned if she did and damned if she didn't.

"First," Emilian began, "I have to see a demon about a contract."

Betrayal knifed through her.

Emilian started to chant and she felt the corporeal world around her fade into nothing. She could still see Falcon, but Tally was sure he could no longer see them and she mouthed *I love you*. She was sure it was her last chance to say it and though he'd never know she'd spoken the words, she'd know. It would have to be enough.

They materialized in a familiar tea shop, where an equally familiar demon sat eating a scone and drinking a steaming cup of tea. Tally gritted her teeth so hard she was surprised they didn't all snap off in her mouth. She tasted blood and knew the lamia had caused fangs to descend from her gums. She'd known Ethelred was evil, but how could he do this?

"I see you've captured my errant parolee," Ethelred said with no evident emotion.

"The bone dust you gave me worked," Emilian said, his features completely humanoid again, all but his eyes.

"Everything I give you works. This time you thought to specify *how* you wanted it to work." Ethelred still didn't look at Tally. She wanted him to; she wanted him to see the darkness in her eyes and the reckoning she'd bring to his door.

She blinked as her vision blurred and she began to see all of the occupants in the room in terms of their heat signatures, where the meat was. Tally was watching them like prey. They weren't men, or angels, or demons: They were prey to be devoured. They were enemies to be destroyed.

"Would you look at that?" Emilian grinned. "Something pissed her off."

"She's hungry," Ethelred said. "You should find something to feed her. Lamia are easier to control when they're full."

"I thought you used food to reward them."

"Yes, you do. But a nearly sated lamia has logic. If she's too hungry, you'll have to use aversion training with pain."

"We like pain, don't we, dove?" Emilian asked her solicitously. "Such pretty eyes. What magick can be wrought with lamia eyes?"

"Much, but she's more valuable to you alive."

Tally would have exploded with her rage; the lamia would have filled her skin and killed them all if not for that titanium cuff on her wrist. As soon as he took it off and *he would take it off* if he wanted to use the lamia's power, she'd kill him.

"Do you still want demonhood, Emilian?" Ethelred asked.

"No, I'm happy with what I am."

"Then why are you here?" The demon asked the question as if the answer didn't matter, flipping casually though a gardening magazine.

"To make sure the Powers That Be don't vote to end me. Something they can't do if they're all dead." He clasped Tally tightly and pressed her against him. "I'll enjoy watching her kill them. I've never seen a lamia in action."

"There aren't many who have. For so large a creature, she's very stealthy. The Angel of Death never saw her coming, did he, Tally?" Ethelred replied.

"No, he didn't." She left the rest unsaid. *He* wouldn't see her coming, either. The lamia rallied at the thought and Tally ran her tongue over her fangs.

There was something in Ethelred's voice, something about the set of his mouth, that told Tally maybe things weren't as they seemed.

In all the darkness, Tally saw a tiny candle flame of hope.

"So again, why are you here, Emilian, if you don't want what I've offered? I don't see how I can help you with the vote." He continued to thumb through the magazine as if he didn't care one way or another about the things going on around him.

"My sister. Where is she?"

Ethelred narrowed his eyes momentarily, then sighed. "I wouldn't know. I'm not her keeper."

"Oh, but I think you are. I could make you tell me."

This time Ethelred put the magazine down and looked up to give Emilian his full attention—his eyes blazing with hellfire. "Listen to me well, you whelp of a whore. I've been a demon since mankind was nothing but squirming things in the dirt. When this world ends, I will still *be*. Perhaps you will swallow the sun, but my origins are older, deeper than you mewling things that struggle to keep your faces in the light."

"Such posturing." Emilian laughed. "If you could end me, why haven't you? Why don't you save the world?"

"Because I don't wish to." He accentuated each word and Tally believed him. His gaze slid to Tally and it seemed to say: *That's your job.*

Tally remembered her lessons with Ethelred on the nature of Hell—adversity. It wasn't to hurt humans for the sake of hurting them; it was to make them grow, to make them reach their potential for goodness, sacrifice, love.

"That doesn't change the fact I want my sister, demon."

"Why?" He went back to thumbing through the magazine.

"She's the other half of my soul and I need it to finish what's begun."

"I'll be sure to pass on the message." Ethelred looked him up and down for a moment and, obviously deciding he was lacking, went back again to his gardening magazine.

"She's probably back at the house. You know it would be just like this demon to hide her from you in plain sight," Tally whispered in his ear. "And you don't need him to help with the vote. Like you said, you've got me. Let's go."

Emilian looked at her, the beast staring out from behind his eyes, and wrapped his arms around her to teleport back to the beach house.

When the beach house became solid around them, Tally realized it had become her anchor somehow. The realization was all the more stark because she knew after what was coming, she'd never be able to return.

"Your angel is long gone," he sneered.

"I already told you I don't care."

"I can see the lie on you. Smell your pheromones. The way your heartbeat accelerates in your chest."

"Because I'm *hungry*."

"Soon, pet. I need to find my sister before we end the Powers That Be."

He was still mortal! He'd be mortal until his sister was infected, too. Only then would they become the invincible beast the Powers feared. Why hadn't she seen it before?

She had to get that cuff off.

Tally felt her consciousness slipping away, the now familiar touch of the lamia's presence filling her.

Sleep, Tally. Sleep and let me bear this burden.

No, together. We'll do it together, Tally thought.

"If I uncuff you, I want you to swear on your magick you'll do as you've promised."

She smiled. "I swear on my magick, I'll do everything as promised." If she didn't follow through, she'd lose her magick, but she didn't specify which things she'd promised. The binding settled over her, but it was an easy weight to bear.

The cuff disintegrated into granules of sand, sliding from her wrist. The skin was red and raw underneath, burned from just those few minutes of contact.

He still had his arms around her from teleporting and Tally returned the embrace, locking her claws into his shoulders. With that, the lamia burst into the front of her awareness and began to feed.

But it wasn't like it had been before—it was more metaphysical. It took something from him, something vital and hot. It filled her veins like a molten river of gold. It was bliss unlike anything she'd ever experienced.

He fought her, struggled in her grip, but he'd already lost too much of himself by the time he realized what was happening. The beast shifted as he invaded her, all of that fury and hunger. She knew those sensations, but they were nothing like the power of the lamia.

The punisher inside her consumed the beast easily, greedily, swallowing everything that made him powerful and deadly like some succulent meal.

She tried to stop when she sensed the pure things— Emilian's willingness to sacrifice himself, his love for his sister, even his forgiveness of Tally herself for what she was doing.

But the lamia wouldn't stop. She thirsted—said they had to be sure. Emilian had to die to break his curse. Tally flailed for control, but part of her didn't want to stop. His essence tasted too good, sated her in ways she'd never known, filled pieces of her that she thought would always be empty.

The body of the gypsy prince crumpled in her arms and then, only then, did she release him.

Tally sagged to the floor with him, hot tears burning down her cheeks.

CHAPTER TWENTY
A Falling Star

D read choked Falcon as he paced back and forth in front
of the beach house. Tally's fear was as strong as if it had
been his own. All he knew was that he had to get to her.

His heart had torn itself from his chest when he'd seen
Tally with Emilian. The things she'd said—if he hadn't
known better, her words would have broken him. He'd
never get the sight of her like that out of his head; it would
be there until his next turn on the Wheel scrubbed it from
his brain like baked-on barbeque. He'd see it every time he
closed his eyes, but he couldn't hold it against her.

Falcon was the Angel of Love. Now that he'd finally accepted love, he could see Tally's true feelings for him in a
bright starburst in her aura; he could also see what she'd
done to herself. There was a darkness hovering over her. It
was something strange and new that had merged with her
aura—it could only be the lamia.

He was afraid for her now, but he was also so proud of
her for doing what she thought was right even though she
was terrified. Falcon wished he could have spared her that,
the fear. The lamia could, though; it would make her
stronger, help her survive, and because of that, he couldn't
fault her or the creature inside her.

But Falcon knew he had failed her. If he'd been strong
enough, she never would have had to go through this.

Falcon wished like hell he could slay the monster. All he could think about was that night at the beach house when they'd been watching *The Howling*. She kept hiding her face in his shoulder, looking to him to save her from the monster, even though it was only on a screen.

This was real. The monster had her and she had to fight it without him. He couldn't ride to the rescue. Damn, he couldn't even fly. His wings had burned and it had been agony. He knew he'd heal, but what about Tally? What was this going to do to her?

He sank to his knees, at a loss. For once in his life, Falcon didn't know what to do. He didn't have a plan, or direction. Logically, he knew he needed to go petition the Powers That Be for another vote, but he couldn't abandon Tally to Emilian. He couldn't leave her there, hopeless and afraid. Falcon didn't even know how to find her.

He looked up at the sky. "Merlin? Are you listening?" Falcon had so much to say, but not enough time to say it. "I'm sorry. I screwed up. Don't make her suffer because of what I did. Please. This time, I mean it. Help me help her. Not so I can get in her knickers, but so I can save her life. Her soul." Falcon waited. He knew the Bigger Boss liked to say he worked in mysterious ways, but there was no answer forthcoming.

Falcon, being a Crown Prince of Heaven, had expected one. Immediately, considering the fate of the world was at stake.

Someone had to be at the wheel, didn't they? That left only the Big Boss—Caspian. Falcon had met him a few times since his ascension. Wasn't really a bad guy—he'd helped Dred out with his sister. Maybe he could help Falcon?

"Okay, who else is listening? Anyone? Caspian? Look, I don't know if I have anything you want. Even though I'm already a Crown Prince of Heaven, my soul is a little dirty. No, I lied. It's a lot dirty. It's dirty like a—"

"Yes, I get it. Do stop carrying on so." A voice rumbled from the ether of the sulfuric cloud that bubbled and boiled in front of him. It stank like rotten eggs and convenience store burritos.

"Uh, you don't look like Caspian," Falcon said to the debonair man with a sharply groomed goatee who appeared in Caspian's stead.

"That's because I'm not, genius." The newcomer rolled his eyes.

"Well, who are you?"

"The Devil." He spoke as if that should have been obvious. Falcon didn't have time for games.

"Last time I checked, Caspian was the Devil," Falcon said, not liking this guy at all.

"Last time you checked, your girlfriend wasn't the great and terrible evil. Things change."

"So, do you have a name or do I call you the Thunder from Down Under?"

"You're quite the smartass for being the Angel of Love and . . ." He trailed off. "What the fuck happened to your wings? Holy Me, it stinks like that time my granddaughter tried a summoning and lit her hair on fire."

"Stink? Have you smelled your mode of transportation? I almost puked."

"Eh, sorry about that. I had burritos for lunch." He shrugged. "That still doesn't explain your wings or your stench."

Falcon thought he was going to be sick. "The dickbag formerly known as Emilian Grey shat all over my corn-flakes. He warded me out of the house I was sharing with my parolee with a bag of bone dust and stole my woman."

"So, your parolee and your woman are the same person? Is this the lamia/Drusilla Tallow/Ethelred debacle?"

"Those people are involved, so I'm going to go with yes."

He looked at his watch. "Hmm. This is getting down to the wire, isn't it? Do you want to kill him?"

"Yep." He was glad the Devil understood. It made things so much easier.

"Well, you can't."

"Damn it. Why not?" Falcon snarled. So much for easier.

"I said so."

"Like I said before, who the hell are you?"

"Exactly." He smirked and then sighed. "Fine, I'm Hades. Merlin retired. Caspian ascended. I thought they were supposed to send out announcements or something, have a party, have cake. Someone gets drunk and photocopies their ass. You know the drill."

"I guess he was too busy with this whole destruction of life as we know it thing."

"I suppose that's a reasonable excuse for missing social obligations," Hades acknowledged.

"Do you think I can hitch a ride? I have to find Tally."

"I guess, but you'll have to hold on to me. It might feel a little gay," Hades shrugged. "All hard bodies pressed together and such."

Falcon coughed. "What?"

"You know, man flesh rubbing against man flesh." Hades smirked.

"It's not like I asked to ride you like a pony."

"You kind of did." Hades examined the end of his tail for a moment.

Falcon considered what he'd said. Maybe he had. Fuck it. It didn't matter. He had to get to Tally. "Yeah, okay. Whatever. If that's what it takes to get it done."

"I think I like you." Hades grinned. "I wasn't sure I would, you know with the pink wings and everything."

"Why does everyone feel the urge to comment on the wings? Doesn't the shade come with the office?" Falcon sighed.

Hades cocked his head to the side as if he were considering the juiciest bit of gossip this side of *Desperate Housewives* and then leaned in toward Falcon as if he was going to share said tidbit. "The last guy?" The Devil looked around to see if anyone else was listening.

"Go on," Falcon said, not liking where this was going.

"His wings were red," Hades said in a conspiratorial tone. "Of course," he added as he straightened, "we all gave him tons and tons of shit about his"—Hades paused to snicker—"*red* wings."

"Cupid just can't win."

"Nope, but you've got to understand, we all feel we got gypped by love at one time or another, so we all figure fair is fair since you, or your office, has it in for us."

"That has nothing to do with me. It's Fate, not Cupid," Falcon protested.

Hades held up a hand. "Preaching to the choir, man. You know how much shit I get on a daily basis because I'm the oh-my-god-devil?"

"Yeah, I bet everyone blames everything on you. If it's not the tidal wave on some island nation, it's a serial killer next door," Falcon sympathized.

"Exactly. I can see this is going to be a beautiful friendship. Of course, you know everyone also thinks Cupid is already in league with the Devil."

"If I'm already doing the time, might as well do the crime, right?"

"You sound like an old pro. I can hardly believe you've only been in office for a few months."

Falcon inspected what was left of the tips of his wings and was less than pleased with what he found. He wondered how long it was going to take for them to grow back. "Only a few months and I've already lit my wings on fire."

"Technically," Hades said, "it wasn't you."

"Since you're the Big Boss, do you think you could fix them?" Falcon asked hopefully.

"Why does everyone think I have magick?"

"Don't you?" Falcon gave him a sly look.

"Not unless you want black wings."

"I'll take 'em!" Falcon tried not to sound too excited.

"Yes, but your kisses taste like cotton candy to your woman, right? That comes with the pink. If I change your wing color to black, you'll taste like licorice. Does Tally like licorice?"

"No." Falcon would have stomped his foot like an eight-year-old girl throwing a tantrum if he'd been any less of a man.

"Red tastes like cherry. I could maybe do red, but I think you'd taste like Twizzlers. They'd look pretty fucking cool though, with black tips."

"So Tristan tastes like licorice?" Falcon asked hopefully.

"No, he's Death. He will taste like ash and despair to anyone who hasn't known death intimately."

"Intimately? That's disgusting."

"It can be," Hades said with a shudder. "Are you ready to go?"

"Yeah, I guess. How do we do this?"

"We have to spoon."

"What?"

"I told you it was a little gay."

"Whatever. Let's get on with it."

"So, of course, you know I'm kidding. I just wanted to see what you'd say."

"Thank Merl—uh, Caspian for that."

"Good save! Every time you do that, you solidify his power base."

"You're full of fun facts, aren't you? Anything I should know about Cupid?"

"You can't be shot with your own bullet," Hades said with a meaningful look.

Falcon felt sheepish for a moment. The Devil sure did know a lot about him. "Can we go?"

"Yeah, I'm getting to it."

"Do you need wing clearance?" Falcon asked with a sigh. "No."

"Fine." He moved to stand behind the Devil, because one didn't want the Devil looking over one's shoulder and Falcon wrapped an arm around his waist.

"Is that a love gun, or are you happy to see me?" Hades laughed.

"Considering the situation, I'm very happy to see you," Falcon tossed back.

"I'll say this for you—you're a guy who can give the Devil a run for his money. Hold on tight. You've missed most of the big show. We'll catch her at the Hall of Gods."

CHAPTER TWENTY-ONE

Cuffed and Stuffed

He'd taken the cuff off, the stupid bastard. Her intent had been to separate the beast from Emilian, but in the end, Tally couldn't stop and she'd absorbed both life forces.

She'd knowingly killed a man.

Granted, he could have been the harbinger of the apocalypse, but he was still a man inside. A person with thoughts and feelings, dreams and hopes. Someone's child. Someone's brother. Someone's lover. And all that he was, all that made him unique was now gone—swirling inside her like some kind of Samhain candy treat.

She slipped into the shower, knowing her hands, her body, her soul, would never be clean again.

Tally sat down as the hot water pummeled her skin and watched it run down the drain. It should have been bloody. She didn't understand how she could take a life without any blood or gore to scar her memory. Not that she'd ever forget it, but there should have been red and instead it was all gray. She felt dirty and Tally didn't think there was enough hot water in the world to wash the feeling away. She'd never be able to scrub his stench from her body or the memories of what she'd done from her mind.

Tally felt her chest tighten and tears burned like acid, but she didn't want to cry again. She didn't want to feel sorry for herself.

The world was still turning. She'd traded one life for many—Tally had made the hard choice.

You're human, it's okay to cry.

The lamia tried to comfort her. It was a strange alliance, Tally thought. That alien presence inside her mind had once been so foreign, but knowing it was there now brought her an odd peace. Its voice was familiar to her, something she knew amid a sea of unknowns.

Finally, she knew what it felt like to sate that gnawing hunger. She'd thought the lamia could only feed on purity, but the beast had been anything but pure. He'd been a blight of malevolence on the warlockian and mortal world alike. She'd done a good thing. Perhaps it was the purity in the act that sated the hunger?

That's what she kept telling herself.

All she wanted now was to sink into Falcon's embrace and forget everything, but that was impossible now. He was an angel and she was . . . something else. Her heart burned more than her tears. It was full of him and empty at the same time.

I won't hurt him. He makes it warm here for me. You don't even have to tell him I'm inside you.

"If I didn't tell him that would be a lie. We don't lie to people we love," Tally said aloud.

After all Middy had sacrificed to separate her from the lamia, she'd invited the creature back in with open arms. She'd hoped her best friend would understand, but Middy had almost died, and so had Dred. All to save her and it was like she'd thrown that sacrifice back in their faces.

No, you were the only one who could stop him. They'll understand. Stop being unhappy. It's uncomfortable.

It *was* uncomfortable. Tally looked at her hands, and

down her body at the expanse of seemingly clean skin, and bit her lip. She couldn't stop thinking there should be blood. "I'd like to be alone, please."

She felt its presence withdraw to a dark, private corner of her mind. It sent out waves of pleasure as it left to calm and soothe her. Tally could see why the women of yore would have been willing vessels. No matter what horrors they committed, if they surrendered to the lamia, it filled them with bliss.

If only she could surrender her conscience to that feeling, but she couldn't. She knew what she'd done would have consequences.

Falcon. Oh, Merlin, Falcon. If she really loved him, could she be strong enough to let him go without explaining herself? Her explanations wouldn't ease his pain, just her own. If he hated her, if he believed she'd betrayed him, he'd let her go easily.

The thought of never seeing him again was like poison, and she couldn't stop the tears from falling. She sat under the spray until the hot water ran out. She waved her hand and used her magick to renew the hot water and cried a little bit more.

"Hey, kiddo. You've got to come out of that shower sometime." Tristan's voice startled Tally out of her thoughts.

Rather than screaming at him for coming into the bathroom uninvited, she said, "I don't want to."

"I know, but you need to. The Powers That Be need proof that Emilian Grey is no longer the eater of worlds. Before they vote again on his existence."

"They're the Powers That Be! Aren't they supposed to know that stuff? Emilian is dead."

"One would think," Tristan agreed.

"I'd like to stay here for a little bit longer. I can't seem to get clean," Tally confessed in a small voice. The world waited outside the shower curtain. It was stupid to think a piece of plastic could be a veil between worlds and dimensions, but it seemed to Tally that it was. She was safe in the steam and the water. There were no mirrors there—either metaphorical or real.

"I know, but I promise, it will pass." He was silent for a long moment, but when he spoke again, his words didn't comfort her. They were knives. "Falcon loves you."

"That just makes it worse."

"Why?" Tristan asked.

"That's going to make it so much harder to walk away," Tally said through the curtain, using it like a confessional.

"Why do you have to walk away? He's the one, girl. He's it for you, in case you didn't know."

"No, I know all right." Tally felt miserable. "He's always been the one. I've loved him since I was a witchling."

"So, why the big good-bye? He loves you, you love him—sounds like simple math to me." Of course, it would, he was male.

"I can't ask him to give up so much for me."

"What would he be giving up?" He sounded confused.

"Sex."

"Why? Don't you like it? Because if that's the case, you know I'm still single. I won't pass out between your thighs." He rustled the shower curtain playfully.

"No, damn it. You know the lamia is like a succubus. I could end him just from a single touch."

"He's an angel. He has regenerative powers. I'm sure you guys could find a way around that. I mean, it's True Love. You can't let a little thing like death ruin your Happily Ever After. Or, you know, *Death*." He laughed at his own joke. "Just like I told him at The Banshee's Bawl, he's not on the docket to be reaped. Any reaping of someone with Crown Prince status requires my personal appearance. He's not scheduled. It's going to be fine. Really."

"That's because I'm not going to be weak. I will never

see him again if that's what it takes. I don't think I'm one of those. I'm not the kind of girl who gets a Happily Ever After." Tally was resigned to her fate.

"If you don't believe you'll get it, then you won't. Everything you've ever wanted is there for the taking. All you have to do is reach out with both hands and hold on."

"Tristan, not that I don't appreciate your help, but why do you always manifest when I'm naked?"

"Because Death is a pervert?"

She laughed. "Don't make me laugh right now. Everything is still so raw. I failed, Tristan. Emilian is dead."

"No, he's not. I brought a friend to help. If you still have Emilian's life force, if you can convince the lamia to give it up, she can put it back in his body."

"That easy, huh?"

"I never said it was easy, but come on. Get out of the shower and mope later. There's still work to do."

Tally sniffed. "Is Ethelred okay? What happened to Luminista?"

"He made a side deal with Emilian and you're asking if he's okay?"

"He's wormed his way under my skin. Like a tick. I know Ethelred was hurting, and sometimes people do stupid things when they hurt."

"Interesting observation. He's a demon, though, not a people," Tristan said with a smile.

"I think he's more a people than he'd want anyone to know. These demons and angels, the ones who didn't start out being one of us, their emotions and thought processes seem to be like ours, only exaggerated. Like they don't know how to process what we do every day."

"Another astute observation. It takes them time to learn, but eventually they do," Tristan said. "Eventually, we all do."

"I think that's a gift for us, for humans. It's so ugly and messy, but beautiful and perfect all at once."

"Perhaps that's why the lamia wanted to come back to this plane. Why it wanted to stay with you."

"How did you know that?" Tally stuck her head out from around the curtain.

"I'm Death, dummy. You had to pass through my realm to get to the Abyss. I see all, hear all, and know all."

"Yeah, you're definitely still a know-it-all. Death hasn't changed that any."

"And look, you're still Tally." He swiped his finger down the tip of her nose.

"After all of this, huh?" She sagged back in the shower. Tally switched subjects.

"The lamia said Falcon made it warm for her."

"Perhaps you'll change her as much as she's changed you." Tally didn't say anything.

"Now, are you coming out or what? We have a gypsy prince to bring back to life."

"Depends. Are you getting out of my bathroom?"

"It's not like I haven't seen it before." He wagged his eyebrows suggestively. Tally narrowed her eyes at him and he held up his hands in mock surrender. "Fine, I'm going. But hurry up. His soul may decide it doesn't want to come back. We have to catch him while he's still confused. Or so my source says. Move it!"

The door closed and Tally swallowed hard. Tristan was right, she couldn't stay in the shower forever, couldn't hide from what she'd done and what she'd become. For better or worse, this was the path she'd chosen. It was just like what she'd told Falcon. She had to make do with what she had—not only make do, but make the best of it. A life.

That started by facing the corpse in the living room.

Resolved, she turned off the shower and slipped into the filmy pink maxi dress she had hanging on the back of the door. Tally caught a glimpse of herself in the mirror and she stopped to look.

She almost didn't recognize the woman looking back at her. She was a hundred million miles away from how she thought she'd turn out and even further away from who she wanted to be.

Then she smiled because that was wrong. Drusilla Tallow was exactly who she wanted to be. It had been a shit-ugly journey to get there, but she was there and that's what mattered. She'd loved someone else more than herself, put him before her own needs, and she'd been brave enough to face her fears—all of them to do the right thing. That was a woman worthy of her Second Chance and maybe even redemption.

"Tally, move your ass or I'm going to spank it!" Tristan demanded.

"Damn it, I'm having a moment, Tristan."

"Have it later." He popped the door open and she threw the mouthwash at him.

"Tristan," a sultry female voice interrupted, "I think you can let the woman have her moment after what she's been through."

Okay, so maybe Tally wasn't as evolved as she thought. She hated the owner of that voice with a singular burning intensity simply based on the fact that she had a voice that screamed fuck me now. Her jealousy doubled when she saw that the woman was insanely beautiful *and* had bigger breasts that she wasn't afraid to display in a tight T-shirt. She was everything that Tally always wished she was.

Thanks, Universe. Why is it every time I think I'm getting somewhere you—oh, right. She was tired of being tested. Life was just one big pop quiz and Tally always felt like she hadn't studied the material.

"Is this your friend?" Tally asked. *Duh, who else would she be?* She needed something to say and the obvious seemed the only thing available. Tally pushed all those feelings down. This woman had come to help her; so what if Falcon looked at her rack? Did it really matter? He was going to be doing a lot more with other women besides looking because she couldn't be with him.

"Hi, I'm Ghislaine. I'll be your Zombie Master today. Buckle up and keep all hands and feet inside the ride." The woman laughed.

"Thank you for doing this," Tally managed.

"Sure, anything to get Death off my ass. Is he always so bossy?"

"Afraid so. Comes from being an ex–war hero and Academy football star. Thinks he's entitled."

"Uh, no," Tristan interrupted. "What makes me feel entitled is that part where you killed me. Horribly. Remember that?"

"Yeah, but you love me anyway." Tally smiled.

"I do." He nodded with a sigh. "But you and The Diapered One have Happily Ever After on the horizon. So I'll just have to suffer without you."

Tally snorted and Ghislaine rolled her eyes. "I don't know how you stand him," the Zombie Master said.

"Mostly, I don't. We broke up a hundred years ago, didn't we?"

"Yeah, because I'm an asshole. I know the song and dance."

"Wait, wait. I need to record this for posterity. Death admitted he was an asshole?" Ghislaine fake gasped.

And suddenly, Tally smiled. Death and a Zombie Master. What better couple? She supposed it was a leftover impression from Falcon's cupidity that let her see it, but she knew they belonged together.

"I thought this corpse reanimation was time sensitive, Hissy Ghissy. Can we get on with it?"

"Call me that again." Her eyes narrowed.

A look came over Tristan's face and Tally knew he'd accepted her challenge. "Hissy. Gh—"

Tally popped up and slammed her hand over his mouth. "Do this later. Like you said, *Time sensitive*. Right?"

"Right. And if Death were all that, he'd be able to do this himself, wouldn't he? We'll have to excuse him since he's got a raging case of scythe envy." Ghislaine turned on her heel and sauntered back to Tally's living room.

"I'm gonna kill her. I am." Tristan nodded emphatically.

"I hate to break it to you—" Tally began, but Tristan held up a hand to cut her off, shaking his head.

"I don't want to know."

Tally shrugged and followed Ghislaine to where she stopped at Emilian's body.

"This won't do. We need a bed."

"I've got that covered," Tristan said and teleported them all to Tally's bedroom.

Emilian looked so . . . *wrong* lying there on her white quilt, the tiny pink flowers cross-stitched to make a larger flower design. It looked like a pyre rather than a bed, the flowers spread out to follow him into the afterlife. His face was so drawn and gaunt, his silvery eyes open, but unseeing, and his lips shriveled away from his mouth, making him look like he was screaming. His hands were curled into fists at his sides and his broad shoulders and powerful chest were shrunken and wasted.

"Do you really want to put a soul back in that body?" Tally shuddered.

Ghislaine took her hand. "Yeah. But you have to be willing to give back what you took."

"That's a problem, because I'm not." Tally sighed.

"What?" Tristan demanded.

"Shh. The adults are talking." Ghislaine turned her attention back to Tally. "Not the cursed part of him. If I'd been here while you were draining him, I could have separated the essence of the beast and Emilian's. If *your* curse is willing to let it go, I can do this."

The lamia had been strangely quiet. So, Tally would just assume it was willing. "I believe so. But if not, if I sprout wings or anything other than my eyes change, you need to go, okay? Promise me."

Ghislaine flashed her a warm smile. "I'm not afraid of you, Tally. My *grandmère* told me stories of women with power like yours. In ancient times, some women actually sought out the power you have to punish those who wronged them or someone they loved. My *grandmère* would have wanted to meet you and I am honored to help you."

Tally felt guilty for hating the Zombie Master on sight. All she could do was smile and nod. "Okay."

"This may be uncomfortable," Ghislaine warned as she directed Tally to kneel on the other side of the bed and they linked hands over Emilian's body.

"What do you need from me?" Tristan asked, serious.

"When you see Emilian's life force, don't give him any opportunity to go with you."

"So, basically sit down and shut up?"

"Yeah." Ghislaine smiled.

Tally reached inside herself, seeking the alien presence of the lamia to reassure it that she wasn't trying to oust it, only give back what didn't belong to them, but she got no response.

Again, another test, Tally realized. She had to face herself. All of herself. She felt like a witchling who was ready to cry because she didn't want to go to school. She didn't think she could stand any more lessons. She'd learned enough for a hundred turns around The Great Wheel.

Tally relaxed and opened herself, bringing down the last wall between herself and the lamia inside her.

At first, there was the incredible bliss that was second only to the way she felt in Falcon's arms. As the lamia merged with her on a cellular level, filled her with knowledge, power, strength, Ghislaine reached inside her and ripped something away. Pain swelled and ebbed, like a tide of suffering, but the lamia didn't rise to protect them, because Tally had become the lamia and the lamia Tally.

And Tally had offered this piece of them to Ghislaine.

When she drifted back into the world, she realized the man she'd killed, Emilian Grey, held her against his chest and she was sobbing.

"Merlin, but I can't seem to turn off the waterworks," Tally blubbered.

He felt so real and solid against her, and she could sense there was nothing in him but the heart of a noble gypsy prince. Relief seemed to melt her bones and she couldn't hold herself up.

"Thank you," Emilian whispered. "For everything. You were so brave. And I'm so sorry."

"We can play the blame game later. You two can apologize to each other until shit sticks to the moon. After Tally puts in an appearance at the Hall of Gods. They're still voting on whether to wipe out your existence."

"If they're really all that powerful, they should know they don't need to do that."

"No, I've come to realize they're not that powerful, all-knowing, or all-seeing. It's more like a supernatural government than anything. There are bigger forces at work than the Powers That Be. But that doesn't change the fact that now, Tally, you're a threat to them."

"You know, I was tempted to ask what else anyone or anything could expect from me after I've saved the world, but there's my answer."

"You know better than to tempt Fate, don't you?" Tristan eyed her.

She sat up. "Let me put on something a little more . . ." Tally struggled for the word.

Ghislaine offered her a hand and helped her stand. "I like

it. You save the world and you're still stylish. Let's go see what's in your closet for your moment of triumph."

Triumph. As she went in search of the perfect outfit, Tally wished she felt that way.

"Shit," she cried out as a familiar ripping pain stabbed through her back. The only time she'd ever felt that pain was when the lamia had erupted from her body. "Run, Ghislaine."

"No, I told you I wouldn't." The other woman locked her hand tighter around Tally's. But Tally's hands didn't change to claws, and her body didn't change into a predator's. Instead, gold wings exploded from her back, knocking books and knickknacks off shelves and filling the hallway around them.

"Oh," Ghislaine gasped.

Tristan and Emilian came running, but stopped short when they saw her.

"Wow, Tally. I think you just got a job," Tristan said, and led her into the bathroom where she could see a mirror.

Tally was almost afraid to look, but when she did, she didn't see any sort of beast looking back at her. Only her own face. Her own eyes.

And a crown of fire on her head. Within the spires of her crown, four letters burned brighter than the flaming jewels: LUST.

"Congratulations. You're a Crown Princess of Hell—the Angel of Lust," Tristan said.

Ghislaine sighed happily. "Isn't it great when Lust and Love go together? How perfect."

"It can be perfect later. We still have to get to the Hall of Gods before the vote."

Hope surged in Tally. "Let's go."

CHAPTER TWENTY-TWO

A Demon's Heart

Ethelred had been a demon since the early days of man, forged from the black soot of a dark heart. He'd never been human. Yet, he was now plagued by human emotion. Uriel blamed the gardening. He said that nurturing things, caring for them while they grew was a distinctive trait of a Crown Prince of Heaven and dealt with one of the softest of human emotions.

Ethelred thought his old lover was full of hyena dung. It was that fucking arrow.

Both sides were riddled with human emotion; it was simply that Ethelred had been exposed to the more unsavory, yet necessary aspects of the thing.

He'd been a bit infatuated with Uriel. Ethelred could own up to that, but what he'd thought could have been love had only been a passing obsession. Intense, to be sure, but love? No. It was nothing like what he felt for the gypsy princess.

So with everything that had happened, Ethelred didn't see that he had any other choice but to take desperate measures. He'd hidden Luminista away in Hell. A big step to be sure, but they were already living together at the beach house and there was no way he'd let Emilian anywhere near her until Tally had done her job. At least while Luminista was in Hell, he felt like he had some control.

As soon as she'd popped through his door, she'd started

pawing through his CD collection and taking everything off the shelves, which he'd had in ABC order. She was a frustrating little baggage—most of which he assumed was on purpose. It had to be. No one creature could be as difficult without intent.

He knew Tally was pissed about the double cross, but he couldn't help himself. He had to test her to her limits. It was part of his job. Maybe she was off parole, but she hadn't reached her full potential and she wouldn't until she had no one and nothing to rely on but herself. Of course, he also had to have insurance. Ethelred simply couldn't allow anything bad to happen to Luminista. Well, nothing bad except him. He'd tuck her away like a dragon guarding gold if that's what it took to keep her safe.

Ethelred stepped through the door to his quaint Victorian to find the girl sprawled where he'd left her—her pretty silver hair a tangle around her head, looking like she was trying to make a snow angel on his Aubusson rug.

Merlin! Not only had she taken every CD off the shelves, but she'd dug through his old picture albums as well. He was not pleased.

"Stop playing Sleeping Beauty and sit up. I can't scold you properly if you're asleep." She lay there like a recalcitrant slug. "Fine. You can call me Ethel. If you must." He heaved a great sigh. When even that didn't rouse her, Ethelred crept closer, his steps hesitant.

Every single scenario running through his mind was completely and totally unacceptable. He toed her gently in the ribs. She didn't move. He sank down onto the rug next to her, unmindful now of the mess of CDs and pictures.

He leaned down close to her bow mouth, but there was no sound of breath, no warm rush like butterfly wings against his ear. Ethelred couldn't process that and rested his hand over her heart. Surely the thing would be thumping away in defiance of him and everyone else.

Nothing.

She was dead.

With her death, he should have been free of the arrow. But there was no freedom in this. Only a rage unlike he'd ever known before fueled by what he could only assume were the fires of endless torment because he'd failed to protect her. It was as if his heart had been ripped out of his chest and shoved into a blender.

He'd promised her. Falcon's arrow or no, he'd promised her he wouldn't let the Powers That Be wipe her out of existence.

Ethelred hadn't been blowing smoke up the beast's ass when he'd confessed his origins in the Abyss. He was darkness that had been molded into a man, that had submitted to this new belief system, this Heaven and Hell.

They obliterated Luminista? It was their own ethos that determined his next action. Do unto others . . .

Ethelred would do unto every last one of them the way they'd done unto her.

Wreathed in flame and vengeance, Ethelred flew to the Hall of Gods.

Perhaps it wasn't his place, but he didn't give a shit. Was one woman's life worth an apocalypse? Luminista's was.

He felt a hand on his shoulder, but he didn't turn. Ethelred knew who touched him with such familiarity. He'd scented the angel before he'd felt the touch.

"Don't do this, I beg of you," Uriel entreated.

"I have to."

"Please, Ethelred. Do you know what will happen if you fail?"

"You should fear what will happen if I succeed. I'm going to burn them all."

"It was never love between us, but I care for you. Don't damn yourself." Uriel rested his forehead against Ethelred's back, but the demon remained stoic and unmoving.

"I'm already damned either way," Ethelred whispered.

"You and I are eternal, Ethelred. We are more than these gods and goddesses. Which is why we can't interfere. I hope you can forgive me." Uriel clamped a magickal cuff around Ethelred's wrist.

Ethelred turned to face the angel slowly and smiled. It wasn't his usual gleeful malevolence, but sad and soft.

The shackle dissolved into salt as they both watched— Ethelred with certainty and Uriel with disbelief.

"Your cause is righteous! You truly love her," Uriel whispered in awe.

"I do."

Uriel seemed to deflate, looking weaker, smaller. Almost mortal. "Then there's nothing left for me to do"—he looked up at Ethelred and searched his face for a moment— "but ask how I can help."

"You would do that for me?"

"Ethelred, when it's love, what can Heaven do, but offer a helping hand? I don't want to see any more destruction, but the shackle proved your righteousness. My sword is yours. While we are no longer lovers, I'll always care for you."

"And I you, my friend. Thank you," Ethelred said, humbled by Uriel's offer and admission.

It had been a long game between them, spanning several centuries—each interaction loaded with innuendo and sexual tension. They'd never bonded on a deeper level or gotten to know each other as individuals. It had been all about the sex and getting one up on Heaven, or Hell, depending on who was talking.

Uriel hadn't really been the jealous type; it had been an act that suited both of their purposes for the game. Ethelred hadn't expected any tenderness before, during, or after their relationship and Uriel hadn't been inclined to show any.

Until now.

Ethelred wasn't sure he ever remembered having a real friend. Not until he'd fallen in love with Luminista. The gypsy princess had become his friend and now suddenly, he had another one in Uriel.

There was a warmth inside Ethelred that hadn't been there before, or perhaps it was something he'd never noticed. It had sparked when Caspian had fallen in love and the neighborhood had gone to shit right after, filling up with the softer emotions and feelings. It made Ethelred a little nauseous, to be honest. It felt like a roller coaster after too much popcorn and funnel cake.

Overindulgence was a particular talent of Hell, so Ethelred figured in for a penny, in for a pound. What else did he have to do with eternity, anyway?

"We need a plan, you and I," Uriel said. "You can't just show up with guns blazing. You'll end up in the Abyss."

"Chances are, I'll end up there anyway."

"The Powers aren't going to give up without a fight," Uriel warned.

"Good thing I'm not asking them to give up, isn't it? I'm going to crush them beneath the boot of Hell."

"You should know, Tally is in there right now telling them they have nothing to fear from Emilian or Luminista."

"Then why is she dead?" Ethelred growled, and the flames of his rage danced around him like a mad circus troupe.

Uriel took his hand. "Because Tally broke Emilian's curse. In doing so, she took his life and the twin souls left this plane together."

A howl of pain was ripped from Ethelred's body. "I am not the one who sacrifices to save the world. That's not me. They can all burn, Uriel. All of them."

Cupid had given him love and his woman had taken it away.

Ethelred would make sure Cupid felt the same sting.

CHAPTER TWENTY-THREE

A Date with Fate

Drusilla Tallow had a newfound confidence when she entered the Hall of Gods to address the Powers That Be. Tristan walked her to the archway of the ancient door, but she wasn't afraid. She'd found her big girl panties, so to speak, and she'd pulled them up. The burning crown on her head didn't hurt, either. Someone thought she'd done something right.

There was nothing any of these gods or goddesses could do or say to her that would change anything. She was strong in her convictions and Tally was prepared to take whatever punishment she had to endure for allowing the lamia into this plane of existence.

She came. She saw. She kicked the ever-loving hell out of the biggest, baddest, and nastiest evil they couldn't. All in all, she was proud of herself. No matter what happened, they couldn't take that from her.

If Tally had one regret, it was that she wouldn't be able to be with Falcon, but she'd saved him along with everyone else. That was a heady sort of accomplishment to put on her résumé. Even if she'd failed by the Big Boss and Bigger Boss's standards, she'd found her own redemption and she'd forgiven herself. Who were they to judge her?

They were human or had been once and were fallible. Only The Great Wheel could judge her guilty or innocent and mete out her punishment. Not these small, yet eternal creatures.

But that didn't mean she thought she was any better than they were. She was simply Tally.

She didn't wait for them to call her, to invite her to address them. Tally had done this thing, this service, and she wouldn't wait on their pleasure. She walked into the large meeting hall, the Hall of Gods, with her head held high and her spine straight as a broom handle.

Tally saw many unfamiliar faces, strange and alien faces, but those were the most comforting to her, proof that there were others like herself in the world. The red-tinged woman with all the arms appealed to her the most. Her jet-black hair hung straight and perfect, but when she smiled at Tally, her sharp fangs were revealed and her many arms moved in a graceful dance. Tally had read about the legends and myths of many cultures and it occurred to her the woman must be Kali and the man next to her Lord Krishna.

Then she saw the goddess with the hair that was like the night sky and she felt the first stirrings of awe. She saw Odin and Freya, and the Valkyries the guys were always on about, but she kept her eyes away from Falcon. She wasn't ready to look at him, to meet his eyes, but she would be.

"So this is your great werewolf slayer? The girl doesn't look any bigger than a minute," Odin said.

"I daresay we need proof," a male version of the pretty-haired goddess put in.

Tally recognized a few others in the room. She spotted the Greek and Roman gods, but they weren't allowed to talk while the adults were talking. At least, that's what it looked like with them all crammed together at the kiddie table. Tally wondered if they got to use big forks or if they had to have finger foods.

Upon further consideration, she recognized the Morrigan, too. Her hair was blue-black and she wore a dress that was spun of dark cobwebs and peat moss. The raven combing her hair with its beak was a nice touch and the woman gave her a kind smile.

The most brutal of the goddesses were the ones who had the softest smiles. Perhaps in Tally they saw one of their own?

"What proof do you have to offer the Powers, young woman?" Kali asked kindly.

"We're all still here." Tally realized it sounded smug, but she didn't know what else to say.

"I see. Tell us how you defeated him," Odin prodded. "I find it hard to believe a mere slip of a girl bested the wolf that was supposed to be *my* undoing."

"So, what, you think the beast let me go out of the goodness of his black little heart? Hmm?" Tally tossed back.

"Perhaps you're the precursor to whatever he has planned. Yes, the thought crossed my mind," he said.

"You've been the most vocal, Odin. Perhaps it's time to let someone else speak. Enki, you've been quiet," directed the guy at the head of the table

"It's something that comes with age, son. I have nothing to say on the matter just yet," Enki replied. "That and living with Inanna since the first granule slipped through the hourglass. When she wants my opinion, she gives it to me." He winked at Tally.

The lamia stirred and stretched. It liked this god; it could sense his power. A wink meant to soothe and comfort was like a match to kindling. Tally felt heat curl around her spine until she heard Falcon's voice in the background. It was like tossing that ember out into the snow, where it was kindled again by everything she felt for him.

"Well, will you look at that," Enki replied. "It likes me." The swarthy god smirked.

"Everything with a vagina likes you," Inanna sighed. "The lamia can taste your power and she probably wants to eat it." Inanna turned her head to address Tally. "It's okay, honey. If he's stupid enough to fall for it, you have my permission to eat him."

The lamia purred with the anticipation of pleasure, but was again slapped on the nose like a naughty puppy by Tally's conscience.

Fine. I'm just saying he could be a lot of fun. We even have permission.

"See? She doesn't love me," Enki said as if he didn't care one way or another, but the look he and Inanna shared said it all. They were madly in love.

Tally thought it was lovely to see a couple who'd been together so many years and were still in love. It warmed her heart and the lamia purred again. It liked it when Tally was warm.

"Drusilla, if you don't mind, the Powers would like you to recount how you defeated the beast and what your assurances are to this council that the creature inside of you can be controlled," someone asked.

"I do mind, actually. It was horrible and after this moment, I never want to think of it again. Suffice it to say, he put a magickal cuff on my wrist that controlled the lamia and then the idiot took it off. I absorbed his life force." Tally was proud her voice only shook a little as she finished what she had to say.

"I know this is hard, but it's important we understand what happened. Please tell us how the lamia came to be in your body," someone else asked.

"Which time?" Tally asked and lifted her chin a notch.

"Both," he supplied.

"The first time it was forced on me by nefarious parties who wanted to raise a lamia to destroy the warlockian world. This time, I invited her in to fight the beast. I knew it was the only thing that could defeat him."

"What guarantees will you give the Pantheon?" Odin said. "Will you wear the cuff the beast used to bind you?"

"She will not," Falcon said for her. "This has gone on long enough. You will not bind Tally, or cage her in any way. After all she's done? Why would you ask her to put that back on when it represents something so horrible, something she doesn't want to remember?"

"It's okay." Tally smiled at her white knight. He wanted to rescue her, but she could do this herself. "No, I won't wear the cuff."

"Then will you take steps to banish the lamia again?" It was Freya who asked this time. "I like my way of life and I don't want to worry you're going to change it."

"Change happens to us all, goddess. Even you are not immune. No, I will not banish it. I gave my word. It lives in submission to my will, my conscience, and it may stay inside of me, here on this plane," Tally confessed and the howling inside her head quieted.

"Soon, neither of you will be aware of the line between you," Hades warned.

"I don't care. I paid my price for what I had to do. I'm not going to go back on my word. She's lived up to her end and it was a deal sealed in blood," Tally said quietly.

"Then we have no choice," Freya said. "I've heard enough. I'm ready to vote."

"What is there to vote on?" asked the handsome man who appeared to be running things at the head of the table.

"She has to go to the Abyss with the lamia, if she won't banish it," Freya proclaimed.

Who are they to judge us, Drusilla? I punish the evildoers. It's what I was made for. The Mother Kali knows this. Who are they to say we must go? Perhaps they should be the ones to go. Their power wanes and they cannot judge us if we do not judge ourselves. What was done was righteous. Tell them!

"No. There will be no vote. You all know what I did. You're all still here because of me. I'm explaining my actions to you as a courtesy. You have no power over me," Tally said calmly.

And it was her undoing.

She'd been winning them over slowly with her casual manner and honest explanations. It was that last sentence that did her in, because it was what they feared. They feared the loss of power, the loss of control, the loss of their place in the world. If humans were shrugging off their yoke, their power would fade into nothing.

"I don't need your forgiveness or your permission. I've forgiven myself."

Her open defiance and bone-deep belief that they didn't have any power over her shattered something that seemed to bind them together. They all spun their magick, shooting power at her to force her compliance, but nothing touched her.

Except for the men who sat at each end of the table. Both of them had nothing but kind smiles for her. The one with the goatee even had a wink.

She couldn't help smiling back. She turned to leave, but the way was blocked by a long shadow that bloomed into a wall of flame. The flame re-formed into a body—Ethelred. The whole plane shook with his fury.

Tally was again reminded that Luminista was the other half of Emilian's soul. When Emilian had died, he must have taken Luminista with him.

Great chunks of the hall crumbled into dust and columns cracked as it became clear the Powers That Be had been dismissed by Fate herself. Tally had never had a kind word to say about her, but she thought perhaps that had changed.

It was pandemonium, gods and goddesses and their entourages all scrambling to flee the disintegrating hall with their powers intact. She couldn't bring herself to fight

Ethelred or the destruction he brought because she imagined she knew his pain well. Falcon wasn't dead, but he was still just as lost to her.

Falcon fought his way through the debris and dust until finally he flew across a terrible crack in the floor that pushed the rock up at a vertical angle. Tally was unafraid. She knew she'd be safe—she was a Crown Princess of Hell now. But she'd let Falcon save her one last time.

He took her in his arms and carried her from the wreckage of the hall. The scent of him was so pure; it was home, not just for her, but the being inside her, too. She wanted to touch her lips to his, but she knew down that path lay only more pain. She loved the feel of his arms around her, the way she fit against his chest.

Tally memorized every second of what it was like to be held by him, to be close enough to touch him since it could never happen again. It was all so bittersweet.

It seemed so long ago that he'd come through the door with a case of beer and a pizza. It was only Falcon, only her best friend's older brother and her parole officer. What was between them had become something else so very fast, neither of them had had time to breathe. Well, she was breathing now and she was thankful for every breath she took.

She hadn't even realized they were flying. They were in Captiva again, her toes were scrunched into the warm sand, and Falcon was holding her in his arms. If only this were the end of her story. If only this was where she could say they did live happily ever after.

"Tally, thank Heaven and Fate you're safe." He clutched her to him.

She wondered if he'd still be thankful she was safe when she told him what she'd done. When she confessed the price she'd paid for her victory.

He touched the side of her face and kissed her reverently. Tally melted under his kiss, opened her mouth for him, and sighed, breaking the kiss, turning away from him before she could hurt him. Falcon touched his forehead to hers. "I'm so sorry I failed you."

"What do you mean?" Tally asked, not wanting to talk. She knew when they started talking, it would end with one of them walking away. If Falcon was too noble to end it, even after what she'd done, she would have to be strong enough to do it.

"What happened with Emilian. If I'd been stronger, he never would have been able to take you."

"Oh, Falcon." Tally sighed. "No, you didn't fail me. I chose this. Merlin told me if I took the curse, I could save you."

"You shouldn't have had to," Falcon replied.

"No one should have to, but I owed a debt and I paid it," Tally said.

"Did he hurt you?" Falcon asked, almost so softly she couldn't hear.

"No," she said.

He kissed her again. "I love you, Drusilla."

The lamia sang inside her. It urged her to touch him, to taste him, to be with him in all ways. It could feel his power through his kiss; his touch and his warmth were like a drug to it.

She pulled away from him. "I'm sorry, Falcon."

"For what?"

"I can't do this." For all of her bravado and newfound strength, she couldn't look at him. She didn't want to see the pain in his eyes.

"What do you mean?" he asked.

"I have to tell you things, things I'd rather forget. But if I don't tell you, it's the same as a lie."

"Then tell me." Falcon sat down in the sand and pulled Tally down next to him.

"You might not want to touch me after I tell you." Tally tried to pull her hand away from his.

"Don't be stupid."

"Look, this isn't easy for me."

"I never said it was. If you don't want me to touch you, fine. But there's nothing you could tell me that would make me push you away."

"Never say never," Tally said, looking down at her feet.

Don't cower. Tell him. And look him in the eye while you do, damn it. You're strong. You're a warrior, a goddess, a Crown Princess of Hell, and a woman who knows herself and her worth. Hold your head up!

Tally didn't know if it was the lamia talking or her own inner voice, but it was loud and strong. She looked up into Falcon's eyes and the only thing she saw reflected there was herself. He saw *her*.

She wasn't the means to an end for him—she wasn't the latest on a long list of conquests. He saw her and wanted her for Tally, for who she was, and what she was. All of it. That scared her more than the lamia did.

"I was released from parole," she began with a deep breath to signify she was only getting started. Falcon waited patiently for her to continue. "I used magick and I invoked the lamia. I bound her to me and she's never leaving. She's inside me; she's part of who I am now forever." Tally took another breath. "I meant what I said. I won't cage her. I can't and I won't go back on my word and try to push her back into the Abyss."

"She made you strong," Falcon agreed. "She nurtured the strength already inside of you. She kept you alive. I'd never ask you to cage her. Maybe ask her not to eat people and use their own bones as utensils, but no, I'd never ask you to betray her."

She took another shaky breath and looked at him again.

She wanted to remember what his face looked like when he loved her.

"I had to . . ." She trailed off and took another steadying breath to try again.

"Tally—" Falcon brushed his thumb across her cheek. "It doesn't matter. I know what you did. You don't have to tell me. It's not a lie, because I already know."

Her eyes filled with tears, but she was determined not to let them fall. She had to be strong. If she was never strong another day in her life, she could live with that, but for this day, her resolve was iron.

"It's important to me that you know I don't want this—" She bit her lip as quiet sobs shook her.

Her resolve was iron, all right—after it had been left to rust in a field for a hundred years. He was so close and so eager to keep her from the ugly things in the world that she wanted to let him.

"Tally, when I saw him take you, I knew what you'd have to do and I know you did it for me. We can still be together, if you'll have me."

Sweet Heaven, she could end him, consume his life force, and he was asking if she'd still have him. Tally couldn't ask for a better man, a stronger man, or a more honorable one. He was a hero in every sense of the word and he didn't deserve to be chained to someone he couldn't be with in every way.

"Falcon, I want you to know I love you." Tally closed her eyes, as if that could somehow add strength to her resolve.

"It sounds like you're about to do something that's going to kill me," he said with an uncomfortable laugh. "Don't you know you changed me? You made me believe in Love. You made me love you and now you're going to take that away?"

"It's for your own good, Falcon."

"Didn't you once tell me that I didn't get to make that choice for you about what was good for you?"

"It's not the same."

"No? Why not, because it's you doing the choosing?"

"How is it you can make me feel like hell for doing the right thing?" Tally whispered.

"The right thing for who? You? Is this what's right for you? If you don't want me, Tally—"

"Falcon, what if I told you we could be together, but we'd never have sex again?" She waited a moment for it to sink in. "Yeah, that's what I thought. You'd be too noble to tell me you didn't want to live that way and then you'd hate me."

"Hey, I'm not going to lie and say I want to live without sex, but, woman, I love *you*. I didn't whisper sweet nothings into your vag. Well, maybe I did when I was drunk, but I was talking to your face when I told you I loved you. I even made eye contact instead of ogling your rack."

"Stop trying to make me laugh. This is serious."

"So it's serious. So what? I love the sound of your laugh. You should do it more often." He reached out a hand to touch her, but she shied away.

"You don't understand. The lamia is part of me now. She loves your warmth and I know she'll try to suck it all out of you."

"That scares the shit out of me—I won't lie. But I have regenerative powers, fuck it." He shrugged. "I don't care. Why won't you give me a chance to prove we can do this?"

"Because it's better to make a clean break so we can both heal rather than dragging out an impossible situation. I'm trying to make this easy for you."

"I thought we'd already established I don't like easy?"

"Please, Falcon. Just take me home."

"I'll take you home, but this discussion isn't over."

"It has to be. Don't you understand that sex with me

could kill you? I absorbed a man's life force just because he was close enough for us to breathe the same air. If you were actually inside of me?" she said into his chest.

"I'm holding you now and it's just fine."

"But you smell so good and I know you'd taste good, too."

"Like cotton candy."

"It's more than that. I'm a predator now," she cried.

"Let me be the judge of that. And hey, if you do consume me, we'll be together forever. Maybe not like we planned, but I'll never leave you, Tally. Never."

"If I didn't love you"—she gave a watery laugh—"that would be scary. The rest of that goes something like you'll never let me leave you and you rock back and forth in the corner saying things about your mom."

He tightened his arms around her. "It's good you understand the lengths to which I'm willing to go." Falcon gestured toward the sea and sand. "Here is where you tried to redeem yourself and here is where I failed you. Let this be where I have my redemption and prove to you that I'm worthy of you."

"Oh, Merlin, damn it." Tally sniffed. "You can't say those things to me. This isn't going to happen, don't you understand? Ethelred is up there ending the Powers and we did nothing and now we're—"

"Maybe they had it coming. You didn't see Caspian or Hades doing anything to stop them, did you?"

"Where was Merlin?" Tally asked.

"He retired. Anyway, if they'd wanted to stop it, they could have. And I don't care about them. There's always something falling off this stupid world or breaking down. It's like a classic car that's been taken to a lazy mechanic. Something else will be broken tomorrow. Right now, it's about us. About Love." He rubbed his cheek against hers.

"And Lust. I saw your crown, even though you tried to hide it. We'll have forever now, Tally. I swear."

"Forever is a long time with no sex. No touching."

"I'm touching you now."

He eased her down into the warm sand and she was suddenly naked. "I don't know whose fantasy you're in, but having sex in the sand is not on my list. It's not *your* orifices that will intrigue the sand crabs," she said, laughing, all the while struggling for control. Searching for another way to make him go. Tally knew she could tell him that she didn't want him, but that would be a lie. Tally didn't lie. She had to make him understand, but she was weak, so weak. Her defenses crumbled with every breath, every second she spent with him touching her. Maybe just one last time?

Falcon knew she loved him and he loved her; why was she being so difficult? He was the one who didn't believe in Love, or he hadn't until Drusilla. Maybe she didn't believe he'd really changed? Maybe she thought the bullet Ethelred had shot him with was responsible for this and not his genuine love for her?

Maybe he could show her with touch.

He eased his knee between her thighs and shifted his weight so he didn't crush her beneath him. Falcon buried his face in her hair and inhaled the scent of her. He pressed his lips to her temple before kissing her mouth. He loved this Crown Prince gig—he could strip them both at will. His uniform dissolved, leaving him naked with his cock thick and ready, poised to enter her. She'd wrapped her legs around his waist and urged him to take her with the bucking of her hips. Tally moved beneath him and shifted to angle his cock for entry.

He held his hips rigid—Falcon was determined to go slow, to show her what she meant to him. But she was so wet, the scent of her taunting him to fill her, to drive into her, and find his release. It was what she wanted, too; he could tell from the small sounds she made, the way she pleaded with him to touch her.

Tally nipped at the lobe of his ear and dug her nails into his shoulders to force his compliance to her pleasure, but Falcon wanted to slide his tongue into her slit before his cock. He wanted to taste her again, she was so sweet. What he loved most about using his tongue was the way she screamed for him as her orgasm shook her, the hedonistic look on her face when she came.

"Give it to me fast and hard," Tally demanded.

His intentions and softer feelings were no longer in the fore of his awareness; not to say they were gone, but he wasn't a man to argue with a woman when she demanded to be fucked. He'd seek his own pleasure again with softer seductions after he'd given her what she wanted.

Falcon entered her and felt her hot sheath clench around his cock. He thrust inside her and she bucked to meet him. She dug her fingers into his biceps and pleaded for more. Always harder, faster, deeper.

He loved the way her breasts bounced when he drove into her, the way her slit tightened around him to keep him from withdrawing, and the half breaths she took while she bit on the swollen flesh of her bottom lip.

Her eyes fluttered closed, but Falcon wanted her to look at him. He wanted to see her face, watch her eyes.

"Open your eyes," he said as he leaned in to her.

Tally's lashes fluttered open and Falcon cupped her cheek and looked into her eyes while he thrust into her heat with long, sure strokes. She tried to look away again, to avoid this last intimacy, but he wouldn't allow it. If she'd gotten so deep under his skin that he'd fallen in love with her, there would be no walls between them. He needed her to know the truth and it was there, in his touch, his kiss, and the fire between them.

"Tally," he said as he nipped at the soft skin of her neck.

"Hmm?" She tightened her legs around his waist and closed her eyes.

"Ethelred did as you asked. He told me to love myself. But I love you more." He cupped the round globes of her ass and guided her hips to meet his thrust.

Her eyes flew open and she tilted her head up to look at him.

Falcon took advantage of the shift to pull one leg up to rest on his shoulder and kept the other around his waist. She cried out when he hit the core of her and Tally shuddered when he swept his thumb over her clit.

He was already swelling inside her, his cock surging and straining to come, but Falcon wanted to watch her first, wanted to see the wanton abandon on her face, and know he'd aroused every shudder and every cry that echoed through her.

Her body tightened as she neared her release and he had to use his magick to keep from spilling before she'd peaked. He moved slowly now, every movement eliciting another gasp or shiver from her. If they had more time, he would have muttered that charm for hours to keep her on the brink and push her past the edge, only to do it again and again.

"Come inside me," she whispered, her breath warm and soft on his ear.

No charm or spell could fight the magick of Tally's voice. He bore down and buried his face in her hair again as he spilled inside her.

He hadn't even caught his breath when Tally straddled him.

"Sweet hell, woman."

She rolled her hips so her wet slit teased his sensitive member.

He groaned as his cock stiffened in immediate response. Falcon could usually go for a couple rounds, but he liked to breathe in between. What Tally was doing now was almost painful, but it was good. He loved how wet she was. He could feel the mingled evidence of their pleasure slicking down to his sac and he found his body shifting up into her in an involuntary motion.

Falcon gritted his teeth and did it again, but she raised herself away from him.

"This is why, Falcon. I am Lust," she said in a singsong voice.

"I have to confess, I do like your methods."

She slid down his length and impaled herself fully, her eyes fluttering closed as she sighed, but it only lasted a moment before she withdrew. "I can't stop."

"Let the torture continue."

Tally didn't move, but shook her head. "No." She grinned.

"I've already told you something. It's your turn," he said and flexed his cock so it moved against her.

"What did you tell me?" She brushed her breasts against his chest.

"You want to hear it again?"

"Yes." Tally sank down and filled herself with his girth.

"I love you," he said simply.

"Why here? Why now? When it's too late?"

"I can think of other things we should be doing with that pretty mouth of yours besides asking questions."

"Please, Falcon."

He knew she wasn't talking about the timing of his thrusts. "It's never too late for Happily Ever After. You may be Lust, but I'm Love. The strongest magick of all."

"Oh." It was a sound of revelation and a breathy sigh of pleasure.

"Admit we belong together," Falcon demanded, ceasing all movement.

She continued to rock her body, seeking the fulfillment only he could give.

"I can't—oh!" she interrupted herself and rode him harder.

"Not what I wanted to hear." He grasped her hips and forced her compliance.

Tally ground herself against him and gritted her teeth. "Falcon, this game is dangerous."

"Very. How good you feel may kill me," Falcon managed, though coherent thought was almost beyond him.

"It might!" she cried as she bent down to him, her hair brushing his cheek.

He pushed the damp strands of hair away from her brow and cupped the back of her neck to keep her near. Falcon kept eye contact as he found his release.

She slipped a hand between them to bring herself off, but his fingers covered hers. Tally took control again and used his hand to come. She pushed his fingers inside her and if he hadn't already come twice, he would have been ready to fuck her again from the sensation of her body pulling his fingers deeper inside.

His fingers were covered in her sweetness and he wanted another taste, but she was riding his hand, seeking her own release again. Falcon tugged her down to him and kissed her hard, his tongue pushing past the seam of her moist lips and exploring the cavern of her mouth. She made soft mewling sounds against the onslaught, but he didn't stop. He crashed into her again and increased the pressure and the pace until she was writhing and screaming his name.

"It would serve you right if I buried my face between your thighs this very moment," Falcon said in a ragged whisper.

Tally collapsed and nestled herself in the crook of his arm. "I can take it."

"Not for another thirty minutes." He cringed, thinking how sore his cock was going to be.

"Why do they always have so much sex in books, but in real life, it seems once is enough?"

"A real man gets it done right the first time."

"We did it twice."

"As a real man, I'm not averse to practice."

Just as Falcon believed everything was going to be okay, he realized Tally's fears weren't to be taken lightly. Something wrenched at his insides and the blissful expression on Tally's face was more than postcoital ecstasy—it was the same one she wore when he made her come.

"So good," she sighed.

It morphed from a tugging in his gut to outright pain, a hundred knives flaying him. Fear welled in a fountain from the most primal part of him—the thing that every man dreaded deep inside—that this woman would devour him. Yet, his fear was founded in truth.

This was his sacrifice to be with her, he realized. He'd meant every word he'd said. She'd sacrificed so much, been through so much, and he hadn't been there to slay the dragon. He had the power of regeneration, but he wasn't sure how that worked with this creature she'd become.

In that moment, Falcon surrendered. He opened himself to whatever she wanted to take from him.

That was the miracle of love: His heart would never run out, never be empty. There was always more. A new kind of bliss washed over him, and eased his pain. It was like cold water on a burn and he was prepared to follow it as deeply as need be.

The connection between them was severed with a snap that jarred him into reality. The horror that twisted Tally's lovely face told him everything she was thinking.

"It's okay, Tally. I'm fine."

"No." She shook her head slowly, as if that would somehow make it all go away as she scrambled away from him. "No."

"It's what you are. I accept you. Love is endless. Boundless. You can't hurt me. Take all you need." He held out his hand to her.

"No, that's not true. It's part of the lamia's power to make you think that. It's—"

"Drusilla. You are the lamia, now. It's part of *you*."

"That's why we can't be together." With those words, Tally ran back up to the beach house and all Falcon could do was let her go.

CHAPTER TWENTY-FOUR

Love in the Time of Lust

Tally felt that a part of Falcon was still inside her. His essence filled her up, sated her, and made her hungry for more all at once.

She'd felt what he'd felt in those moments she'd been taking from him. His fear was bitter ash, but there was something beneath that. The truth of his words. The bright beacon of his love for her. The breadth and depth of his love was more than she could fathom—seemingly eternal and endless.

He'd struggled when she first started taking from him and she'd tried to stop, but couldn't, not until he surrendered. That acceptance of what was happening had jackhammered through her haze of pleasure to make her very aware of what she was doing.

And it was all Tally.

The thing inside her, its voice was quiet and still. She couldn't blame it for what she'd done. Only herself. She'd known better and she'd slept with him anyway.

Because Falcon fed more than the lamia—more than any supernatural hunger. He fed her heart, her soul, her very self.

Again, she was reminded of the nature of sacrifice and redemption—the kind of witch she wanted to be. But she wasn't a witch anymore, was she? Drusilla Tallow was a

Crown Princess of Hell, the embodiment of Lust. It was in her nature now to want, to desire. Yes, it was better she part from Falcon now. Her heart only wanted Falcon Cherrywood, but what about the rest of her? What about her demon magick? Would Lust be content with only one lover for eternity?

"You're giving up, Tally," Ethelred said from Luminista's bedroom.

"Says he who just obliterated the Powers That Be." Tally snorted and leaned against the doorway, his familiar presence actually comforting to her.

Ethelred shook his head. "No, Uriel stopped me." He flexed his fingers in the thin nightgown that had been spread across Luminista's bed. "I allowed the deities themselves to leave with only a ward on their magick."

"Why?"

"He's an angel." Ethelred shrugged and looked at his hands for a moment, still buried in that soft nightgown. Then he looked back up at Tally, his eyes raging with the fires of Hell. "But I will still have my vengeance."

"On me?" Tally asked.

"Why would you think I want vengeance on you? *What did you do?*" he asked, although it was obvious he already knew.

"You know what I did. I broke Emilian's curse. I killed him."

"It wouldn't have mattered if it wasn't for Cupid and his fucking self-righteous arrow, would it?" he snarled.

"Oh, I see. You're going to hurt me to punish Cupid for giving you Luminista, only for you to lose her."

"Glad you understand."

"I do. More than you know, Ethelred. For all the lessons you're so quick to hand out, this one is yours. We, humans, witches, all of us with the capacity to love also have the capacity for the pain you're feeling right now. And we feel it every day. All of those little accidents you like to engineer? People lose the ones they love because of you."

"But it makes them great!" His flames licked the bed around him, crawling up the wall.

"How do you know this isn't to make *you* great, Ethelred?"

He roared, the flames reaching out to her, enveloping her, but she didn't feel the fire. "Don't you spew the company line at me, little girl."

"Then put away the horns and the tail. We're working for the same company now." Tally revealed her crown and her wings.

"Damn you."

"Damn me? No, Ethelred. Damn *you*. You can take that same objectivity and shine it on yourself. Can't accept that sharp knife digging into your soft places?"

"She's dead, Tally! Do you know what that means?"

"Yeah, I know what that means. Do you? Do you really? What you're feeling now is pain. And it's all yours. You want someone to blame? There's no one to blame. Just Fate. Just another spoke on The Great Wheel."

"I don't feel this, Drusilla. This is not me. This is not . . . I'm a demon. I was born a demon, not with all of this putrid humanity."

"Now you get to roll in shit with the rest of us." Tally sat down on the bed with him as the flames receded, leaving the room as it had been.

"It's not fair."

"It rarely is."

"I hate Love."

"Hate Love if you want, but don't hate Falcon."

"He did this to me!" Ethelred said again as if Tally just didn't grasp the concept.

"You did this to you. Remember, we have to take responsibility for ourselves. You told me that. He doesn't get his Happily Ever After. I'm the Angel of Lust now and I've got all the baggage that comes with the title."

"Good," Ethelred growled, still looking at his feet.

Tally leaned on his shoulder.

"Stop that." He was suddenly scandalized instead of raging. "We're not friends."

"Yes, we are. You just don't know it yet. You changed my life, Ethelred. You did everything that you said Hell is supposed to do. You pushed me. You made me become greater than I was. So now you're stuck with me."

"I could end you," he said, without conviction.

"Maybe you could. Maybe you couldn't." She sighed. "But if you did, I would forgive you."

He shoved her off him. "That burns, Drusilla. Why would you go and say a thing so horrible? Forgiveness? Are you sure you're a Crown Princess of Hell?"

"Yeah. You're the one who told me Hell is relative."

"And I regret it. I hate you."

"No, you just *want* to hate me."

"Look, I don't like this teacher becomes the student bullshit. I don't have time for it. I'm angry. I want someone to pay. I don't want redemption. I don't need it. I'm a fucking demon."

"Yes, you're a demon. Why do you feel like you need to keep reminding *me* of that fact? I'm not a witch anymore."

"Shut up."

"Okay."

"Still talking," he grumbled.

"Yep."

He sighed. "Might as well make some tea."

"Hey, Tally, I thought I heard—" Emilian stood in the doorway. But there was something more on his face than surprise when he saw Ethelred. "You."

"Luminista," Ethelred mumbled in return. "But you're not you. You're him. And you. And him," he said dumbly.

"One soul instead of two," Emilian said.

Tally realized they had a lot to discuss and she backed out of the room quietly toward her own. She didn't know how they were going to work it out, but it was obvious that when Emilian had been resurrected, the two halves of the twins' soul had been joined. Ethelred saw Luminista, or some piece of her, looking back at him from Emilian's eyes.

What was Tally supposed to do now? Was she supposed to fly around and inspire lust? Was she supposed to make deals and sign contracts for souls? Was she supposed to stay in the mortal world? All of these questions fogged her brain like a sandstorm, little gravelly bits worming into her soft places.

But the most important one of all was more than uncomfortable sand gravel and it would be a billion years before Tally could make that pain into a pearl.

How was she supposed to live without Falcon?

CHAPTER TWENTY-FIVE
Conversations with Kali

Falcon Cherrywood may have let Tally run, but he was not going to lose his woman.

He didn't give a good damn about what she needed to take from him. She could have it. He loved Tally, everything about her. Love meant accepting all of her. He'd admit, knowing that she was no longer a girl of sugar and spice and everything nice was a little intimidating, but Tally had always been more snakes, and snails, and puppy dog tails. So, a Crown Princess of Hell really wasn't that much of a leap. It scared him at first that she could feed off their sexual energy.

Living without her scared him more.

He remembered Kali saying she'd given the gift of the succubus and the lamia to many of her devotees who wished to remain untouched. If she could give the gift, then perhaps she had some advice for Tally on how to live with it.

Falcon had willed himself to materialize in one of her temples. He made it a point to hide his wings—there would be profound religious implications if an angel appeared in Kali's temple.

Thankfully, it was empty, though incense offerings burned, making the air thick and sweet.

"Mother Kali, I ask you to bless me with your presence,"

Falcon said humbly. He didn't actually expect her to appear, but he hoped against hope she'd come. Or send him smoke signals, or a pictogram in some chapati—it didn't matter. He didn't know what else to do.

"Ask and you shall receive, Cupid," a deep, yet still feminine voice responded.

Falcon looked up to see a woman with dark skin in a dress of crimson rose petals. Her skin had been red in the Hall of Gods; now, it looked like black marble. Power thrummed through the room and Falcon bowed at the waist and presented his own offering of marigolds.

She accepted them with a smile. "So polite. I see you even took the time to research what I'd like. What is it you want from me? Have you come to ask me to take the lamia out of your little witch?"

"No. As easy as it would be, I wouldn't ask that. Tally gave her word."

"Interesting. Then what?"

"How does she get past her hunger?"

Kali laughed and the bells tinkled with her mirth. "You don't want it to go away for always, only when you want to have sex."

"It doesn't need to go away. I just want her to believe that she won't hurt me."

She laughed some more.

"Kali, I've told her it doesn't matter to me. She doesn't believe me."

"I wouldn't, either," Kali replied. "What are you going to do if I have no answer for you?"

He sighed. "I don't know. Be that guy in her bushes? I can't let her go."

She snorted. "I'm sorry, I know this is serious, but you're too funny."

"Now I know what Tally meant."

Kali laughed harder. "Oh, you're wonderful, Cupid. Really. You're a good man and I can see you do love her. Are you sure you don't want me to banish the lamia? I can do that, you know."

"No, no. The lamia kept its end of the bargain and Tally made her bargain in good faith. I won't interfere with that."

"Are you afraid to kiss her?"

"No, why would I be?"

"That's the question of the hour, isn't it?" Kali grinned. "Are you afraid if she wants to give you oral sex?"

"No," he said hesitantly, unsure of where this was going.

"You're not afraid she'll bite you? You don't fear her mouth? The lamia uses Tally's body the same way. To take nourishment. If you would let her lick whipped cream off you, then you have nothing to fear from the lamia. Only it eats your life force instead of whipped cream. And with you, I imagine it would be your sexual energy. Of which you have plenty to spare."

"Kali, you mistake me. I don't fear her or what she would take from me. *She* does. She thinks she'll hurt me, but I've told her Love is eternal."

"And so it is." Kali smiled. "She needs to believe that. Understand it. You must prove it to her."

"How do I do that?" Falcon asked, at a loss.

"Take her home to the people who love her. Women, are at their core, the same. All we want is to be loved. A simple concept, but not so simple in execution."

"Thank you, Kali."

"Now, go get your woman before the Powers That Be can mobilize. You should know they won't take what's happened lying down. They'll blame Tally as much or maybe even more than Ethelred. You, too. Love gets blamed for everything." Kali kissed him on the cheek and marigold petals began to drift down from the ceiling in blessing. "Take her some flowers when you go. Try foliage before kidnapping."

"I wasn't—" Falcon started, but the look on Kali's face told him that she knew exactly what he'd had planned and didn't care for it. "Okay, I was. I don't know how else to make her listen to me."

"Try listening to what she says first. Really hear it. Don't just wait for her to be done talking so you can say what you want to say."

"She keeps running away."

"Well, then maybe you'll have to kidnap her after all." Kali winked at him as the marigold petals continued to fall. The petals of her dress began to blow away and with it, the vision of Kali herself.

CHAPTER TWENTY-SIX

They Say You Can Never Go Home

Falcon gave Tally a day and then decided he could try talking later. After he'd kidnapped her. Although, kidnapping was such a harsh word. He preferred the phrase "borrowing her presence without permission." After all, it was easier to ask for forgiveness than permission. He knew that wasn't very Heavenly of him, but he didn't care. Because another common saying was that all's fair in love and war, and Falcon wasn't sure which this was yet. Either way, he planned on going home with the prize.

The stupid beach house was still warded against him.

He crept around to the back of the house, peering inside the kitchen window.

"Well, if it isn't King Creepo of Creepstania. What the fuck are you doing here, Falcon?" Tristan hissed in his ear.

"I could ask you the same, Peeping Tristan. What are you doing in Tally's bushes?"

"Making sure she's okay." Tristan looked at him, obviously waiting for an answer as to why Falcon was there.

"She's going to be a long way from okay for about an hour. Maybe more, maybe less. Depends on how pissed off she is about being kidnapped."

"You've lost your mind. I'm not going to let—"

"What you're going to do, Death, is mind your business," Falcon interrupted him.

Tristan laughed so hard he started to snort like a pig. "Why would I do that? You're getting too big for your leathers, Falcon."

"That's what she said." Falcon winked.

"Yeah, your mom."

"You know what? If you have the stones, give it a shot."

"You're awfully fucking cheery. I don't like this plan."

"I don't care if you like it or not. There's not shit you can do about it."

"I'm Death—" Tristan began as if Falcon didn't know who he was, or his power.

"Right you are. And throughout all of history, when has Death ever been able to stop the power of Love?"

Realization crossed Tristan's face. "Oh, you smug bastard," Tristan growled.

Falcon suddenly felt a twinge of pity for him and turned to really look at the Angel of Death. He wore his heart on his sleeve, contrary to his claims that he had no heart. He loved Tally; Falcon could see that. They could have had a good life together, but just like the woman he and Tally had seen on the bench, she could bloom so much brighter and so could Tristan.

"I'm not going to hurt her, Tristan. I love her."

"Are you two going to make out or get a room?" Ethelred demanded, opening the door.

"Well, the closest rooms would be upstairs and since the house is still warded against me . . ." Falcon shrugged.

"Well, if it were just me, I'd leave you outside. I'd never want Love to think he was welcome in my house. He's a sloppy bastard and doesn't clean up after himself," Ethelred drawled. "But apparently, the lady of the house would like a word."

Tally stood in the living room, her heart in her eyes and her soul on her sleeve. She'd never looked more beautiful.

Or hot.

She'd adopted a red uniform like his, but hers was satin. It was a form-hugging dress that revealed her curves and would have shown lots of leg if not for the red leather boots laced up to her knees that left only the tops of her thighs showing like some kind of illicit peepshow. She'd also cut her long, curly blond hair into something short and spiky, focusing attention on her sweet face and bow mouth.

A diamond angel wing charm hung from a bracelet on her wrist and Falcon couldn't help hoping that it was for him.

"What are you doing here, Falcon?" she asked quietly.

"I like your hair." He stopped in front of her and reached out a finger to touch the shorn golden locks. "What, no horns?"

She gave a weak laugh. "Living in this house? Can you imagine all the 'horny' jokes? No thanks."

"I miss you."

"Don't do that."

"Don't what? Don't miss you? Don't need you?" He tugged her against him and the feel of her small palms splayed against his chest, her cheek resting over his heart, it was so right. So perfect. "Don't love you?" Falcon finished.

"Yeah," she sniffed. "Don't do any of those things. It just makes it harder."

"Harder?" he teased.

Instead of laughing, she started crying.

"Oh, shit, don't do that. Come on, baby. I'm taking you home." He tightened his arms and they teleported to the front porch of his mother's house.

Tally looked up at him in horror. "What are you doing?"

"You asked me the other day to take you home. I took you to the wrong place. Home is where your family is, and this is your family. Your home."

"I know what you're doing, Falcon. And it's for this very reason that we can't be together. I love Raven and Hawk, Stardust, Midnight. Dred. *You*. I love you all too much to—"

"Falcon!" Stardust popped her dark head through the door. "I'm so happy you've brought our Tally home. Hurry up! Your brother and his girlfriend brought homemade fried chicken. That girl does know the way into my heart."

But Falcon wasn't looking at his mother. He was watching Tally and the play of emotion over her face. Watching her pain was like feeling it himself, but he hadn't brought her here to hurt her.

"Family, Tally. Yours. Mine. Ours," he whispered against her ear and dropped a kiss on her head.

The door flew open behind Stardust and Midnight ran out from behind her mother. Tally found herself lurching forward into Middy's steady hug.

"Oh, Goddess, I've missed you." Middy squeezed her.

Tally squeezed back just as tightly. "Me, too." Tears threatened and Tally sniffed irritably. Damn, it seemed all she could do was cry these days.

"Upstairs. Right now." Midnight grabbed her hand and dragged her past Stardust. "We need a moment before dinner, Mama."

"You go on. But don't be too long or the boys will have eaten all the chicken," she said.

Tally turned to look back at Falcon and the smile on his face was nothing short of gold. It lit up his face, even the air around him. It occurred to her that she was the cause of that smile. He'd brought her home, not as the poor little girl who was his sister's best friend, or as his parolee, or even as his friend. He'd brought her here as his woman, his partner. *His*. He was looking at her with everything he felt for her shining on his face. Just like she'd always dreamed.

It occurred to Tally that this moment was perfect. Everything she'd ever let herself want in the darkest and most secret part of the night.

If only she wasn't Lust. If only—

"Oh, hell, Tally. Make googly eyes at my loser brother later. We have approximately ten minutes to catch up before Mama hunts us down and drags us to dinner by our hair." Midnight jerked her up the stairs to her old bedroom.

"So, how was the honeymoon?" Tally asked.

"Perfect. Dred is still disgustingly perfect. Everything about my life is perfect. *Except you.*" Middy narrowed her eyes at her.

"I know, and I'm so sorry," Tally blurted, still fighting tears.

"Don't be stupid." Middy's words were soft, but her hug was strong and fierce. "It's not your fault. It's because you're not happy. This is my attempt to beat some sense into you the same way you did to me about Dred."

"I feel like I failed you," Tally confessed. It hurt to speak the words, but it had to be done. Middy deserved to know.

"For what? The lamia? I know you did what you had to do. That's over. You've obviously kicked ass, taken names, got the T-shirt. It's the rest of the story you're having trouble with. See, in all the stories what happens after the sacrifice? What happens after you slay the dragon?"

"Happily Ever After?" Tally mumbled.

"Right. And you're throwing it away with both hands. Falcon told me everything that's happened." Middy blushed. "Even being a married witch, let me tell you I was heartily sorry for using my magick to check in on you that one time."

"Yeah." Tally swallowed hard. "Sorry about that. You did only give me permission for a one-night stand."

"I've always wanted you and Falcon to end up together. You've always fit. You're the sister of my heart, Tally. Be my sister in the eyes of the law, too, okay? Do you know that Falcon has never brought a witch home? Ever?"

She'd already marveled that he'd made such an obvious statement to his family that they were together.

"You know my mother already approves. I hear she was already trying to plan your wedding—if not to Falcon, then to any one of my other two brothers." Middy laughed and the sound reminded Tally again that she was *home.* This was where she belonged, her place in the world.

"This is everything I've ever wanted, Mids. Everything."

"Then what's the problem?"

"I'm a Crown Princess of Hell. The Angel of Lust."

"Isn't a relationship all that much stronger when both Lust and Love are present? You belong together."

"I . . . I'm not a witch anymore. My magick requires certain energies."

"Just like Falcon. He gets stronger when people love. You'll get stronger when people lust." Middy said it as if it were the simplest thing in the world and didn't matter one way or another.

"I'm going to hurt him. My magick is parasitic. It will feed on him, don't you understand?"

"Yeah. And so does he. He wants to feed you and give you what you need. He wants to provide that for you. Why don't you let him?"

"It will hurt him, Mids. I could kill him."

"I doubt it. Because then you couldn't have your Happily Ever After. And they're real, Tally. You just have to have faith."

"I don't know if I have any."

"Falcon has enough for both of you." Middy hugged her again. "Let's go down to dinner."

Tally was aghast at how much faith Middy had in *everyone,* but it shouldn't have surprised her. Midnight had always been an idealist.

She followed Middy downstairs and made small talk with

everyone before they sat down to dinner. It was good to see Middy's husband, Dred, again. The love they had for each other burned brighter than any fire, any star, any sun. It was obvious in every touch, glance, and laugh. Hawk and Raven were the same prankster troublemakers she'd always known. Hawk's very pregnant girlfriend was mortal and a little blown away by their world, but seemed happy and eager to adapt. Stardust clucked over her like she was some foundling kitten until they shuffled into the big dining room and gathered around the table.

Again, it occurred to Tally that Falcon was right. This was home. This was family. But that had never been in doubt. She loved the Cherrywoods, so she had to protect them from what she'd become. It was really that simple.

She looked across the table at Middy, who shook her head vehemently, as if she already knew exactly what Tally was thinking. She probably did, since they'd known each other for so long.

"I have a card, Tally. Don't think I won't be mercenary enough to play it," Middy threatened.

But just as Mids had known what she was thinking, Tally knew what was going on in her best friend's head. It was the *You almost killed me and my husband and I'm only asking you for this one thing* card.

"I think I'd prefer the cat litter," Tally grumbled.

"I know," Middy said cheerfully.

"What are you talking about?" Dred asked, as he shoved a biscuit in his mouth.

"Who knows? They've always had their own language. They probably had half this conversation in their heads." Falcon shrugged.

"That's disturbing. They could be crafting all kinds of devilry." Dred looked back from Tally to Middy.

"There's no could about it, Mordred. Everyone always

said my boys were such a handful, but they didn't know about my Midnight and Drusilla." Stardust winked at them again. "They give the term 'wicked witch' new meaning."

Falcon grabbed her hand under the table. "We love you, Tally."

It amazed her how sometimes he knew just the right thing to say.

The whole table stopped, forks paused halfway to mouths, and Hawk choked on his chicken, coughing and spluttering into a napkin.

"Don't choke your chicken at the table," Raven snickered, but slapped his brother hard on the back.

"I don't need the fucking Heimlich. I need a replay. Did you hear what Falcon just said to Tally?" Hawk managed through watering eyes and coughs.

"Yes, he said that your family loves her," Hawk's girlfriend replied. "It's not like he said there's a human head on the table." She shoveled a bite of mashed potato into her mouth.

"No, he said that *he* loves her. Out loud. In front of everyone," Midnight explained. "Falcon has never brought a woman home to Mama. None of my brothers have. You're a first, too."

Stardust beamed. "Does this mean we can plan the wedding now? I have a whole tub of *Witch's Bride* I've been saving for the occasion!" Then she scowled. "I had one for Midnight and one for Tally."

One for her? Just for her? Tally felt like she was going to cry again. Damn it, she was going to get her tear ducts surgically removed. She couldn't handle all of this sniffing, sniveling, and general overemotional nonsense.

Suddenly, Falcon turned her chair to the side and he was on his knees in front of her.

"Oh, dear Merlin, don't do this, Falcon. Don't do what I think you're—"

He didn't let her finish; instead, he kissed her. "I want you with me forever, Tally. Be my mother's daughter. My sister's sister. Be my wife."

Starbursts of joy and hope exploded inside her, but she knew her answer had to be no. "Falcon," she began.

"We'll figure it out. I swear to you. If the worst happens, it will still be the best thing that ever happened to me. I want all of you."

Her mouth opened, but instead of saying no, she whispered, "Yes."

Oh, hell, what had she done? She couldn't do this; she couldn't saddle him with a wife he couldn't touch. Tally knew he'd push and push until they had sex and then she'd kill him and—Stardust squeezed her so hard every last thought was smooshed up and out of her head.

She was lightheaded, dizzy, terrified, and gloriously happy.

Tally's whole body went numb when Stardust slipped the garnet–and–diamond ring off her own finger and handed it to Falcon, who in turn put it on Tally's hand.

"It was my mother's and her mother's before her. It was always meant for you." Stardust kissed her cheek. "You're marrying the whole family, you know."

"I know, Mama Stardust."

"We'll start planning tomorrow," she said, obviously decided.

"No, Mama. Give Tally a few days. She's still settling in to her new job, aren't you?" Falcon said, running interference.

She nodded dumbly.

"Fine." Stardust turned her attention to Hawk expectantly. He kept chewing. "Don't you have something to say to the girl?"

The girl in question put down her chicken leg. "Yes, Hawk. Don't you have something to say?"

"No, not really. Except maybe I'll be glad when our son

is born, so you'll stop putting your cold feet on my ass in the middle of the night."

She flung her chicken wing at him, her missile crashing into his forehead. Tally and Middy both looked at each other simultaneously and added a little magickal kick to that leg, knocking him back in his chair and over.

"You're in trouble now, buddy." Dred nodded. "Middy tried to kill me with a cranberry bullet she shot out of her nose into my eye on our first date. You may as well give up and marry her."

His girlfriend got up and stomped out of the room, Stardust on her heels.

"It was really shitty of you to put me on the spot like that," she whispered in Falcon's ear.

"Yeah, it was so horrible to tell my family that I love you. It was so horrible to ask you to spend your life with me. Yep, I'm an asshole," he said happily.

"You know what I mean."

"I will use anything in my arsenal to keep you, Tally. It took me long enough to see what was right in front of my face. I'll utilize kidnapping, bribery, peer pressure, my mother, anything at my disposal. I love you."

"I kept trying to get away from you because I love you, idiot. But you know what? You deserve anything you got coming for this little stunt."

"Good, I'm glad you see it that way. Because you know what I got coming?"

"A horrible, grisly death at the hands of the woman you love?" Tally retorted.

"No, baby. You." His hand crept up her thigh.

She gasped and slapped his hand away. "Stop it."

"Surrender and be happy. We'll work everything out later. I swear."

He was right. She didn't know what tomorrow would bring. Maybe they wouldn't be able to be together. That was more than possible, it was likely, but he loved her. Everyone at that table loved her and she loved them.

This was her family.

She was home.

So, for the moment, she'd let herself wish, she'd let herself dream, and she'd have just a little faith.

In Love.

CHAPTER TWENTY-SEVEN

A Bad Idea or Happily Ever After?

Tally was sure that out of all of the bad ideas she'd ever jumped into with both feet, this was probably the worst. She'd let Falcon talk her into this and she still wasn't sure how he'd done it. That man could talk a demon into buying a space heater.

It helped that she loved him more than Godiva.

The beach house was still her safety net, so they'd decided to try their first experiment there. With Death in residence, if he was willing.

Which was more than a little weird and not simply because he was Tally's ex-boyfriend. He'd know what they were doing. Of course, they'd been to tons of parties together where everyone was having sex everywhere—Academy parties were just like that. But Tristan had said he still loved her, so Tally didn't really want to ask him to keep an eye on the outcome of their experiment.

She had no other choice though. She had to make sure if things went poorly that Falcon would be okay—it was either this, or nothing.

Tally paced back and forth, waiting for Tristan to appear after she summoned him.

When he finally did, Tally was so happy to see him that she flung herself against him for a hug.

"Whoa, did you change your mind? Finally kick Falcon to the curb?" He laughed and hugged her back.

"No. I have to ask you a favor. It's sort of a favor to trump all other favors."

"Bringing back the dead isn't a good idea. You have to know that. Your mother was in a lot of pain."

She shook her head. "It's not my mother. I want to make sure Falcon doesn't die."

"He's a Crown Prince of Heaven. He believes in Love, obviously. His job is secure. He's not going to die." He released her.

Tally swallowed hard and blushed. "No, when we . . . um."

"When you . . . um . . . what?" he prodded.

"You know."

"I don't. You have to tell me. I'm not psychic." Tristan rolled his eyes.

"You just want to embarrass me."

"I swear, I have no idea what you're talking about, Tally." He held up his hands, as if to show her he wasn't hiding anything.

She exhaled heavily. "When we have sex, Tristan. I don't want my fiancé to die when we have sex. Is that clear enough for you?"

"Oh. Since you're Lust now. I see. Well, you're planning on doing this soon, right? He's still not on the docket to be reaped. And I can tell you, I check daily." He winked at her.

"Not funny."

"So, was that it? I do have some things to do other than sit here and talk about the woman I love banging someone else."

"Shut up. You don't love me."

"I do, Tally. But maybe I'm not *in* love with you. And

you're right, I love to needle the shit out of Falcon Cherrywood. It just makes my day brighter somehow."

"What I want is for you to sit here, to be within emergency response distance, in case."

"While you have sex?" Tristan arched a brow. "Are you kidding me? I'm never going to let him forget it."

"Nope. That's something else. You can never, ever hold this against him. See, it's not Falcon who wants you here. It's me. I won't condemn him to a life with a woman he can't have sex with."

Tristan searched her face for a long moment before responding. "Yes, Tally. I'll do that for you. But I gotta say, I think you're both going to be fine. He told me something that I think you need to keep in mind because it's true on so many levels. Death can never stop Love." He swiped his finger over her nose as he would a child's. "If you tell him I admitted that, you'll think Middy's cat litter curse is Hex 101."

"Thank you, Tristan."

"I'm not going to say 'anytime,' because I am never doing this again. I trust you're ready now?"

Tally bit her lip and nodded.

"Get your ass in gear then." He flopped on the couch. "No tantric shit, either. I've got stuff to do. If it works out, you guys can do that on your own time. Got me?"

"Yeah, Tristan. I do."

She scurried up the stairs and told Falcon she was ready. Tally lay down on the bed to wait for him. She felt like a virgin sacrifice, lying there on the bed. In any other circumstances, she would have found the analogy hysterically funny because Tally was about as far from virgin as one could get on this side of prostitute.

It will be okay, we love him. The voice was soft and distant now, its separateness fading a little more every day.

Its word choice was comforting, but no, it wasn't *its*

word choice, it was *her* word choice. The lamia was part of her, now and forever. Tally couldn't believe Falcon accepted that. He still wanted to make love to her, knowing what horrible fate possibly awaited him.

"You don't hurt me when I hold you. Why should sex be any different?" he'd said last night, after he'd maneuvered her into bed with the age old "just wanna hold you." To his credit, he'd done as he'd promised and only held her.

Yes, he'd held her while he stroked her back, kissed her with such passion and intensity, he'd made her burn. Tally ached for him, for his touch. It was casual, the caress of his fingers down her arms, over her hip and her leg, but she wanted more.

She'd been pleading between his kisses for more, but he'd refused. It wasn't that he was afraid, or didn't want to. He'd said it was because he'd promised her. Damn the man and his sense of right and wrong.

She realized now it had been to prove something to her, to her and the thing that had become a part of her. He was a man of his word. He wouldn't try to force anything, or demand anything that wasn't given.

He'd also made her promise while she was desperately grinding herself against him that she'd let him try to make love to her today. She'd promised, and she was a creature of her word as well. It was just further proof Cupid was a sneaky bastard.

"Why are you covered up to your chin?" Falcon interrupted her thoughts as he came into the bedroom.

"I'm feeling shy." Tally blushed.

"You don't need to hide from me."

"I'm scared, Falcon. I don't want to hurt you," Tally said.

"I trust you. If something happens, it's only temporary. We'll try again." He made it sound so easy.

"Aren't you afraid?"

"No," Falcon said as he pulled the sheet back and exposed her bare skin to his roving gaze. "Like I said, I love all of you, Tally. Sure, there might be some new challenges, but we'll work through them." He moistened his lips. "All night if we have to."

Tally's skin grew warm where he looked at her and the heat suffused her body when she thought about what exactly working though it all night would entail. Her slit ached with desire and the lamia was strangely silent. She didn't know whether to be thankful or to panic.

"Do you trust me?" Falcon asked as he brushed his knuckles across the top of her thigh.

She shivered at the sensation and had to fight the urge to spread her thighs for him at that moment. Tally still wasn't sure they were doing the right thing. She nodded; she did trust him.

"And I trust you, so trust yourself." Falcon's caress slid nearer to the origin of the throbbing ache.

He splayed his fingers over her lower belly, the heat from his hand like a brand on her skin. Falcon leaned down and took her mouth, his tongue tracing her lips and the tips of her teeth. His erection was pressing into her thigh and Tally was thrilled to discover he meant every word he'd said. If he was afraid, he wouldn't be so ready to be inside her.

She drew her legs up and relaxed her thighs so her knees were slightly parted, a tentative invitation. Yet, he didn't move his hand. He continued to kiss her and stroke her hair as he had the night before.

Tally tried to shift, to urge his hand down, but he was frustratingly stubborn. He kissed where her pulse thrummed like a hummingbird on her neck, her collarbone, the valley between her breasts, and she arched her back, pushing herself toward his mouth. He complied and took the tight bud of one nipple into the hot cavern of his mouth. As he sucked and nipped at the sensitive flesh, each act flared sensation from deep in her belly to her clit.

Still his fingers made no move to descend, but he pushed a leather-clad knee between her thighs. Goddess, but the man was sin personified in his leather pants and no shirt. If he'd had his guns strapped to his thighs, she might have come right then and there.

He moved to the other nipple, licking and sucking while using the hand that wasn't on her abdomen to continue his attentions to her breasts. She loved to look down and see his dark head bent over her flesh, and run her hands over the wide expanse of his back as he pleasured her. She tugged the leather lower on his hips, but he moved down her body and pressed his lips to her inner thigh.

She felt exposed and vulnerable—frightened, but he'd stirred a need in her too hot to be denied and Tally made no protest when he slipped his tongue inside her. He worked her clit with his thumb in a motion that slowly increased in intensity.

He licked her slit like he was savoring an exotic fruit, making sure not to lose a drop of ambrosia. He sucked her labia minor into his mouth and eased his tongue between them. She sighed as she gave over to mounting pleasure.

She was wet for him, but she felt something new. He was exploring her slit just as he had her mouth, with the same sure confidence. It was divine! Her hips jerked, prompting her to push up to meet his caress in an involuntary movement.

His weight on top of her was a welcome pressure; skin on skin—she opened for him and drew him inside her body. He pushed deep inside with one sure stroke and he stopped moving, his eyes closed.

She thought for one horrible moment that something had happened, but the look on his face was sheer bliss. Tally tightened carefully to pull him deeper inside her. This felt new to her and she realized she'd merged completely with the lamia. It had never experienced this, not for pleasure.

It was wondrous and wild, all of the things she'd never known. Tally felt her love for Falcon well up like a spring and fill her alongside the ecstasy. She hadn't known she could have both.

His hands circled her waist and he shifted her to get his forearm beneath them, angling her for maximum penetration.

And something else she loved, he wasn't asking her if she was okay. He really wasn't afraid. She hadn't been ready to believe it, even when he was hard for her. It wasn't until he'd entered her that his words became real. That in itself was an aphrodisiac and it meant she could stop being afraid as well. She could surrender and ride the waves of delight he'd loosed.

His hand slipped between them again to continue stroking her clitoris, his fingers keeping time with his hips as he thrust into her. Falcon rolled them over mid-thrust so she was riding him. It was her favorite position because his cock hit a place inside her that was so good, it was almost pain. She liked to tease him this way, too, to slide her slit up his shaft and sink back down the hard length until he was buried to the hilt. When she rocked her hips forward, she could push her nipples past his lips.

Tally pulled away and turned so her knees were braced behind his shoulders and she could suck his cock while he licked her clit. She bobbed down the length of his shaft and tasted herself on him. She loved the taste of their mixed fluids on her lips—it made her feel naughty and very good all at the same time. She used her tongue to lave at the velvety tip, moving faster in response to Falcon when he took her clit between his teeth and tugged softly.

His hands were moving up her thighs and cupped her ass

to hold her where he wanted her; to expose her hidden flesh to his eyes and mouth. He didn't use his fingers as he had before; it was only his tongue. She felt a hot rush between her thighs and he moaned, his cock jerking in response.

Tally took it in her mouth again and wrapped her hand around the shaft, moving up and down slowly. The faster his tongue flicked, the slower she moved her hand. He'd told her he liked to come after she did. He liked to feel her spasming around his cock, and loved how wet she was.

She cried out as his tongue pushed her over the edge and, as she came, he lifted her easily and moved her down the bed. Falcon entered her from behind and held her up on her hands and knees while her orgasm rampaged through her.

Tally bit down and tensed as the crescendo didn't explode and ebb, but exploded again and again with his every thrust. Falcon eased her forward and grazed his teeth along her earlobe and the tender part of her shoulder. He marked her like an animal and the lamia accepted him as her mate.

His breath was harsh against the shell of her ear and the break in his rhythm signaled he was ready to come. She pushed back and clenched around him to hold him inside her when he would have withdrawn to stave off his orgasm.

He spilled inside her and after he was spent, Falcon pulled her into his arms.

"Are you okay?" she asked tentatively, looking deep into his eyes.

"What did you think was going to happen?"

"We both know the answer to that."

He laughed. "Sweetheart, I gave you a part of me, but I'm still whole."

"You never doubted, not for one minute?" Tally asked as she laid her head on his shoulder and traced nonsense symbols over his skin with her forefinger.

"Not for a second."

"I think you just wanted the street cred," Tally teased.

"What do I need street cred for?"

"You've got to do something to make up for your pink wings."

"I think I'm good with them, actually. Hades offered to make them red or black, but he said it would change how I taste to you."

"Don't tell me—licorice?" Tally wrinkled her nose.

"Yeah, or cherry Twizzlers. What good are black wings if you won't make out with me?" Falcon said in all seriousness.

"I must admit, keeping the pink was a good choice," she giggled. "I've become even more fond of cotton candy. You might even say I love it."

"That's good because you're stuck with it."

"So, since Tristan's wings are black, does he taste like licorice?"

"That's not a question you need an answer to, little witch," Falcon growled.

"I don't know, call me curious. I might have to ask him," she taunted.

"You'd break the poor guy's heart."

"Right," Tally snorted. "Tristan doesn't love me. He only thinks he does because I'm suddenly unattainable. He'll find the right woman. I know he will. Especially now since he's got the whole super-broody Death thing going on. There'll be some poor sop who won't be able to resist thinking he's a DIY project."

"Was I a DIY? A fixer-upper?" Falcon asked, teasing her.

"No, you were always Prince Charming."

"Even when I was trying to get into your panties on graduation night?"

"I wasn't wearing panties," Tally confessed.

"If I'd known that then, perhaps this would have turned out differently." He smirked.

"I kept leaning over, trying to show you, but I didn't think you were interested. I thought you were doing the Big Brother shtick."

"Oh, I think we can say with a definitive certainty that my feelings for you are nowhere near brotherly."

"Hmm," Tally sighed. "I think you need to explain those feelings to me. In vivid, physical detail." Tally pressed a kiss to his chest and then licked his flat nipple.

Falcon clasped her tightly against him and laughed. "That tickles."

"So it's another round of the tickle game? I seem to remember owing you—" Tally found herself flat on her back again and Falcon pressing her down into the mattress.

"You owe me, do you?" He captured her wrists and held them over her head with one hand, running the other down the length of her.

"How do you feel about a payment plan?" she asked breathlessly.

"Depends on what terms you're offering." Falcon dipped his head to kiss her collarbone.

"A decent rate, but the duration of the deal is what those in the business would call extended."

"Yeah, we don't usually go in for such a long payment plan, but in your case, we'll make an exception."

"What kind of exception?" Tally laughed. "Seventy-two months instead of sixty?"

"How about forever?" Falcon raised his head to look into her eyes. "I meant what I said when I asked you to marry me."

Tally smiled. "I know."

"But you didn't mean your acceptance. I know I pressured you into it in front of my family. Say yes again, now.

Be with me forever. Say yes and fight with my mother about what your dress is going to look like, how many tiers on the cake, and if our first dance should be to 'Last Worthless Evening' by Don Henley or 'You're So Cool' from the *True Romance* soundtrack."

"I don't care about the cake, but I want a champagne fountain and a carriage ride in one of the Cinderella Pumpkin carriages and then I want to go to Venice," Tally blurted out.

"You don't want to fight with my mother?" Falcon smiled.

"No, Stardust can have whatever she wants because she made you." Tally bit her lip and sniffed.

"Are you crying? I thought this was a Good Thing?"

"It is. But I can't believe I just said something that hokey."

"Me, either, but it's adorable on you." Falcon grinned before kissing her.

"You still didn't actually say the words again."

"Are you going to make me?"

"I haven't decided yet." Tally tugged on a lock of hair as if she was deep in thought.

"I thought that was pretty damn cool as far as proposals go. Slick, too. And you didn't only get asked once, but twice."

"How long did you practice with Dred?" she laughed.

"No longer than you practiced saying yes through the mirror with Middy."

"Do you always listen at the door when I'm in the bathroom? What if I'd been doing something unladylike?"

"Like demanding that time of the month not begin until tomorrow?"

"I shouldn't even be surprised." She rolled her eyes heavenward.

"I love you, Tally."

"Don't think that's always going to get you out of trouble," she warned.

"Why not? It's what always gets me in trouble. I think it should work both ways."

"I don't know, try it again and we'll see."

Falcon cupped her cheek and brushed his fingertips down the side of her face. "I love you."

"It definitely works." She gave a dreamy sigh. "I love you, too. So much it hurts. I'm scared though. Are we those people? Do we get the Happily Ever After?"

"Happily Ever After happens one day at a time, sweetheart," he said before kissing her again. If there'd been a sunset, he would have carried her off into it like any conquering hero. Instead, they had to settle for making love until dawn.

After the Curtain

The Powers That Be are still *really* pissed, but like Tally said, they have no power over her because she chooses to believe they don't. Much like the goblin king Jareth at the end of *Labyrinth,* only not as sexy. Fate has its own design for the Powers, much to their chagrin.

Merlin retired with Nimue, having had enough of the Bigger Boss gig. The invitations to his retirement party did, in fact, get lost in the mail. Because he never mailed them. Merlin wanted to retire quietly and sneak away for that honeymoon he and Nimue never had a chance to have. He knew everything would work out in the end; he kind of planned it that way.

Falcon's father, Orion, invited the family to a group therapy session and to his surprise, everyone came. Stardust has agreed to lunch once a week, but nothing more. The cooking classes she was taking with Roderick Snow ended and she's not spending as much time with him as before, but Rod hasn't given up. He knows he's the rich Prince Charming to Orion's worn-out bad boy.

Tristan, a.k.a. the Angel of Death, loves that his black wings get him in with chicks, but his newest assignment, Miss Ghislaine Grisly, is unimpressed. Tristan is thankful Merlin is out of office; he has a feeling she's the kind of ghoul who would inspire a dream where he'd have a conversation with his own cock and he's fine with their non-talking relationship the way it is. It goes where he tells it to and that's the end of it. Though the Zombie Master might have something else to say about it. Death is most definitely not "the boss" of her. She's currently taking every opportunity to tell him so.

Ethelred found redemption in love, but he's not sure what to do with it. He still gardens and thought it would make a nice birdbath. Falcon offered him a shot of Lethe to forget his pain, but Ethelred knows he needs to remember. He's been assured that eventually, it won't hurt anymore, but Ethelred thinks that's probably everyone blowing smoke up his ass. He'll believe it when he sees it. He goes antiquing with Uriel; he has a better eye anyway. He doesn't spend much time with Emilian because it's too painful for them both. Fate has a surprise in store for them, but the author can't talk about it. Cryptic crap again, a pet peeve of Tally's.

Hawk and his baby-mama drama won't resolve itself for some time. See, his girl may have been a mortal, but she was a gypsy and she's an Olympic grudge holder. It's not all her fault, though; Hawk is just as stubborn. Cupid has been forbidden to interfere, but they forgot to demand that Lust mind her own business, too, and Tally is all about being helpful.

Falcon and Tally? We're getting there. Don't you want to know what happened with the Trifecta of Doom and their sexy calendar?

No?

Fine.

We already know Falcon and Tally lived Happily Ever After with the capitals. Stardust demanded a fancy wedding, and Middy was maid of honor. Falcon *did not* pass out between Tally's thighs in a pergola. What else do we need? Okay, so you want to know about the succubus/lamia gig?

It didn't just magickally go away. Tally made her own choices and did what she had to do to save her loved ones and find redemption within herself.

Falcon loves her, all of her. He's not afraid. Knowing that her power could drain him dry is only a physical manifestation of what most men have feared from the beginning; once a woman gets her teeth into you, it's all over. Falcon may have pink wings, but he's all man. He's definitely earned his cupidity, or so they say in the gym when he's hitting the showers after a good game of hoops and everyone can see he's still all man.

And of course, they lived Happily Ever After.